At last, they reach parked in front of the house and cut the engine. He turned and in a somber tone said, "I'm sorry if I said anything to upset you. I wanted you to enjoy yourself today."

"I'm sorry I caved in like I did," she said with a calmness that amazed her. "Getting out was a real treat. Thanks so much."

"You're welcome. I promise next time we get together—" He tilted his head. "What? You look really distressed now."

Maybe she hadn't been as calm as she thought. She hesitated, and then said, "Mike, do you think there should be a next time?"

"Of course, I do." He reached out and tipped up her chin, forcing her to meet his gaze. "I could say, 'Doctor's orders,' but I hope we'll get together again because you want to."

The longing reflected in his eyes reached deep inside Rose. At that moment, she knew with all her heart and soul she wanted to be with him. They were so perfect together. Always had been—except for the one thing that kept them apart.

"You do want to come out with me again, don't you, Rose?"

"I—yes, I do," she whispered.

A slow, sexy smile tipped the corners of his lips. "I knew I was right on with that diagnosis."

When he leaned closer, she didn't move away. Softly, gently, his lips barely touched hers. And yet the effect, at first a shiver of delight and then a wave of pure desire, spread all the way down to her toes.

He deepened the kiss, rubbing his lips back and forth over hers.

She savored the touch of his warm fingers on her shoulder, the scent of his aftershave, the slight bristle of beard along his jaw. All so familiar and yet at the same time new and exciting.

Praise for *FINDING SARA*

"A modern Western, packed with secrets, intrigue and old-fashioned romance. *FINDING SARA* is a story that won't be forgotten..."

~Joanne Hall, Writers and Readers of Distinctive Fiction

~*~

"Lee takes a cowboy and an heiress and combines them into a refreshingly sweet tale. Readers can easily relate to the main characters as Sara searches for herself while Jackson overcomes a devastating loss."

~Karen Sweeny-Justice, Romantic Times (4 Stars)

Loving Rose

*The Red Rock, Colorado Series,
Book Two*

by

Linda Hope Lee

Linda Hope Lee

This is a work of fiction. Names, characters, places, and incidents either are the product of the author's imagination or are used fictitiously, and any resemblance to actual persons living or dead, business establishments, events, or locales, is entirely coincidental.

Loving Rose: The Red Rock, Colorado Series, Book Two

COPYRIGHT © 2011 by Linda Hope Lee

Contact Information: info@thewildrosepress.com

Cover Art by *Kim Mendoza*

The Wild Rose Press
PO Box 708
Adams Basin, NY 14410-0706
Visit us at www.thewildrosepress.com

Publishing History
First Sweetheart Rose Edition, 2011
Print ISBN 1-60154-963-6

Published in the United States of America

Dedication

For the Flexers:
Karen Muir, Liz Osborne, and Joanne Otness,
with thanks and appreciation
for their friendship and invaluable help.

Chapter One

As Rose Phillips made her way down the aisle of the TransAmerica Railroad coach car, a bolt of lightning pierced the dark sky, followed by ear-splitting thunder. Heavy winds buffeted the train, and driving rain obscured the spectacular view of Colorado's Rocky Mountains. Rose shuddered and hugged her arms. As the railroad's Quality Control Manager, she'd traveled this route many times and through many storms, but none as violent as this one.

The car was about half full, which was usual for early May. Once tourist season began, more passengers would be booked on this cross-country route.

Reaching her window seat, where the air was cooler than in the aisle, Rose sank onto the cushion. She glanced at her wristwatch. Ten-thirty a.m. In another half hour, the train would arrive at her hometown of Red Rock, thirty miles east of Denver, where she'd detrain for a weekend off. Come Monday, she'd be traveling again.

Despite today's unsettling storm, she loved her job. Being on the go helped to keep painful memories at bay, including her breakup with Dr. Mike Mahoney. Although two years had passed since she'd told him they had no future together, their paths crossed all too often. Each time she saw him, her heart twisted. Each time, she had to tell herself all over again that saying good-bye had been not only the right choice, but, given the circumstances, the *only* choice.

1

Deciding a change of residence would allow her to truly move on, last week she'd applied for a transfer. She had no particular place in mind; she'd consider anywhere, as long as it was away from Red Rock and Mike Mahoney.

Rose flinched at another round of lightning and thunder. She needed a distraction, both from the storm and from her troublesome thoughts about Mike. Digging into her purse, she pulled out her PDA and switched it on. Since one of her tasks was to monitor the railroad's food service, she began making notes on the breakfast she'd had earlier in the dining car. The omelet was superb, but the toast was a little dry. She filled in the rating form accordingly.

Five minutes later, lightning again lit up the sky. Rose scrunched her shoulders while she waited for the inevitable thunder. Sure enough, the loud peal began. But, instead of fading away, the sound grew into a shuddering, deafening roar.

Not only thunder. Something else.

Rose's blood went cold.

The train began to vibrate and for a moment she feared an earthquake was in progress. Then a horrendous crash brought them to a screeching halt. The coach car swayed back and forth like a drunken sailor. Women screamed and babies cried. Passengers leaped into the aisle and ran toward the exits.

"Stay calm, everyone!" Rose shouted. She lurched from her seat, but before she reached the aisle, the car gave an agonized groan and toppled onto its side. With a gasp, Rose thrust out her arms to grasp the seat ahead. Her fingers connected but another jolt ripped her hands away. Something heavy smashed into her left side. Sharp pain arrowed up her leg and her knees buckled. Arms flailing, she fell, hitting her head on the armrest of the seat across the aisle. Black dots swept across her vision, and then she lost consciousness.

****

"Do you think it's my liver? Or my gall bladder?" Tugging at the neck of her paper gown, Eleanor Donnelly shifted her weight on the exam table.

Dr. Mike Mahoney gave his middle-aged patient what he hoped was a reassuring smile. "I don't know yet. I'll order some tests that should tell us what's going on."

Eleanor had arrived at the Timber Ridge Medical Clinic this morning complaining of pain in her upper right abdomen. Palpating the area turned up no masses or swelling. Nor did he see any signs of jaundice. She wasn't a hypochondriac, though. Chances were, something definite caused her discomfort.

Mike stripped off his latex gloves and tossed them into the trash. A sudden crack of thunder drew his attention to the room's one narrow window. For the past hour, a violent storm had been raging over the area. Rain beat against the glass, and in the parking lot, the aspen trees swayed under a vicious wind.

"That's a wild storm, isn't it?" Mike nodded toward the window.

Eleanor's brows drew together. "Worst I've seen in a long time."

Mike made some notes on his clipboard. When he finished he set the clipboard on the counter and approached his patient. "I'm sending you to Valley General for some blood tests and an ultrasound. When I get the results, I'll call you and we'll go from there."

Pursing her mauve-shaded lips, Eleanor nodded. "Okay. But I sure am tired of this pain."

Mike patted her shoulder. "I know. But don't worry, we'll find the cause. You take care now, and

I'll talk to you soon. Oh, and be careful driving home."

"Don't have to worry about that." Eleanor waved a hand. "My daughter's picking me up. She can drive in anything."

"Good. Then I won't be concerned about you." He stepped from the room, and as he closed the door, thunder again boomed in the distance. Yes, this was some storm, all right. Worst he'd seen in his thirty-four years in Colorado.

On the way to check with his nurse, Lucy Alvarez, he glanced through the open door to the waiting room. Patients filled more than half the seats, and several children clustered around the corner aquarium. Mike smiled to himself. Establishing the clinic with his associate, David Genoa, had been a great idea. The three specialists who had since joined them, plus their up-to-date medical equipment, made Timber Ridge one of Red Rock's most highly rated clinics.

So far, his career as a small-town doctor was a success.

He wished he could say the same for his personal life.

At the nurses' station, Lucy was on the phone. "What? Oh, that's terrible! Yes, he's right here." Her brown eyes wide, she said to Mike, "It's Susan at Valley General. There's been a train wreck, and they're rounding up everyone who's available. I told her David was out of town, but that you're just finishing up with a patient."

Shock rolled through him. In all the years he'd lived in Red Rock, there'd never been a railroad accident. But, given today's storm...

"Reschedule the rest of this afternoon's appointments and tell Susan I'll be there as soon as I can. Does she know which line it is?"

"TransAmerica."

His gut clenched. Rose Phillips worked for TransAmerica. He hoped she wasn't on the ill-fated train.

A scant ten minutes later, Mike hunched over the wheel of his SUV as he sped across town to Valley General Hospital. Even with his windshield wipers at full power, the heavy rain blurred the road ahead. After skidding around the corner of Fourth and Aspen, he sucked in a deep breath and eased up on the accelerator pedal. He wouldn't be much help to the train wreck casualties if he had his own accident.

He couldn't stop thinking about Rose and wondering if she'd been on the train. When he'd seen her brother, Jackson, in Red Rock yesterday, Mike asked about her. He always did, even though their relationship ended two years ago. Jackson said she was doing well. She'd been traveling and was due home soon for a weekend off.

Why Rose had ended their relationship remained a mystery. She'd said she wasn't ready to settle down, but he'd never quite accepted that. He'd always suspected something deep and troublesome weighed on her, but to this day, he had no idea what it was.

Pulling into the hospital driveway, he shook his head. He couldn't dig up those old bones now. He had a train accident to deal with.

****

Rose's eyelids fluttered open. Her head throbbed and sharp pain radiated up her left leg. A blast of cold air swept over her. Where was she? What happened?

Then she remembered. The train...the storm...the crash. Oh, God...

Raising her head took great effort, but she managed to survey the wreckage of the coach car's interior. The car had toppled, but not completely

5

over, resting instead at an awkward angle. Seats were uprooted like trees, with cushions scattered about. Above her head, rain mixed with smoke spewed through a broken window into the coach. Holding up her head made it throb harder, and, oh, the pain in her left leg. Excruciating. Glancing at her leg, she saw that rubble buried it from the thigh down.

Someone nearby moaned and from farther down the car came a baby's mournful cry. An agonized shriek rent the air. Rose's heart squeezed. Other passengers were hurt, too. She looked around for train staff that might help, but none was in her immediate sight. She'd been prepared for emergencies such as this. If only she could free herself, she could assist the injured.

Bracing her arm against the wall of the car, she managed to raise her upper body, but no way could she budge her leg, and the pain of trying made her gasp for breath. Sweat beaded her forehead. Exhausted from even such a simple effort, she eased back down. She lay there, trapped and helpless, praying rescuers would soon arrive.

****

At the hospital, Mike plunged into caring for the wounded train passengers. Disasters such as this were rare at Valley General, but everyone knew the drill. A sense of urgency hung in the air, and aides sped gurneys down the hall with practiced efficiency. Doctors and nurses hurried from room to room, stopping to consult with one another in the hallways and at the nurses' stations.

As Mike assessed patient after patient, treating everything from superficial cuts and bruises to the more serious broken bones and internal injuries, he continued to worry about Rose. He took every opportunity to check the updated computer list of admissions. Not finding her name, he then scanned the faces of the walking wounded that crowded the Emergency waiting room.

He didn't see her anywhere, but a foreboding kept his nerves taut.

After Mike finished attending a six-year-old girl who'd sustained severe lacerations from broken glass, one of the hospital's resident doctors stopped him in the hall.

"Fractured leg in twelve," his colleague said. "Can you take it?"

"Sure."

As he entered Room 12 and glimpsed the dark-haired woman lying in the bed, Mike's heart flip-flopped. Rose? Holding his breath, he stepped closer.

He hadn't made a mistake. His next patient was indeed Rose Phillips. After a quick check of the monitors to be sure her vitals were stable, he bent over the bed. Her eyes were closed, dark lashes resting against pale cheeks. Her full lips moved slightly, in sync with the slow rise and fall of her chest. Rain-matted hair clung to her forehead, and a purple bruise bloomed near her hairline. As his gaze traced the contours of her blanketed body, he saw the bulge of the temporary splint on her left leg.

Her right hand lay atop the bedcovers, close to her side. On impulse, he reached out and touched her fingers, then the back of her hand. The contact with her smooth, cool skin sent his heartbeat into high gear. He hadn't been this close to her in two years, and yet it seemed like only yesterday. He leaned closer and whispered, "Rose?"

Moaning softly, she rolled her head side-to-side and stirred under the blanket. Then her eyelids fluttered open, and she peered through her thick lashes.

Shadowed by the room's dim light, her eyes appeared darker than the warm brown he remembered. Despite the bruise, the pale skin, the rain-matted hair, to him, Rose was as beautiful as ever. He ached to take her in his arms and hold her tightly, to feel her softness, the beating of her heart against his chest.

But, of course, he dared not. Keeping his voice light, he said, "Hey, it's me, Mike."

Recognition flashed in her eyes, and a wan smile touched her lips. "M-Mike. I never thought y-you'd be the one to come."

Her confusion brought a momentary smile to his lips. "You came to me."

"Oh. Where am I?" Raising her head from the pillow, she blinked and gazed around.

"You're safe now, Rose. You're at Valley General."

"Hospital? Oh, no. My leg...hurts. Bad." A grimace twisted her features.

"Your leg is broken. But don't worry. I'll take care of you." *Like I've thought of so many times.*

Her smile returned, wider this time. "Oh, I'm so *glad* it's you!"

Sinking back onto the pillow, she gazed steadily at him. Her eyes shone with the bright fervor of...what? He searched his mind for the right word. Finally, the answer came.

Rose had the unmistakable look of a woman in love. *Yes, love.* He was sure of it. His heart soared and he suddenly had trouble breathing.

But that couldn't be, his rational mind told him. If she still loved him, why had she left him? The answer to that question didn't seem important now, not when her glow surrounded him with warmth he hadn't experienced for a long, long time. "I'm glad it's me, too," he said when he found his voice.

"Mike, it's so good to see you."

Despite her injury and the need to get treatment underway, Mike seized the unexpected opportunity. He grasped her hand between both of his and leaned closer. Resisting the temptation to press his lips against her cheek, he whispered instead, "I've missed you, Rose."

"I've missed you, too. More than I ever thought I would. But, how can we—" Tears filled her eyes as she continued to gaze at him.

He gave her hand a reassuring squeeze. "We'll work everything out. Don't worry. Right now, I'm going to take care of that broken leg."

****

"There she is!"

The familiar voice awakened Rose from a light sleep. She opened her eyes to see her brother, Jackson, and his wife, Sara, step into her hospital room. Jackson carried a vase of red and white carnations, while Sara's arms were full of magazines.

Warmth and affection filled Rose, lifting her spirits. She and her older brother had always been close. And, since Sara had come into their lives, she'd been like a sister. Rose took credit for bringing her and Jackson together. After Sara had been mugged while on a layover at the Red Rock train station, Rose insisted she recover at Jackson's ranch.

"Hello, you two," she said. "Thanks for coming. And for the lovely flowers and the magazines."

"Of course, we'd come." Jackson grinned from under the brim of his tan Stetson as he crossed the room to place the flowers on the tiled windowsill.

When he passed her bed, their sweet fragrance floated to Rose's nose.

"I'm sorry we couldn't get here sooner." Sara stacked the magazines on the bedside table. "We had to wait until Molly came home from an appointment in town, so she could watch Ryan."

"How is the baby?" Rose asked, always eager for news of her nephew.

Jackson pulled up two metal straight chairs and

sat in one. Removing his hat, he ran a hand through his dark hair. "Growing like the proverbial weed."

"In a few months, we'll be celebrating his first birthday," Sara added as she settled into the chair next to her husband's.

Sara wore her blond hair pulled back in a ponytail, emphasizing her high cheekbones and wide-set blue eyes. Rose always admired her sister-in-law's taste in clothing and today was no exception. Her light blue Capri slacks and matching jacket worn over a white T-top were casual yet elegant.

"How're you doing?" Jackson asked Rose. "Are you in pain?" Eyebrows pinched together, he nodded at her left leg encased in a blue fiberglass cast.

Rose shook her head. "Not too bad, but of course the pain meds help."

"Mike said the break's a simple fracture and should heal fine," Sara said.

"Yes, he told me, too." Much to Rose's dismay, after setting her broken leg, Mike remained her attending doctor. Considering their past history and stressful breakup, she'd expected him to turn her care over to a colleague. She wished he had. His frequent visits knotted her nerves and flooded her mind with memories she'd rather forget.

"Awkward having Mike as your doc?"

Jackson spoke as though he'd read her mind. Which wasn't unusual—they often were on the same wavelength. She shrugged. "He's as good as any, I suppose."

Sara leaned forward and patted Rose's hand. "The accident must have been horrible, Rose. I'm so sorry you had to go through such a terrible experience."

Recalling the chaos and terror of the wreck, Rose shivered. "Thanks, Sara. You're right; the wreck was a nightmare. The storm was the worst

I've seen. Still, I never thought there'd be a landslide."

"Doesn't the railroad keep an eye on potential hazards?" Sara asked, settling back in her chair again.

"Oh, yes. They're very diligent about safety."

Jackson fingered the band on his hat. "I'm sure they do the best they can, but sometimes old Mother Nature gets the upper hand."

"Do you know how long you'll be here?" Sara asked.

Rose lifted a hand and gently touched the bandage covering the cut on her forehead. "I'm not sure. Mike said I also have a slight concussion, so they're keeping me for observation. I hope not more than a few days."

"Whenever you're discharged, you're coming to the ranch to recuperate." Jackson wagged a finger in her direction.

"No!" Rose burst out. Then, realizing how rude she must sound, she added in a calmer, though firm, tone, "I mean, no, thank you."

Sara frowned. "With your cast, you can't possibly stay alone in your apartment. We've a room downstairs we can fix up for your bedroom, so you won't have to climb stairs."

"That's thoughtful of you," Rose said, smoothing a wrinkle from her bed sheet, "but I'm sure I can manage at my place."

"Come on, Sis. You're always helping other people. Why not let someone help you?"

Reacting to her brother's cajoling tone, Rose crossed both arms over her chest and lifted her chin. "I like to be independent. I'll be fine."

****

After Jackson and Sara left, Rose took a couple deep breaths, attempting to untie the knots in her stomach. She regretted her outburst, but they'd caught her off guard. No, she did not relish recuperating at the Rolling R.

She enjoyed visiting the ranch for an afternoon or an evening. But, although anxious to leave Valley General, the idea of staying at the ranch for days, and in this case, weeks, held little appeal. Sara and Jackson, and their foreman, Buck, and his wife, Molly, were happily married. Each couple had a child they adored. Rose had neither husband nor child. She'd be an outsider, an oddball, a misfit.

You and Mike could've had what they have.

No, no, not possible. And all because of a mistake I made years ago. A mistake I dare not confess to anyone, especially not to Mike.

Pushing away the past, she lay back against the pillows and closed her eyes. A cart clattered down the hall, and voices rang out. Then all was silent.

She'd almost drifted off to sleep when footsteps moving closer signaled someone's arrival. She opened her eyes as Mike strode into the room. Gripping the bed covers, she let out an audible sigh. The last thing she needed right now was a visit from *him.*

Yet, there he was, as handsome as ever, filling the room with his commanding presence. Thick, reddish-brown hair topped a strong, masculine face of angles and planes. Broad shoulders more than filled out his white doctor's coat, and although the coat hung almost to his knees, she could easily imagine the flat abdomen and muscular thighs underneath.

Brow furrowed, Mike studied her monitor for several seconds before his forehead smoothed and he turned to her. "How're you feeling?"

Feigning indifference, Rose studied her fingernails. "Pretty good, considering the circumstances." She hoped he wasn't going to take her vitals. If he did, her heart rate would shoot off the chart.

He stepped closer, blotting out her view of the doorway. "How's the cast feel?"

"Like I stuck my leg in a bucket of cement."

His laughter echoed around the room. "I'm glad you haven't lost your sense of humor."

"If I don't laugh, I'll break down and cry. And I may cry, anyway."

"Go right ahead. You're perfectly justified."

She lifted her chin and met his gaze. "When can I be discharged?"

Pushing back his coat, he planted his hands on his slim hips. One expressive eyebrow peaked. "In a hurry to get out of here, are you? What's the matter? Is it the food? The help? The room service?"

Rose had to bite her lower lip to keep from laughing. How easily they'd slipped into the banter they'd always enjoyed when they were together. Had they really been apart for almost two years? "Neither," she said, maintaining a serious tone. "I need to get back to work."

"Too bad." His head shook side to side. "Your body is the boss now and will heal in its own time. I want to keep an eye on your concussion until I'm sure you're out of danger. Still, I'd say you'll be enjoying the sunshine on the Rolling R in a couple of days."

Apprehension grabbed hold. He must have been talking to Jackson and Sara. They all were conspiring against her. "Who says I'm going there instead of to my apartment?"

"Jackson did."

"Hmmph. We'll see about that."

"I recommend you take him and Sara up on their offer."

"I don't think so." Bracing herself for more argument, she met his gaze head on. As far as she was concerned, his role as her doctor went only so far. Once discharged, she was on her own, and if she wanted to recuperate at her apartment instead of at Jackson's ranch, that was her business.

Instead of arguing, he leaned over and patted her arm. "You have a couple more days to think about it. I'll let you get some rest now."

His patronizing tone set her teeth on edge. And, although he surely meant the gesture to be impersonal, his touch hinted of the intimacy they'd once shared. She struggled to keep her voice steady. "Thanks. That's what I was about to do when you came in."

"Sorry about that. But my job is to keep an eye on my patients."

He was right, of course. Mollified, she said, "Hey, I'm sorry to be so crabby. My broken leg isn't your fault."

"No problem. I'm used to crabby. I'll see you later." He headed for the door.

Ah, rid of him at last. Settling back into the pillows, Rose took a deep breath and prepared to resume her nap.

But then, before stepping into the hall, he turned and pinned her with a sober gaze. "Rose..."

Rose tensed and gritted her teeth. What now? "Yes?"

"Do you remember my visiting you in the E.R. before your surgery?"

She searched her mind, but her recollection of being brought to Valley General was hazy. "Not really."

He took a few steps toward her bed then stopped and rubbed his forehead. "You don't remember what we said to each other?"

What was he leading up to? "No, I don't. Why?"

Several seconds passed, and then he said, in a low tone, "Never mind." Wheeling around, he headed for the door again.

14

Alarm arrowed through her. Whatever she'd said must have been important. To him, anyway. "Mike!" she called after him. "What did I say?"

Without stopping or turning around, he gave her a dismissive wave over his shoulder. "Nothing important."

"Mike!"

But he was gone. His footsteps echoed down the hallway then faded away.

****

A couple hours later, Mike grabbed a cup of coffee in the hospital staff room. Instead of joining one of the groups at the round tables, he strode to the window and gazed out. Although rain still pelted the asphalt parking lot and the maple trees still bent under the wind, bits of evening sky peeked through the gray clouds. Finally, the storm was almost over.

After a couple sips of his coffee, he set the cup on a nearby table. He really didn't need the stimulation. Adrenalin fueled him, not only from responding to medical situation after situation, but also from his unexpected and startling encounter with Rose.

He should have turned over her case to someone else. Instead, he'd let those few moments in the E.R. sweep him back in time, back to when they were deeply in love. Responding to the love he'd seen in her eyes and heard in her voice, he'd vowed to take care of her and her injury.

Then later, when he'd dared to ask her about their conversation, she claimed to not remember it. Had he only imagined she'd said she'd missed him? Had he only imagined the love he'd seen shining in her eyes?

No, the words were uttered, the emotion expressed. She still cared for him. He knew it all the way down to his bones.

The question was, what to do about it?

Go after her, man. You know you still love her. True, but she'd sent him away once. Did he want to risk being rejected again? But if he pursued her now and won her back, he'd be the happiest man on earth.

Chapter Two

Three days later, Rose found herself where she'd vowed she wouldn't be—at Jackson's ranch. She'd finally given in and come to the Rolling R to recuperate. Deep down, she knew Sara and Jackson—and Mike—were right; staying alone in her third-floor apartment would be a struggle. As promised, Sara and Jackson fixed up a first floor room, so she wouldn't have to climb the stairs to go to bed.

She'd spent this afternoon sitting on the ranch house's front porch. The warm summer breeze, thick with the sweet smell of meadow grass, lifted strands of her hair and fluttered the pages of the book on her lap. Her broken leg lay propped up on cushions covering a log footstool. At her side, a log table held a glass, a pitcher of lemonade, and a plate of Sara's peanut butter cookies.

Jackson was out on the range, tending to his business of raising and training quarter horses. He'd been up and gone long before Rose awakened. Sara was working in her bakery, a business she'd established soon after she and Jackson married. He'd remodeled an unused building into a modern kitchen with all the latest equipment. Sara spent most of her days there, aided by two employees, while Molly Henson cared for Ryan.

Anna Gabraldi, the Phillips' middle-aged housekeeper, would have provided Rose some company, but today was Anna's day off. So, Rose was left to herself—and her thoughts.

Uppermost in her mind this morning was the

conversation she'd had with Mike in the E.R. *The supposed conversation*. She'd wracked her brain, but still couldn't remember what she'd said that he'd found so important. Rose heaved a deep sigh and shifted in her chair. She hoped her words wouldn't come back to haunt her. She already had enough ghosts of the past to deal with.

Returning to her job with the railroad would solve everything. Well, not exactly solve, for she couldn't change what had happened those many years ago. But being on the go, traveling across the country, was the best remedy for coping with her troubles.

Her roving gaze fell on the pots of geraniums lining the porch, which reminded her of the geraniums in her Red Rock apartment. Thanks to her neighbor, Nancy Reese, they were being cared for. Several other friends had phoned, including two men she sometimes dated. Both hinted they'd be glad to pay her a call. Rose thanked them and told them she'd be in touch. *Maybe*, she'd added to herself.

With a sigh, she picked up her book, found her place, and began reading. The historical novel was the current selection for her book discussion group. She needed to finish it in time for their upcoming meeting next month.

Full of political intrigue and romance, the story under other circumstances would have fascinated her. But today she found concentrating difficult. After reading for several minutes with none of the words sinking in, she gave up. Snapping the book shut, she leaned her head back against the cushions and closed her eyes.

A few minutes later, the rumble of an approaching vehicle jolted her awake. Opening her eyes and gazing out over the porch railing, past the stone walkway and the weeping willow tree, she spotted a silver SUV traveling along the asphalt road connecting the ranch to the highway.

She sucked in a breath and gripped the arms of her chair. Mike owned a silver SUV. She'd seen him driving one around town. Maybe he'd come to check up on her. No, doctors these days didn't make house calls. The visitor must be someone else. A buyer to see Jackson about his quarter horses, or a sales rep to see Sara about her bakery products.

She waited for the SUV to pass by the house and continue on to the bakery or to the stables. Instead, it stopped in front of the ranch house. Her curiosity piqued, Rose glued her gaze to the vehicle. The driver's door opened and a man leaped to the ground. Sunlight glinted on reddish-brown hair and the clasp of the black bag he carried.

Dr. Mike Mahoney.

Rose steeled herself for yet another encounter with the troublesome man who had so suddenly come back into her life. Even though the black bag indicated his visit was official business rather than a social call, that didn't make dealing with him any easier.

Yet she couldn't take her gaze off him as he strode along the path leading to the porch. No doctor's coat hid his lean yet rugged build today. A tan shirt open at the neck stretched across broad shoulders, and khaki jeans hugged lean hips and topped dark brown, leather boots. Her breath caught.

As he climbed the porch steps, he met and held her gaze. "Hey, Rose."

"Hello, Mike. I didn't know you made house calls." She nodded at his black bag.

"Only for special patients like you. I was in the neighborhood and thought I'd stop by to see how you're doing. I always carry my supplies with me when I'm on the road." A hand patted the bag.

"Never know when they might be needed."

"Does this take the place of my appointment with you next week?"

"Not a chance." With a grin, he wagged a finger. "You're not getting off that easy. I want to see you then, too."

"Well, have a seat." She gestured to a log chair nearby.

"Thanks." He pulled the chair close to her and sat, placing the black bag at his feet.

His nearness sent her heartbeat into overdrive. Her hand trembled as she laid her book on the table.

"How're you doing?" he asked, when she'd finally turned her attention back to him. "Is the cast itching?"

"Yeah, some."

He studied her bare toes sticking out of the fiberglass. "Doesn't seem to be any swelling. Is the cast too tight?"

Feeling vulnerable, she fought to keep from curling under her toes. "Not really."

"Okay, then." He opened the black bag and took out his stethoscope and blood pressure cuff.

"Do you have to do that?" She folded her arms across her chest, a protective gesture she knew in the long run was useless, but one that gave her momentary comfort.

"Checking your vitals is my job. This won't take long." Grasping her left wrist, he stretched out her arm and began to wrap the cuff around it.

She couldn't help flinching at the touch of his warm fingers against her skin. Gentle, yet firm— and so achingly familiar. The scent of his aftershave, too, brought back memories.

"Relax, Rose. You've been through this before."

That was the exact problem. Sucking in a ragged breath, she closed her eyes while he pumped up the cuff.

"Over in a minute," he said.

Just when she thought the pressure would crush her bones, the cuff finally came off. She barely had time to catch her breath before he grasped her arm again and pressed two fingers against her wrist to take her pulse. The sensation rippled all the way up her arm. She gazed at his hand, sturdy and masculine, yet with long, sensitive fingers. The image of him stroking her body, the way he used to, igniting every nerve ending, every desire, flooded her mind.

Why is this all coming back to me? I've been over Mike for a long time.

She focused on the wagon wheel, its old wood bleached almost white, propped against the weeping willow tree. A robin sitting on the wheel's metal rim puffed out an orange chest and chirped to a mate half-hidden in the tree's gently swaying branches.

Finished taking her pulse, Mike positioned the stethoscope in his ears to listen to her heartbeat. "Sit up straight, please."

He slid the scope down the front of her blouse, where it rested at the top of her left breast. Blood rushed to her cheeks. Again, her thudding heartbeat drummed in her ears. She could only imagine what it must sound like through the stethoscope.

"Okay, now lean forward," he said.

"I thought we were finished," she grumbled.

One eyebrow arched. "You know better than that."

"Oh, all right."

Rose leaned forward. As he inched the scope down between her blouse and her bare back, his fingers grazed the back of her neck. Involuntarily, she shivered.

"The metal's cold, huh? Even on a hot day like this. Sorry."

"S'okay," she managed to mumble.

He placed one hand against her blouse to steady the scope underneath the fabric, and the other on her shoulder. "Take a deep breath and hold it."

Rose sucked in a breath, while her heart pumped like a train engine on an uphill climb. Oh, this was going to be an accurate test. *Yeah, right.*

When he finally finished and drew away, Rose sagged back against the chair, as limp as a rag doll. "So, what's the verdict?" she said, hoping to cover her meltdown with flippancy. "Am I still alive?"

"Very much so."

His serious tone gave her pause. She looked his way and their gazes collided. Under long lashes, his brown eyes were dark and intense. Unspoken messages hummed through the air between them, messages she didn't want to interpret—dared not interpret. Still, she couldn't turn away.

Finally, he broke the connection, dropping his gaze to wrap up the cuff and the stethoscope. Leaning over, he tucked the equipment back into the bag and snapped it shut. Then he straightened and smiled at her once again. "That wasn't so bad, was it?"

Now the tension between them had eased, Rose shifted in the chair, searching for a comfortable position. "I'm not used to being fussed over. I don't go to doctors very often."

His eyebrows peaked. "Not even for regular check-ups?"

"I have neglected those," she admitted with a twinge of guilt.

"Still running yourself ragged on your job, I suppose."

Hearing an undertone of censure in his voice, she bristled. "I like my job. I like to keep busy. I can't wait to get back to work—if only this blasted leg would heal."

"Healing takes time. I know you're impatient,

but can't you relax and enjoy these days off?" He nodded toward the table. "Looks like you've got everything you need. A book to read. Lemonade. And cookies. Some of Sara's, I bet."

"Yes. Help yourself...if you have time to stay." *Please say you don't.*

He eased back in his chair. "I do have time...and there's something I want to discuss with you."

Her senses leaped to alert status again. There was no relaxing around this man—not for long, anyway. "About my leg?"

"No, something else. But a glass of lemonade and a couple cookies would hit the spot."

"Sorry I can't be much of a hostess. You'll have to get yourself a glass."

"No problem." He rose and headed toward the door leading inside.

"Glasses are in the cupboard above the right hand counter," she called to his retreating back.

He shot her a grin over his shoulder. "Right. I've been here often enough to know my way around the kitchen. Can I get you anything?"

"More ice would be nice."

"You got it."

Rose tapped the arm of her chair while she waited for Mike to return. What could he possibly want to talk to her about? The mysterious conversation they'd had in the hospital E.R. that he'd later questioned her about? Whatever was on his mind, she had the feeling she wasn't going to like it.

When Mike returned, ice-filled glasses in hand, Rose expected him to launch into the mysterious subject he wanted to discuss. Instead, while pouring them both some lemonade, he talked about the train wreck and the investigation that was underway. "The accident hasn't spooked you about your job, has it?" he asked, reaching for one of Sara's cookies.

Rose made a dismissive wave. "Heavens, no. I'll be back at work as soon as I can."

"Not so fast. You're not going back to work until you get your doctor's okay."

About to shoot back a sharp retort, she caught the twinkle in his eyes. Giving a salute, she said instead, "Yes, sir! But if I die of boredom, you'll be to blame."

A beat of silence slid by, and then he said, "I know something you can do while you're healing."

Expecting his suggestion to be more teasing, she fired back, "Oh, yeah? What?"

"Let me keep you company."

Rose's jaw dropped but she quickly closed her mouth. That was the last thing she'd expected him to say. "I, uh..." Groping for an answer that would stall for time, she finally said, "You can't be serious. I mean, considering..."

He crossed both arms over his chest. "Considering you called off our relationship before?"

Heat flooded her cheeks. "I don't like being reminded of that," she said, biting her lip and lowering her gaze.

"Then put it behind you."

If only she could. If only she could put all the painful memories to rest. But, like slumbering giants, they hid underneath the surface of her mind, ready to pop up and harass her. "I don't know if I can..."

He leaned forward, clasping his hands and propping his elbows on his knees. "Look, I'm not suggesting we plan the rest of our lives, just that we get together while you're healing. A little recreation might relieve the stress of being confined."

His thoughtfulness, a quality she'd always appreciated, chipped away at her resistance. And yet, she wasn't ready to accept his offer. Nodding at her cast, she said, "There's not a whole lot I can do."

"You can go for a ride. That would get you out of the house for a while."

Getting out of the house sounded nice. She plucked at a peeling piece of bark on the arm of her chair. "But you're busy—"

"Not that busy. I don't work twenty-four/seven."

"Oh, Mike, I—"

"Hello, I'm home!" Sara's lilting voice echoed through the house and out to the porch.

Heaving a sigh of relief, Rose sagged back against the chair cushion. Thank goodness someone had finally arrived to interrupt this nerve-wracking conversation. "We're out here!" she called over her shoulder.

Sara's footsteps came closer then the screen door creaked open and she joined them. "Mike! What a pleasant surprise!"

"Hey, Sara." He rose and enfolded her in a hug. "Mmmm, you smell like cherries." Standing back, he reached up to brush a smudge of flour from her cheek.

Sara laughed. "Good nose. I've been making cherry cheesecake. But, what brings you out this way?"

"I was in Forksville for a meeting and decided to stop and see my patient on the way home." He nodded at Rose.

Leaning over, Sara patted Rose's arm. "You must really rate to get a home visit."

"I think he stopped by to sample your latest cookies." Rose pointed at the plate where one lone cookie remained.

"So, how'd you like my peanut butter bars?" Sara asked Mike.

"They're a winner." He patted a hand on his stomach. "When can I look for them in the supermarket?"

Sara brushed back a wisp of hair that had

escaped her ponytail. "It generally takes six months to a year from conception to finished product. And I'm not sure I've finalized the recipe yet. I'm still experimenting. I'll give you a batch to take with you today. Have your office crew sample them and give me feedback."

Mike beamed and nodded. "I'd be glad to."

Rose barely listened to their conversation. Her mind still whirled with Mike's suggestion they spend time together while her leg healed. What should she do? A part of her yearned to say "yes," but the red flags flashing in her mind shouted "no."

"Can you stay for dinner?"

Sara's invitation jolted Rose to attention. Mike stay for dinner? She hoped not. She squeezed her eyes shut and prayed he'd refuse.

"That'd be great," Mike said, and then added, "That is, if Rose doesn't mind."

A sinking feeling invaded Rose. Mind? Of course, she minded. Yet what could she do when Sara had invited him?

Deciding humor was her best defense, she opened her eyes and regarded him from under furrowed brows. "Well...okay, if you promise not to poke at me anymore."

He held up his hands. "You got it. I'm all done with that for today." Turning to Sara, he said, "Now that's settled, how 'bout I give you a hand in the kitchen?"

Sara tilted her head, eyes wide. "Hey, a guy willing to do kitchen duty. How can I turn that down? Okay with you if I take him away for a while?" she asked Rose.

Rose nodded and made a dismissive wave. "I'll be fine."

"Molly and Buck and Karli are coming to dinner, too," Sara said as she and Mike entered the house. "Having us all together will be great fun."

When the screen door shut behind them, Rose ran a hand over her forehead, hot enough to make her think she might be running a temperature. Fun? Yeah, right. Fun for them, maybe, but not for her.

****

An hour later, Rose sat with the others at the round kitchen table. Dishes of food were spread before them, and the savory aromas of pot roast, mashed potatoes, mushroom gravy, and fresh beans from the Phillips' garden filled the air.

Still, Rose only picked at her meal. Sitting next to Mike had proved to be a big distraction. More than once, as she raised her fork to take a bite, her arm brushed his, sending little tingles along her nerve endings. She attempted to shift away, but, like an anchor, the cumbersome cast held her in place.

Neither could she concentrate on the conversation, even while ranch foreman Buck Henson told one of his entertaining stories.

Rose had always liked Buck. A tall, lanky guy with curly blond hair and a generous nature, he was also a born storyteller. He loved embellishing his narratives with facial expressions and gestures, even voice changes, like an actor performing onstage.

"You shoulda seen that little calf," he said as he finished his current tale. "He wouldn't let his momma out of his sight for nothin'." Tossing back his head, he roared with laughter.

The others, Rose included, joined in.

"That reminds me of when the momma herself was a little one," Jackson said. "But she was an orphan..."

Having heard Jackson's story before, Rose let her attention wander. Her gaze landed on Buck and Molly's two-year-old daughter, Karli, sitting in a high chair between her parents. With her mother's red hair and her father's ready smile, the little girl was adorable. Karli aimed a spoonful of mashed potatoes toward her mouth. Not all of the food reached the mark, and a glob stuck to her chin.

Grabbing a paper napkin, Molly leaned over and wiped away the drip. Then she planted a quick kiss on the child's cheek.

Karli gave her mother a big grin in return.

Rose swallowed against the lump rising in her throat. Her gaze swung to baby Ryan in his high chair. A miniature version of his dark-haired, dark-eyed daddy, he clapped his hands while Sara fed him a blender-made concoction of peas and carrots.

Sara fairly beamed with love and pride as she lifted each spoonful to the baby's lips.

A familiar ache began in Rose's stomach and snaked its way up to her heart. What would it be like to care for a child, to feed him, bathe and dress him, tuck him in at night with a tender kiss?

Fifteen years earlier, she'd had the opportunity to know. Then, like a leaf chased away by the wind, the opportunity vanished.

She had only herself to blame. If only she could forget, but that time was forever etched into her heart and soul. There would be no forgetting.

Or forgiving, either.

A ripple of laughter signaled the end of Jackson's story. Rose's attention snapped back to the present and she forced a smile.

"Hey, Mike," Jackson said. "See what you're missing by not being a rancher?"

Shifting in her seat, Rose glanced at Mike and waited for his reply.

Mike shook his head. "No way. You ranchers have my greatest respect, but ranching's not for me. I'm much better at working with humans than with animals."

"And we're thankful for that, aren't we?" Sara gazed around the table. "Everyone here has benefited from your doctoring skills, Mike."

"Amen to that." Buck raised his right arm and flexed the elbow. "My arm is as good as new, thanks to you."

Catching the quick flash of Molly's green eyes and sensing the conflict to come, Rose tensed.

"If you hadn't insisted on riding in last year's rodeo," Molly said, jutting her chin, "you wouldn't have broken your arm in the first place!"

Buck grimaced and ducked his head. "Oh, oh, sore subject. I had to go and open my big mouth, didn't I?"

Sara and Jackson exchanged troubled glances. Mike cleared his throat. Karli began to cry.

"See what you did?" Buck frowned at his wife. "When you're upset, she gets upset."

Molly put her arm around Karli's shoulders and leaned close to her ear. "Hush, now, darlin'. Momma's not mad at you." Then she leveled her gaze at Jackson. "Did Buck tell you he wants time off to ride in the rodeo at Glennbrook?"

"Yes, he did." Jackson sat forward.

Buck waved a hand. "Aw, Molly, that's between Jackson and me. Don't bring it up now."

Molly pursed her lips and looked away.

Wide-eyed, Rose stared first at Molly, then at Buck. She'd known that, because of the high danger of injury, Molly disapproved of her husband's participation in rodeos. But she hadn't realized the conflict had escalated to such a degree.

An awkward silence fell. Rose searched her mind for something to say to restore conversation.

At that moment, Sara grabbed the platter of roast beef and said, with a wide smile, "More meat, anyone?"

"I'll have another slice," Mike said.

"How are things at the clinic?" Sara asked as she handed him the platter.

"We're looking for one more doc to fill the last

suite." Mike speared a slice of roast beef and transferred it to his plate.

"I know someone who might be looking for a place to practice," Jackson said.

Glad to have Molly and Buck's troublesome conflict shelved, at least for now, Rose took a deep breath and focused on finishing her meal.

When dinner was over, Sara announced coffee and cookies would be served in the family room. Rose longed to plead a headache and escape to her room. But, fearing such an announcement would bring unwanted attention, she nodded her agreement and joined the others.

In the family room, Mike helped Rose to the leather sofa, pulling up a footstool for her leg and placing cushions behind her back. He was about to sit by her when Jackson waved him over to the TV, where he and Buck had tuned in a Colorado Rockies baseball game.

"Go on," Rose told him, fighting to keep relief from her voice. "I'll be fine here."

While the guys clustered around the TV, Sara and Molly spread a blanket and toys on the floor for the children, and then settled themselves nearby. Rose was close enough to join in the women's conversation; but, since they were discussing an upcoming shopping trip to Red Rock to buy the kids new clothes, she had nothing to contribute.

She sipped her coffee and kept an eye on the game. A long-time Rockies fan, she would've been much more comfortable sitting with the men and watching the game than being stuck with Sara and Molly.

The minutes dragged by. To add to her discomfort, Mike kept glancing her way, his brow furrowed. Avoiding his gaze kept her even more focused on the game. She guessed he'd rather be sitting with her, probably to resume their earlier conversation about spending time together while her leg healed.

Certain he'd bring up the subject again as soon as he had an opportunity, Rose considered her response. Saying "yes" sent little warning signals up and down her spine. Her answer should be a firm "no." And, yet, she wasn't comfortable refusing, either. Whatever, she'd have to take a stand. Stringing him along with "maybe" wouldn't be fair.

After a while, fatigue unraveled the tension in her shoulders, loosening her limbs as it spread down her body. Leaning back against the smooth leather, she let the conversation and the sounds of the TV fade into the background. The next thing she knew, someone touched her shoulder. She opened her eyes to see Mike standing over her.

"Hey," he said, and sank down on the sofa.

His added weight sent her sliding into him. The sudden contact jolted her fully awake. She caught her breath and elbowed into a straighter position. "I must have nodded off. How rude of me."

Mike leaned over to steady her cast on the footstool. "No one took offense."

A quick scan of the room told her the others had left. She and Mike were alone—just what she didn't want to happen. Hugging her arms, she shifted more to her side of the sofa.

The low sound of the TV caught her attention. "Did the Rockies win?"

"They did. Seven to two."

"Good for them. Where'd everyone go?"

"Sara took Ryan up to bed. Jackson and Buck went out to the barn to check on a calf. Molly and Karli took a walk to the duck pond." He sat back, brushing her shoulder with his.

Rose shivered. "Are Molly and Buck still angry with each other?"

"I don't know. I hope not."

"Molly hates Buck riding in the rodeo."

Mike wrinkled his forehead. "She hates the sport as much as Buck loves it."

Shaking her head in disbelief, Rose added, "I thought everyone here on the Rolling R was so happy."

"Molly and Buck still love each other, Rose, but they have problems to work out. Every couple does."

She looked away and bit her lower lip. "Maybe some problems can't be worked out."

"You don't know that until you try, do you?"

Rose's chest tightened. They weren't talking about Buck and Molly any more, but about the two of them. And Mike knew it, too.

Not wanting to venture farther down that road, she blurted, "Thanks for coming today. I may not have acted like I appreciate your good doctoring, but I do."

His lips eased into a smile. "I know you do. And, you're welcome." With a sideways glance, he added, "But you still didn't answer my question about us spending time together while you heal."

She sighed and briefly closed her eyes. Like a dog with a bone, he wasn't going to let that issue go. "I don't know what to say. My instinct tells me—"

He held up a hand. "Okay, okay, no decisions tonight. Think about it for a while. I can wait."

Her shoulders sagged. So much for worrying about stringing him along with "maybe." The man had endless patience. "Well...all right."

Neither said anything for the next few moments. The TV news, featuring a blonde anchorwoman with a cheery smile Rose found annoying, filled the void. Finally, she said, "Thanks again for coming."

"All right, I can take a hint. I'm on my way." He stood, but, instead of moving away, lingered, gazing down at her. "I hate to leave you here alone."

Although his concern touched Rose, her patience

tonight had worn thin. Pursing her lips, she said, "I'll be fine, really. I was alone all day, if you remember. I'm not totally helpless. The room they fixed up for me is only a few steps down the hall."

He spread his hands. "I just wanted to make sure."

In the next moment, he was gone, and the room was very empty indeed.

****

On the drive back to Red Rock, heading down the highway into a mellow, red-orange dusk, Mike switched on the radio and tuned in his favorite country-western music station. Increasing the volume, he sang along. His voice was slightly off-tune, but he didn't care. His visit to the Rolling R had left him in high spirits.

Rose hadn't turned down his suggestion they spend time together while her leg healed. Okay, she hadn't given him a definite "yes" either. He had faith the situation would turn out in his favor.

He appreciated Sara's invitation to dinner. The others' presence provided a good buffer, while at the same time allowing him and Rose to spend more time together. Except for the brief argument over Buck's rodeo riding, the evening had been pleasant and relaxing.

Red lights flashed up ahead and a train's whistle sounded in the distance. The railroad crossing came into view. He pulled up behind a short line of vehicles stopped at the lowered crossbars. The train whistled again, louder now. In the early darkness, the engine light glowed like a shiny new moon. Mike turned down the radio and focused on the train. Wheels clacking, cars rumbling, it sped by the crossing.

His grip on the steering wheel tightened. All too soon Rose would return to work, riding the train across the country. She wouldn't be the captive she

33

was now, with her leg in its fiberglass prison. He'd have to work fast. He could stand the separations if he knew she'd be coming back to him.

Fifteen minutes later, he reached Red Rock. Instead of heading directly to his condo, on impulse he turned up the street leading to Aspen Hills, one of the town's newer residential areas. He drove through the adobe pillars set with globe lanterns marking the entrance. Terraced streets provided sweeping territorial views of the town below and the mountains silhouetted in the distance. Lights beamed from porches and patios, from ground-floor living rooms and second-story bedrooms. Families all tucked away in their homes.

He wound his way through the streets until he came to a vacant lot, one of the few remaining. Parked at the curb, he sat there while the moon rose and, one by one, stars filled the cloudless sky. He'd bought the property two years ago when he decided Rose was the woman he wanted to spend the rest of his life with. When she broke off the relationship, he put the lot up for sale. As a result of the area's economic downturn, no buyer appeared, and eventually he took it off the market.

Dare he now think no buyer coming forth had been a good omen? As he stared at the lot, he could almost see the home he'd envisioned rising from the dust.

The two-story, Spanish-style house had wrought iron balconies and a red tile roof. He even pictured him and Rose inside, sequestered in a cozy den, sharing an evening of talk and warming up to the sweet love-making they'd enjoy after climbing the stairs to the second floor bedroom. Down the hall was a nursery waiting for their first-born son or daughter...

Hey, man, don't get carried away! You've barely started to reclaim what you lost two years ago. Take it easy or you'll ruin everything.

Shaking his head to chase away the dream, Mike switched on the ignition and drove off down the street.

Chapter Three

"I can't be pregnant!" Glenna Jordan wailed and banged her bare heels against the side of the exam table. "I just can't!"

Mike finished making a note on his clipboard, and then looked up at his fifteen-year-old patient. "I'm afraid you are, Glenna. Judging by when you missed your last period, our tests, and my exam, I'd say about four weeks. That home pregnancy test you took was right on."

Pushing a strand of bleached-blond hair behind one ear, Glenna gazed at him with tear-filled eyes. "My parents will kill me, especially my dad. He has an awful temper. You aren't gonna tell them, are you?"

"Not if you don't want me to." Mike plucked a tissue from the box on the counter and handed it to her. "You and I have doctor-patient confidentiality. But I recommend you tell them as soon as possible."

Glenna blew her nose into the tissue then crumpled it into a tight ball. "No. I'm going to run away."

"Running away is a bad idea," he said, keeping his voice calm. "You'll need care during your pregnancy. Think of your baby."

"My parents are gonna kill me!"

Mike gritted his teeth to keep from bawling her out for getting pregnant in the first place. No excuse for it. Not these days, with plenty of contraception available. Okay, so no contraception was one hundred percent foolproof. As far as he was concerned, unplanned pregnancies still occurred far too often.

He doubted chastising Glenna would do any good, especially after the fact. Better to use his time and energy encouraging her to care for herself and her unborn child. The children of mothers like Glenna were the ones who suffered. More often than not, they ended up abandoned, mistreated, or stuck with parents who had neither the interest nor the resources to raise them.

An abandoned child himself, Mike knew all too well what happened to an unwanted child. Even now, years later, memories of all the shuffling from foster home to foster home haunted him. Visions of his unknown parents, their heads blotted out with blurry circles, like on TV when someone's identity needed to be kept secret, marched across his mind at the slightest provocation.

Sure, he'd finally gotten lucky when the Mahoneys, an older, childless couple, adopted him. But not even their love and care could erase the damage done by a birth mother who'd left him in a department store restroom when he was only a few days old.

Swallowing down his bitterness, he focused on Glenna and her predicament. "I still want you to tell your parents about your condition. Would you like to make an appointment for all of you, so you can tell them when I'm present?"

Her lower lip pushed out in a pout. "What good would that do?"

"Neutral ground might soften their reaction."

"You don't know my folks."

"But I do, Glenna. I've been a doctor to both of them since I opened the clinic." Mike made a final note on his clipboard and laid it on the counter. "They seem like reasonable people."

Glenna tossed her head. "Hah! Not where I'm concerned. I'm their little girl who does no wrong."

"What about the baby's father, then? Will you tell him?"

"I don't know. And that's another problem. My parents hate him." She gnawed at a thumbnail. "I've decided to run away."

His patience wearing thin, Mike struggled to keep his voice calm. "Before you do that, will you do one thing for me?"

She narrowed her eyes. "What?"

Mike crossed both arms over his chest and leaned against the counter. "Talk to our social worker, Ms. Eagle. She's a very understanding lady. She can help you decide what to do."

"I already know what I'm going to do."

Ignoring her stubbornness, Mike walked to his phone and picked up the receiver. "I'll call her. She may have some free time now."

Luck was with him. Betty Eagle answered her phone, and she had an unscheduled half hour. Mike hung up and told Glenna, "As soon as you're dressed, come on out, and I'll take you to Ms. Eagle's office."

Glenna glared, her lips clamped tight.

When Mike had time for a break, he went to his office and sat at his desk. He leaned back in the chair and closed his eyes, savoring the solitude. Today's patients had taken a toll, especially Glenna Jordan. She was one stubborn young lady. He was glad she'd finally agreed to talk to Betty Eagle, though. Betty was a good therapist.

Still, he found himself wishing he'd been able to send the teenager to talk to Rose. The thought of her brought a smile to his lips. She would have made a good therapist, too. When they were together, she was working on a degree in counseling at Denver U. Then, about the time they broke up, she dropped out of school and took the job with the railroad.

He'd always wondered what changed her mind about becoming a therapist; but, since they were no longer seeing each other, he'd never learned the reason. Her brother Jackson claimed he didn't know, either.

Next time he saw her, maybe he'd ask. Better be careful, though. He didn't want to frighten her off by pushing his own agenda too soon. First, he wanted them to get used to each other again. With an exhalation, he leaned forward to consult his desk calendar. This Saturday would be a good day to start.

****

Anchoring the crutches under her arms, Rose managed to dry a skillet and set it on the stove. "What shall I do next?" she asked Sara.

Sara released the sink stopper then rinsed the dishcloth under the faucet. "That finishes the dishes. Why don't you take a break?"

"This whole week has been a break." Rose hobbled to the towel rack and hung up the dishtowel.

Today was Saturday. Jackson had gone to Glennbrook to meet a potential buyer for one of his quarter horses, leaving Rose with Sara and Ryan. The baby sat in his highchair munching a graham cracker.

Since the night Mike joined them for dinner, Rose had wracked her brain for ways to pass the time. She read her book club book and watched TV. As much as she could, she helped Sara and Anna Gabraldi in the kitchen. She managed to maneuver her crutches outside, but dared venture no farther than the duck pond. Used to traveling across the country, she found her world had shrunk to claustrophobic proportions.

"I don't blame you for being restless," Sara said. "I'd probably be gnashing my teeth, too..." Her voice trailed off as she gazed out the window over the sink. Then she turned and grinned at Rose. "I think you're about to be rescued."

Maneuvering to stand beside her, Rose leaned over the sink and peered out the window. Traveling along the road from the highway, windows glinting in the sunshine, was an all-too-familiar, silver SUV.

Rose pressed a hand to her lips. Oh, no. Not Mike. Again. Darn him, anyway.

At the same time, her heart took an unexpected leap. "Maybe he's here to see Jackson."

Sara laughed, head shaking. "Yeah, right."

"Well, he could've called first. I'm a mess." Rose let go of one crutch long enough to run fingers through her unruly curls and smooth her blue tunic top over her jeans.

"You look great," Sara said. "Saturday casual."

Moments later, Sara let Mike in the back door. "Mike! What a nice surprise!" She threw Rose a sly glance. "Isn't it, Rose?"

Rose grimaced. "Yeah. I'm so bored even you look good, Mike."

And he did, in more ways than one. Underneath his navy jacket, a white T-shirt contrasted with his tanned skin, and blue jeans hugged his flat stomach and long legs. Rose sucked in a breath and steadied her hands on her crutches.

"I'll take that as a compliment. Good to see you, ladies. And you, too, kid." Mike strode to Ryan and tousled the baby's hair.

"Baa baa." Ryan waved his arms at Mike.

"He's sure growing fast."

"Yes, he is," Sara agreed. "He'll be walking in no time."

"That'll keep you busy." He turned to Rose. "So, how're you doing?" His gaze swept over her, landing on her cast.

Straightening her back and lifting her chin, she said, "Fine, although being useful enough to earn my keep is a challenge. They sure got a bum deal when they took me in."

He raised his eyebrows. "Don't take any chances on hurting yourself more."

Rose huffed. "Always the doctor, aren't you?"

"Where my patients are concerned, yes. But I didn't come here today as doctor."

She'd already guessed that—and was relieved. For one thing, he hadn't brought in his black bag, so there'd be no dreaded checking of the vitals.

Ryan began to cry.

Sara went over and scooped him out of the highchair. "Come on, love, I bet you need changing."

When mother and child disappeared through the doorway into the living room, Rose turned back to Mike. "So, why are you here today?"

"I came to take you away from all this."

"Knight in shining armor rescues damsel in distress?"

"Something like that."

"I'm kinda limited," she hedged. "What did you have in mind?"

Crossing both arms over his chest, he leaned a hip against the kitchen counter. "How about taking a drive? Like I said the other night when I was here, a ride would at least get you out of the house."

Her heart skipped a beat. In truth, a ride sounded wonderful. But was being alone with him a good idea? Given her reactions to him lately, she wasn't sure she trusted herself. She really didn't want to start up anything again.

Correction. Didn't dare.

Still, staying in the house held little appeal. This morning she'd wandered around thinking if she had to spend one more day of confinement, she'd go crazy.

"I'll even feed you," he said. "I brought a lunch."

At his cajoling tone, she tilted her head and narrowed her eyes. "You made a lunch? That doesn't sound like the Mike I know." Secretly, though, she was thrilled he'd planned a special outing.

His mouth twitched with laughter. "You know me well, don't you? No, I didn't fix it; the deli did."

"The Pink Cactus?"

"Of course. Best pastrami sandwiches in town."

"Hah. The *only* pastrami sandwiches in town."

"Right. Anyway, I remembered that's what you like." He rubbed his hands together. "And potato salad, chips...the works."

"Well. How can I say no to all that?"

A scowl crossed his face. "And here I was hoping the clincher would be my irresistible company."

"Dreamer. But okay, you're on. I'll get my jacket."

He edged away from the counter and took a step forward. "Tell me where it is and I'll get it. I'll also let Sara know our plans."

She pointed toward the door leading to the dining room. "Jacket's in the front entryway closet. The beige one. And ask her could she please bring my purse from my room."

"Done."

Ten minutes later, they'd left the Rolling R behind and were cruising along the highway. Rose's gaze swept over the sun-drenched hills dotted with scrub pine and sagebrush, over the majestic snow-capped mountains that surrounded them like protective giants. Then she looked straight ahead, all the way to where the ribbon of road disappeared over the horizon. At last, she was free.

Even so, she couldn't completely relax—her awareness of Mike sitting beside her kept her nerves thrumming. He was so close she could reach out and touch his arm or his knee. But why would she want to do that? *Calm down. This is only a get-together with an old friend.*

Rose focused on the landscape again. She had no idea of their destination, only that they were traveling east. She turned to Mike. "I was so eager for this outing I didn't even ask where we're going."

He accelerated as he passed a slow-moving truck carrying a load of hay then shot her a quick glance. "Where we're headed is a surprise. Relax and enjoy the ride."

Settling back against the seat, she managed to do just that. They even kept up a casual conversation as they drove along.

Presently, Mike took the exit to Glennbrook. They entered the town, cruising down Main Street, where brick buildings dominated, and then along tree-shaded residential streets lined with older frame houses. After a couple more blocks, Mike pulled into a parking lot. Beyond the lot, paths wound through grassy areas dotted with stands of trees and shrubs.

"A park?" Rose said. "I don't remember this."

Mike slipped into one of the vacant spaces and cut the ignition. "That's because it's Glennbrook's *new* city park. I spotted it when I was here for a meeting a couple months ago. Rose would like this, I said to myself. At the time, actually being here with you was far from my mind. But here we are."

Mike's remembering she liked parks gave her a warm feeling. When they were together, visiting city parks was a favorite pastime. Little oases of peace and quiet, they provided the relaxation and serenity both needed from their busy lives.

Rose leaned forward and scanned the area. "It's charming! I love the white picket fence with the roses entwined. And I can see a gazebo from here, too."

"We can eat there, if the walk isn't too much for you."

"I'll make it." The challenge filled her with new energy.

With Mike carrying the paper bag containing

their lunch, and Rose managing her crutches, they made their way along a winding, asphalt path leading to the park's interior. Two gray squirrels shadowed them, dodging behind the towering evergreens and clumps of wildflowers. A light breeze blowing off the distant hills swept the area, cooling Rose's cheeks and tossing her hair about her face.

While crossing a wooden bridge spanning a burbling stream, they paused to lean against the railing and watch ducks glide among lily pads in the water below. Continuing on, they found a play area, where children enjoyed a slide, a merry-go-round, and leather-seated swings. Childish laughter and chatter rang out across the park.

At the gazebo, Rose stopped and stared. "Look at the carved eaves and the purple clematis on the posts. And the little cupola on the top. It's like something out of a storybook."

"I thought you'd like it," he said, grinning ear-to-ear.

With Mike's firm hand on her elbow, she climbed the short flight of steps leading to the gazebo's interior with no trouble. They settled themselves and their lunch on the bench encircling the perimeter.

Mike unpacked the bag, arranging food and utensils on the bench between them.

As he unwrapped the sandwiches, and the aromas of pastrami and cheese reached her nose, Rose's mouth watered. "You couldn't have made a better choice."

He grinned and handed her a paper plate with a sandwich and a scoop of potato salad. "I told you I know how to get on your good side."

While they ate, the conversation skipped from subject to subject, including the new shopping mall in Red Rock and the sightseeing she'd done on a recent trip to Boston. All safe, pleasant topics. Two friends sharing news, bringing each other up-to-date on their respective lives.

As the topic switched to hiking, a pastime they had in common, Mike related an adventure he'd had while on a climb last summer to Garvin's Peak. That led to reminiscing about some of the hikes they'd taken together. One especially humorous account of the time Rose mistook a large misshapen log for a sleeping bear sent them both into gales of laughter.

When the laughter died away, they turned toward each other and their gazes collided. As though a match had been struck, heat sparked then flared between them.

"We had some good times, didn't we?" Mike said.

Afraid he'd read something in her expression, Rose lowered her eyelids and looked away. "Yes, we did."

Long seconds passed while he drank his soda and she took another bite of her sandwich. Finally, she cleared her throat and, in a light tone, said, "So, how's your work going? Everything okay at the clinic?"

"Couldn't be better. David's a great partner and all the docs we've added are easy to get along with. What's really got me going now is the new children's wing at Valley General."

Rose clutched her napkin. Children. Not a good subject. But she nodded and said, "There's been a lot about it in the newspapers and on TV."

"Most of our funding is secured, but we're still raising money. I especially want facilities for teen parents. Like the one I saw in my office the other day. Fifteen and pregnant." He shook his head. "Won't tell her parents. Insists she's going to run away."

Her nerves tensed, the bite of apple sticking in her throat. Now, the conversation had veered into really dangerous territory. "So, ah, what did you do?"

45

"Bit my tongue so I wouldn't lecture her, for starters. You know how I feel about what I call 'irresponsible parenting.'" He cast her a sideways glance.

"Yes, I know," she whispered, her stomach knotting with dread. When they were together before, he'd told her about being abandoned as a baby, and how as a doctor, he especially wanted to help pregnant teens, so that what happened to him wouldn't happen to other babies.

"I did get my patient to talk to Betty Eagle, our resident social worker." Mike paused while he helped himself to another spoonful of potato salad. "She's good. But I wished I'd been sending her to you."

Rose started and her head jerked around to stare. "Me?"

"Yeah." He took a bite of the salad then set down his plastic fork and leaned toward her. "I always wondered why you dropped out when you were going for your Master's in Social Work. You'd make a great counselor."

Lowering her eyelids, she whispered, "No, I wouldn't."

"Why not? You're smart and insightful. You're understanding and sympathetic. You like to help people."

"Being a counselor wasn't for me," she said, shifting her position on the hard bench, still not able to connect with his gaze.

"Your quitting sure shot a hole in my dream that we'd one day be working together. I'd send all my patients who needed counseling to you, especially the unwed mothers."

She cast him a sharp glance. He couldn't possibly know she fit into the very category he thought so little of. No one knew. For fifteen years, she'd carefully kept the secret buried deep inside.

"Why on earth would you think I'd be good with u-unwed m-mothers?" she asked, choking on the words.

"Because as a teenager, you were always so level-headed. You were a good student, serious-minded, and moral, if I may use a word we don't hear much anymore. Yep, you were one straight-arrow kid." He picked up his soda and took a sip. "I always wondered what would've happened if we'd dated in high school instead of waiting until we were older."

Yes, that might have made a difference. A big difference.

"I wanted to take you out then," he continued, his gaze narrowing. "You know that."

A smile touched her lips. "I remember Jackson hinting that you were interested."

"Yep. For a long time, you were my buddy Jackson's little sister. Then one day I saw you differently. I wanted to date you. But you had a crush on the football jock with the wild reputation. What was his name?"

A sharp pain twisted her insides. Rose bit her lip and looked away. A robin settled on one of the gazebo's ornate wooden curlicues. The bird cocked his head and regarded her with a beady eye, then took wing and was gone. She wished she were able to fly away, too.

Mike snapped his fingers. "I remember now. Kurt Fuller."

The mere mention of Kurt's name sent a wave of nausea surging through Rose. She hugged her arms and leaned forward.

Mike continued, "Kurt Fuller, the big man on campus. I can see why he turned your head. A lot of girls would've given anything to have been you, wouldn't they?"

Finally summoning the energy to put the brakes

on this out-of-control conversation, she said through gritted teeth, "Could we not talk about this any more?"

He turned his attention back to her and frowned. "I'm sorry. I didn't think you regretted giving up your counseling career. I thought you were happy working for the railroad."

Despite his apology, she bit out the words. "I'm not sorry. I am happy. So, what's the point in talking about the past?"

"You're right." He blew out a breath. "We'll talk about something else. You pick the subject."

Straightening, she crumpled her paper napkin and stuffed it into the empty paper bag. "I think we'd better go home. My energy's giving out."

On the way home, Rose went through the motions of making small talk, even smiling now and then. She wanted to erase any suspicions Mike might have about why the mention of Kurt Fuller upset her. But her insides churned. She should've known nothing had changed since the last time she and Mike were together.

Two years earlier, when the relationship turned serious and she sensed he was about to propose, she'd agonized over whether or not to tell him her secret. She wanted to, but her mother's strong warning not to tell *anyone, ever*, was cemented into her brain like a brick in a wall.

Then, before she could make a final decision, he told her about his abandonment, his foster parent experiences, and then his adoption. He spoke with great bitterness about his birth parents, especially his birth mother.

After that, Rose feared he would reject her if he knew the truth about her past. For several weeks, she struggled with her dilemma. Finally, she made a decision, not the one she wanted but the one she considered *right*. Telling him she wasn't ready for commitment, she'd broken off their relationship.

Now, if they became seriously involved again, she'd find herself in the same situation as before. What to do? Her stomach twisted with anxiety.

At last, they reached the ranch. Mike parked in front of the house and cut the engine. He turned and in a somber tone said, "I'm sorry if I said anything to upset you. I wanted you to enjoy yourself today."

"I'm sorry I caved in like I did," she said with a calmness that amazed her. "Getting out was a real treat. Thanks so much."

"You're welcome. I promise next time we get together—" He tilted his head. "What? You look really distressed now."

Maybe she hadn't been as calm as she thought. She hesitated, and then said, "Mike, do you think there should be a next time?"

"Of course, I do." He reached out and tipped up her chin, forcing her to meet his gaze. "I could say, 'Doctor's orders,' but I hope we'll get together again because you want to."

The longing reflected in his eyes reached deep inside Rose. At that moment, she knew with all her heart and soul she wanted to be with him. They were so perfect together. Always had been—except for the one thing that kept them apart.

"You do want to come out with me again, don't you, Rose?"

"I—yes, I do," she whispered.

A slow, sexy smile tipped the corners of his lips. "I knew I was right on with that diagnosis."

When he leaned closer, she didn't move away. Softly, gently, his lips barely touched hers. And yet the effect, at first a shiver of delight and then a wave of pure desire, spread all the way down to her toes.

He deepened the kiss, rubbing his lips back and forth over hers. She savored the touch of his warm fingers on her shoulder, the scent of his aftershave, the slight bristle of beard along his jaw. All so familiar and yet at the same time new and exciting.

At last, he drew away. Tucking a wayward curl behind her ear, he let his fingers glide along her cheek. "I promised myself I would go slowly, but I couldn't resist."

She managed a wan smile. "You don't need to apologize. But I'd better go in now." Sitting here with him any longer could only lead to trouble. Edging toward the door, she grabbed the cold metal handle as though she were drowning and it represented her only lifeline.

He laid a hand on her arm. "Sit tight until I come 'round and help you out."

"All right."

"But before you go, here's something to think about." Grasping her chin, he turned her face toward him.

"What?" Her mouth dry, her heartbeat skittering, she raised her gaze to meet his. His eyes were as serious as she'd ever seen them.

"I'm not giving up on us, Rose. *We belong together*. Sooner or later, you're going to realize that, and then we can get on with our lives."

Chapter Four

Half an hour after leaving Rose at the Rolling R, Mike stepped inside his third-floor condo. He tossed his car keys into a copper bowl on the black lacquered table in the entryway and hung his jacket in the closet. Crossing the living room, he opened the sliding glass doors leading to the balcony and went out. A cool, late afternoon breeze swept over the tops of the buildings across the street. In the distance, the mountains were purple silhouettes against a bright blue sky ready for sunset.

Mike paced the length of the balcony for a couple minutes, and then sank onto a yellow padded chair facing the view. Maybe staying out here for a while would calm him.

All the way home, his stomach churned as he replayed the day with Rose. They'd started out on a happy note, laughing and joking and talking. Then, somewhere along the way, everything went to hell in a hand-basket, as his adoptive father, Lloyd Mahoney, used to say.

Something about the past upset her, but what exactly? His questioning why she'd changed her mind about getting a degree in counseling? Mentioning he wanted to date her in high school? Or bringing up the guy she had the crush on, Kurt Fuller?

Could she still have a thing for the big jock? Nah, that was ridiculous. What she and Kurt had was only a teenaged crush. He tunneled a hand through his hair. Whatever, something pushed a button.

When they reached the Rolling R, and she waffled about seeing him again, he nearly panicked. And so, he kissed her. He'd ached to kiss her since that day in the E.R. Holding her in his arms and having her sweet lips on his again had been a dream come true. She responded, too, which gave him new hope.

But then he'd crossed another line when he told her they belonged together. So much for taking their reunion slow and easy.

Mike stood, strode to the railing, and gripped the cold metal bar with new resolve. This time, he wouldn't back down. He would forge ahead and convince Rose that, yes, they did belong together.

Taking one last look at the stalwart mountain peaks, always a source of strength, he turned and went inside.

****

We belong together.

As she lay on the living room sofa, Mike's parting words echoed in Rose's mind. After allowing Mike to accompany her into the house, once the door had closed behind him, she'd collapsed and hadn't moved for half an hour. Physical fatigue was only part of the problem. More exhausting was the roller coaster of emotions she'd experienced, ending with Mike's kiss and his declaration that they belonged together.

Closing her eyes, she took a deep breath, held it, and slowly exhaled. Another, and then another. Deep breathing did little good today, though. Her nerves thrummed as memories crowded her mind. Usually, she could stuff them deep down inside, but today, with her low energy they pushed their way to the surface in living, breathing color.

"Are you okay?"

Rose opened her eyes to find Sara leaning close, her forehead bunched into creases. She'd been so immersed in her misery she hadn't heard her sister-in-law approach. "I am tired," she confessed. Reaching behind her, she tugged at the pillows, and then elbowed herself into a sitting position. Glancing at her watch, she added, "It's not five yet. You're quitting work early."

"Yep. I had a meeting with one of my reps, and when he left, I decided to call it a day. I'm exhausted." Sara sank into an overstuffed chair, leaned back, and stretched out her legs, slim and tan in pink shorts.

"Was it a good meeting?"

"Yes, he's found some new outlets for my products."

"That's great, Sara. Soon you're going to need a larger kitchen."

Sara shook her head. "Some expansion is fine, but I don't want to get too big. I like my cottage industry." She waved a hand. "What about your day? Did you have fun?"

"I did. All the fresh air was great. And the new park in Glennbrook we went to was charming." That was enough to tell Sara. She didn't need to know why the outing had turned sour.

"Looks as though you two may be on your way to getting back together."

"Mike wants us to start over and see if we can make our relationship work this time, but I don't think so. He's a wonderful man, but—" Rose choked as her throat closed. Swallowing hard, she finished, "He's not for me."

"Maybe you feel that way because you have unfinished business to take care of first."

Unfinished business. Sara's words hit a nerve. "Maybe," she conceded.

Sara sat up and leaned forward. "I know it's none of my business, but if you ever want someone to talk to, I'll be glad to listen. And whatever you say wouldn't go any farther than right here." She tapped her chest.

Rose's heart warmed toward her sister-in-law. If she'd been able, she would've run over and given her a hug. Sharing her secret with someone as understanding and sympathetic as Sara would be wonderful. But no way would she ever tell Sara, or anyone, the real reason she'd broken up with Mike. "Thanks, Sara. You're the greatest. I'll keep your offer in mind."

A plaintive wail drifted down from upstairs.

"Oh, oh, naptime's over," Sara said.

Anna Gabraldi appeared in the doorway leading to the kitchen. "Shall I see to him?" she asked Sara.

Concern laced the housekeeper's voice. Usually, Molly Henson took care of Ryan while Sara worked in her bakery. But today, Anna had taken over while Molly and Karli went to a neighbor child's birthday party.

"Thanks, but I'll go." Sara stood and stretched both arms over her head.

Anna nodded. With a tug to straighten her apron, she returned to the kitchen.

"We can always talk more another time," Rose said, secretly relieved to have Sara distracted.

"No pressure," Sara assured her. "Just thought I'd offer." She started across the room, and then detoured to an oak parson's table in front of the picture window. "Oh, I almost forgot. I was cleaning out closets today and I found this." Picking up a large, square book lying next to a row of potted house plants, she turned to Rose.

When Rose recognized the book's brown suede cover, she inwardly cringed. Her old photo album, in which she'd faithfully kept a record of her days at Red Rock High. Just what she didn't need, not when memories of the past were already suffocating her.

"I thought you'd want it." Sara carried the

album over to Rose and held it out.

Lest Sara detect her distress, Rose kept her gaze lowered on the album. "Ah, sure. Put it on the coffee table. I'll look at it later."

Leaning over the coffee table, Sara pushed aside the morning newspaper to make room for the album. "Have fun," she said, and left the room to go upstairs.

Rose lay back against the cushions, wishing she could go to sleep, but jumbled thoughts galloped through her mind like a herd of horses. Despite her vow to ignore the album, keeping her gaze away from its brown cover was a struggle. Finally, she sat up and pulled the book onto her lap. Her fingers ran over the soft suede, rough in places where the nap had worn, and then she lifted the cover.

The album was the old-fashioned kind with velvety black pages and triangular corners to hold the snapshots. Those on the first few pages showed her with three of her friends, Kyra and Jolene and Darla, clowning around at Kyra's house after school. Pretending they were models, they'd struck exotic poses for the camera. What innocents they'd been, so full of hope and promise. She flipped through pictures of them at football games, homecomings, school dances, and parties.

A snapshot of Mike standing in front of his new blue sports car caught her attention. Young and handsome, his face lit with a friendly grin, he posed with feet planted apart and hands on his slim hips. She hadn't paid much attention to him then. He was just Jackson's friend, another big brother who bossed and teased her.

Turning page after page, she relived the past. This wasn't so bad, after all. Some good memories had been preserved here. Then she came to a jagged hole where, in a long ago fit of anger, she'd torn out a picture of her and Kurt Fuller. Ridding the book of the photo hadn't purged his memory. In her mind's eye, she saw him clearly, the day he'd first offered her a ride home...

"Hey, Rose, ya wanna ride home tonight?"

Rose stopped working the combination lock to her locker and turned to see Kurt Fuller towering over her. Broad shoulders filled out his football letterman's jacket. Blond hair glistened with gel, and his square-jawed face showed the hint of golden beard, making him appear older than his eighteen years.

At first, Rose only stared. Then her eyes narrowed. "What about Samantha?" Everyone knew Kurt and Samantha Jennings were a couple. The star football player and the star cheerleader. A cliché, but true.

Kurt leaned one long arm against the adjacent locker. "Sam's skipping today. Anyways, I thought you might like a ride home. Can't be much fun ridin' the bus."

"It gets me there."

To give herself time to think, Rose turned back to the locker and completed the combination. The metal door snapped open. She sorted through the books and papers heaped on the shelf inside. She wanted to go with him, and yet, the idea made her knees tremble.

She grabbed her math book and wheeled around. "What if Sam finds out?"

Kurt dropped his arm and shrugged. "If I don't worry about it, why should you? Come on, time's wasting."

Open-mouthed stares followed them as they left the school building. She could imagine the gossip spreading in their wake, like waves behind a speedboat. She held her head high. Nothing to worry about, Kurt said.

He spoke little on the way home, concentrating

on driving.

The interior of his classic red Camaro smelled of the leather seats, but there was another aroma, too. Rose's nose twitched. Alcohol? Surely, not. Athletes weren't supposed to drink. Her brother Jackson played on the basketball team and was strict about abstaining.

As they turned the corner to her street, Kurt said, "Hear you might make Honor Society."

"I hope so."

"That's cool, Rose. I think I might like a girlfriend who's smart."

Her eyes widened and she stiffened. "Girlfriend? You must be joking. You and Sam—"

"We're over. Done. Through." His lips became so thin they almost disappeared.

Rose fingered the strap on her canvas book bag. "You didn't say that before. You only said she was absent today."

"There you go, worrying again."

"What's going on, Kurt?"

He waved a beefy hand. "I'm giving you a ride home, that's all. Why are you making a big deal out of it?"

"Because this is a big deal to me." Heart pounding, she turned in the seat to stare. "You said you might like someone smart for a girlfriend."

He pulled up in front of her house. Leaving the engine running, he stretched an arm along the back of her seat. "Cute. We're having our first argument." Then he leaned over and kissed her.

Rose scrunched up her shoulders until they nearly reached her earlobes. Then, as his lips slid back and forth over hers, all warm and soft and slightly moist, she went limp and leaned into his body.

"Mmmm, you kiss nice," he said, when he finally pulled away. He tapped the tip of her nose. "See ya tomorrow."

Rose swiped the back of her hand over her burning lips. She yanked open the car door. Clutching her purse and book bag, she stumbled out. Without looking back, she ran up the walk to her house. She hoped no one had seen her from any of the windows, especially the bay window in front, where her mother often sat amid her jungle of houseplants.

Inside, Rose met her mother coming down the hallway, her heels clacking on the highly polished wooden floor. In her slim hands, with their perfectly manicured fingernails, she held a stack of envelopes, probably invitations to her latest party. Her mother thrived on parties, her own as well as those of her friends.

Her mother glanced up. A smile curved her bright red lips. "Hey, honey, you're home. I didn't hear the bus."

Avoiding her mother's gaze, Rose picked an imaginary piece of lint from her denim jacket. "I got a ride with a friend."

"Really? Who?"

"His name's Kurt Fuller."

"Does Jackson know him?"

Rose lifted her chin. "Everybody knows Kurt. He's on the football team."

Her mother smoothed back a lock of her dyed-black hair. "What happened to the nice boy in your chemistry class?"

"Nothing happened to him. He's still there." Rose breezed by and mounted the staircase leading to the second floor. "I'm going to study now."

The first thing Rose did when she reached her room was grab the phone, flop on her canopied bed, and call her best friend, Kyra.

"I'll tell you what I heard," Kyra said when Rose had breathlessly finished her story. "Kurt is teed off because Samantha went out with a guy her brother brought home from college over Spring Break. You probably didn't hear because you always have your head buried in books."

Rose bristled at the dig. "So, I like to keep up my grades. Anyway, Kurt's free now."

"Yeah, and you may be his next girlfriend. Lucky you, Rose."

Lucky, indeed...

The sound of baby laughter and Sara's voice jolted Rose from her memories. She opened her eyes to see Sara, with Ryan snuggled in her arms, enter the room. The baby's hair was tousled and his cheeks were still pink from his nap.

"Look, Ryan, here's your Auntie Rose. Isn't it nice she's come to visit us? Can you give her a big wave?"

"Boo boo," Ryan said, and, with Sara guiding his arm, he waved at Rose.

Rose waved back, her heart warming with love. What a sweet little guy. Yet she could rarely be in his presence without being reminded of her own loss. Today, after the vivid daydream of how it all started, the pain was especially sharp.

Sara nodded at the album in Rose's lap. "Hey, I see you're looking at the photos. Kinda fun to relive old memories, isn't it?"

"Yeah," Rose said with forced brightness. "Fun."

After Sara and Ryan swept off to the kitchen, Rose closed the album and put it back on the coffee table. She didn't particularly want to keep it, but neither did she want to throw it away. At least, not here at the ranch. If Sara or Jackson discovered it in the trash, they would certainly want to know how it got there.

While the past continued to haunt her, the present posed new problems. What was she going to do about Mike? She wanted to see him, but could her nerves take many more sessions such as today? And, what if he found out the truth about the year she'd spent away from home?

****

The following Thursday, Rose sat in Mike's office at the Timber Ridge Medical Clinic waiting for him to return with X-rays of her broken leg. Since their picnic Saturday and the heated kiss they'd shared, she'd been reluctant to face him today. But, unless she wanted to change doctors, she must endure these periodic exams. She needn't have worried, though, for here in his office he wore his doctor's persona as tightly as a glove. And, she'd been spared having him do the dreaded vitals when his nurse, Lucy, took over the chore.

As the minutes ticked by and Mike didn't return, the room began to close in. Sweat beaded her forehead and her hands were clammy. Her gaze roved over the spotless counters and stainless steel sink to the narrow window overlooking the parking lot. The aspen trees planted in dividers sparkled in the bright sunlight. Perhaps if she could see more outside, she would feel better. She was about to grab one of her crutches and wobble to the window when the door opened.

Mike stepped in. A large, flat envelope was tucked under one arm. "Sorry to take so long," he said, flashing an apologetic smile. "One of the docs at the hospital needed a word. But, here are your x-rays." He held up the envelope. "Let's see what we have." He pulled out two sheets of x-ray film. Turning his back, he clipped them to a light box on the wall and switched on the light. The bones of her lower left leg and foot glowed eerily.

Rose focused on the illuminated film, but her gaze kept returning to Mike, roving from his thick hair grazing the collar of his white doctor's jacket, to broad shoulders, to long, sturdy legs planted slightly apart on the tiled floor.

She had the sudden urge to step up behind him, throw her arms around him, and draw him close. He'd turn, smile, and then dip his head and part his lips. She'd raise her mouth to meet his...

"You can see where the break is."

Mike's voice snapped her attention back to the x-rays. His forefinger traced a hair-thin, horizontal line halfway down the larger of the two bones connecting her knee and ankle. "My tibia bone, right?"

He shot her a grin over his shoulder. "Right. I'm impressed."

"I got an 'A' in the anatomy class I took at Denver U."

"Ah, good ol' anatomy class. One of my favorite courses."

She stretched her neck to study the x-ray again. "Is the break healing okay?"

He turned, crossing both arms over his chest. "So far, so good. Like I told you, it's a simple fracture."

"So, I'll be out of this cast in about six more weeks?"

"Should be." He dipped his head and furrowed his brows. "Even so, don't expect to be back to normal right away. You'll need physical therapy. Luckily, we have a good rehab facility at Valley General, and you won't have to go to Denver."

"Will I be able to return to work then?"

"We'll see when the time comes. The tibia is an important weight-bearing bone, so we'll want to be sure you're not putting too much stress on it before it's strong enough."

"So what can I do in the meantime?"

"What you've been doing. Stay off your feet and keep your broken leg elevated." He shut off the light box, and then sat on the swivel stool to make notes on his clipboard.

From her seat across the room, she covertly studied his profile—high forehead, straight nose, firmly set jaw. Her gaze moved down to his long fingers deftly writing the notes. Watching him work reminded her of when they used to study together while he was in med school and she was taking grad courses at Denver U. She always admired his ability to concentrate, his dedication to a task.

He stopped writing and swiveled around. "Okay, that about wraps it up for today—" One eyebrow quirked then he finished in a smooth tone, "Unless you have any more questions?"

Embarrassed to be caught staring, Rose's cheeks burned. "No, I'm ready to go." She straightened and wiggled to the edge of her chair.

"I'll see you again in a couple of weeks," he said, rising and approaching her. "I want to keep an eye on your break and make sure the bone continues to heal okay."

"If you insist," she grumbled.

He grasped her elbow and helped her to stand. Taking her crutches from where they were propped against the wall, he positioned one under each of her arms. "There you go. Steady enough now?"

Rose could barely breathe. *No, not steady with you so near.* "Yes, thanks," she managed to say.

Mike crossed to the door, opened it, and stepped aside for her to leave. "Stop by the nurses' station, and Lucy will set up your next appointment."

Rose hobbled from the room, aiming her crutches toward the semi-circular counter where Mike's nurse sat. The corner of her eye captured him heading in the opposite direction.

The distraction threw her off course, and she nearly collided with a teenage girl. "Oops! Sorry!"

"No problem." The girl teetered a moment then regained her balance.

Rose peered at her. "Glenna?"

"Yup, it's me."

Glenna Jordan's appearance shocked Rose. Usually neatly dressed and well groomed, today her blouse bunched over her jeans, and most of her blond hair had escaped her ponytail and hung like commas around her face. Worst of all, her hazel eyes were red-rimmed and tear-shiny.

Glenna gazed at Rose's cast. "Mom told me about your leg. How're you doing?"

"I'm doing fine. Being laid up hasn't been fun, but I'm thankful for nothing worse than a broken bone." She paused then added, "How're you?"

With a shrug, Glenna lowered her eyelids. "Uh, I'm okay."

Rose didn't think so, and she might've asked more, but just then Lucy called from the open door of an exam room, "We're ready for you, Glenna."

"See ya." Glenna offered Rose a wan smile before turning away.

"Take care." Rose stared after the teen, noting the slump of her shoulders and her bowed head. Yes, something was wrong with Glenna Jordan.

****

"You're awfully quiet," Sara said on the drive home from the clinic. "Did Mike give you bad news?"

Rose shifted her cast to a more comfortable position. "Good and bad. He said my leg is healing okay, but I'll probably need therapy once the cast comes off."

Guiding the car onto the freeway entrance, Sara accelerated to merge with traffic. "I understand your disappointment, but you should follow Mike's advice. He knows best."

Rose heaved a sigh. "I know." Turning away, she gazed out the window at the strip malls populating the outskirts of town. Buildings and asphalt glittered in the blazing sun. Ordinarily, all the sunshine would cheer her, but not today. Today her spirits had sunk to basement level. Not only because of her injury, either. Mike's coolness had left her upset and confused.

His attitude was a complete turn around from when he'd taken her to the park in Glennbrook. She reminded herself that today they'd been in his office, and what did she expect him to do there? Take her in his arms and crush her mouth with hot kisses?

Still, a personal gesture, a word, a touch, a look, would have reassured her he hadn't changed his mind about wanting to get together again.

Wait a minute. Last time she'd checked, she was the one who hesitated to see him. Now, she blamed him for backing off. *Make up your mind, Rose.*

Glimpsing a group of teenaged girls leaving a mall clothing store reminded her of Glenna Jordan. Again, she wondered why the teenager needed an appointment with Mike. She hoped the reason wasn't something serious.

Rose and Glenna's mom, Ellie, belonged to the same book club. When the club met at the Jordans' home, Rose usually stayed afterward to help Ellie clean up. Glenna often emerged from her bedroom to lend a hand, and she and Rose had become acquainted. Seeing the young woman so distressed today troubled Rose. Perhaps she'd find out more when the club met in a couple weeks.

"Almost home."

Sara's statement brought Rose back to the present. Up ahead was the exit that would take them to the Rolling R. "I sure appreciate your driving me into town today," she told her sister-in-law.

Sara flashed a quick smile. "Glad to help you out. Gave me a chance to visit the co-op." She tipped her head toward the back seat full of bags of flour, sugar, and other staples for her bakery.

A few minutes later, Sara pulled to a stop at the Phillips' black metal mailbox. "Flag's down. Looks like the mailman's been here." Reaching out the window, she opened the box and pulled out a handful of envelopes. She passed the stack to Rose. "Take a look and see if there's anything for you. The post office seems to be doing a good job forwarding your mail."

While Sara resumed driving, Rose sorted through the stack of mail. "Hmmm, nothing of great interest. Bills, junk mail...oh, here's something for me." She held up a legal-size envelope. "Wonder what this is. The return address is a local post office box, but not one I recognize."

Sara glanced at the envelope. "Oh, I think I know. Jackson received a similar letter last week."

"Now I'm really curious." Rose slid her finger under the flap and opened the envelope. Pulling out the single sheet of paper, she unfolded it and read, "You're invited to the Red Rock High School All Class Reunion."

"Yep, that's what Jackson got."

"But why am I invited?" Rose wrinkled her forehead. "I didn't graduate from Red Rock."

"It's an all class reunion," Sara said, negotiating a bend in the road, "and anyone who attended high school at any time is included. You'll go, won't you? Jackson and I are. It'll be fun."

Fun? Not likely. Although she'd had a few good friends her first couple years at Red Rock, the trauma of her junior year overshadowed all her pleasant memories. "I think I'll pass," she said. "My cast would make getting around difficult."

"The reunion is in the middle of August," Sara pointed out. "You'll be out of your cast by then."

Studying the invitation, Rose found the date. August sixteenth. The festivities began on a Friday with a reception and lunch at the high school. On

Saturday, there was a dinner-dance at the grange hall. "Oh, I see that," she said. "But, no, I still think I'll skip it."

Sara slid a glance in her direction. "You might change your mind when Mike asks you to go with him to the dinner-dance."

A shock wave rippled through her. Rose's fingers tightened on the invitation. "He told you he was going to ask me?"

"He told Jackson. I hope you'll change your mind when he does. The four of us can go together."

Rose gazed out the window, barely noticing the meadow they were passing, or the cows grazing in the knee-deep grass. So, Mike had the occasion all planned. Even before he asked her, he'd put her on the spot by letting Jackson know his plans. Jackson had told Sara, and the three of them were one step ahead.

Would attending the reunion be so bad, really? Maybe seeing her old friends would be fun.

Then a horrible thought sliced through her mind. Her chest tightened. What if Kurt Fuller happened to be there? The mere thought of him made her quake inside.

She had no idea where he lived now, but he wasn't in Red Rock. Thank goodness. If he lived here, she would have moved years ago. No way could she occupy the same geographic space as Kurt Fuller. What if he decided to return for the reunion? Seeing him again, even after all these years, would be more than she could bear.

Sara's voice cut into her thoughts. "You and Mike knew each other in high school, didn't you? Was there an instant bonding?"

Rose returned the invitation to the envelope and tucked it in her purse. "We knew each other then, yes," she said, careful with her word choices.

"I always had the idea he was your first love."

Sara pulled up to the ranch house and cut the SUV's engine.

"No, he wasn't. He wanted to ask me out, but I was, ah, involved with someone else."

"Really?" Sara's eyebrows shot upward. "What happened to the other guy?"

Rose bit her lower lip as she gazed at the willow tree in the front yard. The drooping branches swayed in the breeze, brushing the old wagon wheel leaning against the tree's trunk. Shifting her mind back to Sara's question, she cringed inside. The conversation had taken a nosedive into dangerous territory. She hesitated on the formation of a noncommittal answer.

"I'm sorry, Rose. I didn't mean to pry."

Rose waved a hand. "No need to apologize. A lot of time has passed since then. I'm well over my teenage crush."

Over the crush, yes, but not the consequences.

Chapter Five

"Hey, Rose, thought I'd call and see how you're doing."

Mike's deep, husky voice, so different from the doctor's crisp tones she'd heard earlier that day, startled Rose. Clutching the cell phone to her ear, she searched her mind for a flippant response. "Why, Mike, you saw me a few hours ago and told me I was doing fine."

His laughter rang over the phone. "Right. But that was a professional meeting and this call is personal." His voice dropped a notch. "Seriously, you doing okay?"

Rose closed her historical novel and settled back into Jackson's comfy leather recliner, where she'd been keeping her leg elevated, as Mike had ordered. On the sofa, Jackson perused the *Red Rock Review*, while Sara and Ryan sat on the floor building a house with Ryan's Legos.

"We're all fine, thanks. Just relaxing after dinner."

"Good to hear."

They chatted a few minutes about the weather and other trivial matters. After a slight pause, he cleared his throat and said, "I do have another reason for calling..."

Assuming he meant inviting her to attend the all class reunion with him, Rose tensed, ready with her carefully composed refusal. "I'm listening."

"How'd you like to go to this Saturday's Rockies game?"

Rose's prepared speech died on her lips. "The

Rockies?"

"Yeah. Knowing how you like baseball, I thought attending a game would make a good outing. They're playing the Seattle Mariners."

Mike was right about her affinity for the sport. Not only did she love to watch the pros play, she played herself—on TransAmerica's team. "Boy, that's a tough invitation to refuse."

"I told you I know how to get your attention."

Noticing the sudden stillness in the room, Rose glanced at Jackson then at Sara. They both nodded and mouthed, "Go, go."

They were ganging up on her again. But Rose couldn't summon the energy to be angry. In truth, his invitation held great appeal. For one thing, the game would demand their attention, leaving little opportunity to fall into a dangerous discussion of the past. For another, attending would be a diversion from sitting around waiting for her leg to heal. Yes, accepting Mike's invitation might work out just fine.

Quit kidding yourself. The real reason you'd say yes is because you want to be with him again.

Rose gave an inward sigh. So true, so true. Since her broken leg had brought them together again, he'd been on her mind. Then she glanced at her cast and frowned. "Getting around Coors Field might be a problem," she told Mike. "I've been there many times, of course, but never on crutches."

"Not to worry. We'll be joining my buddy, Carl Stone, and his wife, Patricia. Carl's company has a suite. We can use the elevator and wheelchairs they provide. You'll be as comfortable as in your own living room."

His consideration gave her a warm feeling. "You've thought of everything, haven't you?"

Mike chuckled. "I'm a good planner."

Something else bothered her, though. Taking a deep breath, she plunged in. "After my appointment today, I thought you might have changed your mind about getting together again."

"No way! My office setting has its own rules, as you well know."

Rose's shoulders sagged with relief. "I do know, but I wasn't sure..."

"Don't worry," he soothed. "We'll get everything straightened out. For now, we'll just have fun."

"Well...all right. I *would* like to go." Glancing at Sara and Jackson, Rose caught them high-fiving each other, and couldn't help chuckling.

"Great. The game starts at one. I'll pick you up around ten. We'll have lunch at the ball park."

"I'll be ready...Oh, Mike, one last thing..."

"Yes?"

Sensing a slight ache in her broken leg, Rose shifted to a more comfortable position. "I saw Glenna Jordan in your clinic today. I know you can't talk about your patients, but she's the daughter of a friend of mine. We belong to a book discussion group, and I've gotten to know Glenna."

"Oh?" A cautious note invaded his voice.

"I hope whatever it is, she'll be okay. She looked awful. Not like her perky self at all."

"Like you said, I can't talk about my patients." He paused then added, "But you and she could talk."

Rose stiffened. "You mean as if I had my counselor's degree, after all? No way. I wouldn't ever practice without a license. You know that."

"You're absolutely right. But what's the harm in talking to her as a friend?"

"None, I suppose. We'll see. The club meets at the Jordans' in a couple weeks. I'm reading the book right now." She absently traced a finger over the book's embossed title on the front cover. "Anyway, if Glenna is home, I'll try to get some time alone with her. She's a sweet girl, and I hate to see her unwell." Rose bit her lower lip.

"So do I," Mike said in a sober tone. "So do I."

****

On Saturday, dressed in jeans, a T-shirt, and with her Rockies baseball cap secured over her ponytail, Rose waited on the porch for Mike to pick her up.

At last, his silver SUV appeared. He parked in front of the house and jumped to the ground. Glancing up, he waved.

Her heart fluttering, she waved back.

He hurried up the walk. Taking the steps two at a time, he soon reached her side. "Hey."

"Hey." She gulped in a breath, suddenly tongue-tied. All she could think about was how sexy he looked in a blue T-shirt and tight-fitting jeans.

Was today's outing really a good idea? Each time she saw him, her attraction grew stronger.

And yet, once they were underway, she marveled at how she could sit so close to him, her pulse skittering, her throat a bit dry, and still carry on a casual conversation.

They talked about the upcoming game for a while, and then he said, "Jackson told me you play for TransAmerica."

"I do when I'm in town."

"What position?"

She lifted her chin and grinned. "Pitcher."

"I bet you're good. Once you're back in the game, I'll come see you play."

"Uh, all right..."

He shot her a glance. "What? You don't think we'll still be seeing each other then?"

If the transfer she'd requested came through, she wouldn't be seeing him anymore *or* playing on the team. "Who knows?" she said, keeping her voice casual. "Let's not think past today, okay?"

"Now you're beginning to sound like me. One day at a time." He grinned and lightly slapped the steering wheel. "But, you're right. I'm set for a good time at the game. How about you?"

Rose made a fist and pumped the air. "Go, Rockies!"

As Mike had promised, getting her to the suite at Coors Field proved an easy task. When they arrived, a group of half a dozen people, including the Stones, were already there. Carl, a stockbroker, was tall and thin. Wire-rimmed glasses gave him a studious look. In contrast, his wife, Patricia, was a plump blonde with a dimpled smile.

"I used to be a broker, too," she told Rose while they ate sandwiches and sipped sodas. "But now, I'm staying home with our twins, Damon and Daphne. They recently turned two and they're a handful." She rolled her eyes.

"I'm sure they keep you busy." Rose mustered a polite smile.

"Do you have kids?" Patricia adjusted the straw in her soda before taking a sip.

To keep the painful twinge in her chest at bay, Rose concentrated on the field below where the Rockies' mascot, "Dinzer" dinosaur, cavorted and postured, psyching up the crowd before the game. "No, I don't."

Carl glanced up from studying his program. "When you do, you'll see what Pat means. They're fun. Wouldn't miss parenting for the world."

Patricia elbowed her husband. "That isn't what you said the other day, when Damon dumped his bowl of soup all over you."

Carl ducked his head. "Yeah, well, I was on my way to a meeting. Otherwise—"

"Otherwise, you would have said, 'Hey, Damon, good boy'? I don't think so."

Becoming more uncomfortable by the minute, Rose squirmed in her seat. She took another bite of her sandwich swallowing hard over a dry throat.

Mike sipped his beer then placed the bottle in the seat's holder. "Don't take this discussion seriously, Rose. Carl and Patricia are great parents. All children should be as lucky as theirs."

"Aw, c'mon, Mike." Carl playfully punched Mike's shoulder.

"No, I mean it," Mike said, raising his hand. "Far too many kids are born to parents who either didn't want them or who have no idea how to care for them. The kids end up neglected or, worse, abandoned. Then they get caught up in the system that often fails them."

"You've got a point." Carl pursed his lips and nodded.

Patricia turned to Rose. "I heard on the news today that a newborn was found in a dumpster." Her eyes rounded. "Can you imagine? What a horrible thing for a mother to do."

A wave of nausea washed over Rose. Clutching her stomach, she leaned forward. "N-no," she managed to mumble. "H-how terrible."

Mike put an arm around her shoulders. "Are you okay, Rose?"

"My leg hurts a little."

"I'll get something to prop it up." He jumped up and hurried to the back of the suite.

Near tears, Rose huddled in her seat, wishing she'd never agreed to come today. The outing had promised to be fun and a distraction from her broken leg, but they'd been here not more than an hour and already the conversation had taken a painful turn. There was no escaping her past. No matter where she went, a reminder lay in wait, ready to leap out and grab her by the throat.

Mike returned, carrying a small wooden footstool. He knelt in front of Rose and placed the stool under her cast. "There. That should help."

"Thanks, Mike." She met his gaze and managed

a wan smile.

He sat beside her and put his arm around her shoulder again.

Comforted by his nearness, she leaned against him, resting her head on his firm shoulder.

"Better now?" he whispered in her ear.

"Yes, thank you."

Mike placed a tender kiss on her forehead. "That's my girl."

Grateful for his help and understanding, even if he didn't know the true cause of her distress, Rose smiled up into his face.

A roar echoed around the stadium, drawing her attention to the field. The players ran out and took their positions.

"Here we go." Carl slapped his program against his palm. "I'm betting on the Rockies, but Patricia's going with the Mariners."

Patricia shrugged and wrinkled her nose. "Seattle's my hometown. What can I say?"

"You're outnumbered here," Mike said. "We're confirmed Rockies' fans. Right, Rose?" He gave her shoulder a squeeze.

"You bet," Rose said, the banter having relaxed the knot in her stomach. As she'd hoped, she soon lost herself in the game. The score seesawed back and forth, with the Mariners leading for a couple innings, but the Rockies finally claiming victory. Exhausted, but in a good way, Rose sank back in her seat.

Mike leaned toward her, his brow wrinkled. "Maybe this was too much for you?"

"No, no." Rose shook her head. "I loved every minute."

"The evening's not over yet," Carl said, holding out Patricia's red jacket. "You're coming to our hotel for a drink, aren't you? We're staying at the Commodore."

"Yes, do come." Patricia slipped into the jacket, adjusting the collar and smoothing the lapels.

Rose's shoulders tensed. Without the game to distract them, would the talk again turn to painful subjects? How many more baby-left-in-the-dumpster stories could she stand? Shooting a tentative glance at Mike, she said, "We have a long drive back..."

"That's why we decided to stay over," Patricia said. "My mother is babysitting the twins."

Mike checked his wristwatch. "It's early yet. We have time. Besides, I'd like you to see The Commodore, Rose. They've remodeled since you and I were there last."

"All right," she conceded. "For a little while."

****

Rose remembered The Commodore as elegant but rather dark and gloomy, with heavy furniture and medieval-style wall sconces. Tonight, due to a new, three-story-high atrium, the lobby glowed with light. Their group settled into comfortable, overstuffed chairs surrounding a burbling fountain and gave their drink orders to a waiter who glided out from behind a chrome-and-glass bar.

Sitting next to Patricia, Rose waited with taut nerves for the twins to make their entrance into the conversation. Thankfully, the Rockies' spectacular win captured everyone's interest instead. Even Patricia conceded her team had been outplayed. Rose finally relaxed and joined in the conversation.

When they finished their drinks, Mike suggested he and Rose be on their way.

Judging by the covert looks Carl and Patricia exchanged, Rose guessed they were eager to be alone. A pang of jealousy stabbed her. They appeared to be such a happy couple, and so very much in love.

A few minutes later, as Rose and Mike headed toward the hotel's front door, Mike said, "Maybe that's what we should have done..."

"What?"

He nodded to where the elevator doors were closing on the other couple. "Planned to stay all night."

Her heart skipped a beat, but she said, with a touch of sarcasm, "Oh, right, with me in this cast."

He skimmed a forefinger down her cheek, blazing a heated trail along her skin. "We wouldn't have to do anything more than be together."

"But I don't think—that is—" Rose swallowed hard, searching for the right words and finding none.

"You're not ready even for that?" A shadow flitted across his eyes then he smiled. "Okay, I'll be patient."

They spoke little on the drive home. Moonlight bathed the highway in silver, and the surrounding mountains cast ghostly shadows over the landscape. The peaceful scene should have calmed Rose, but tension kept her nerves thrumming.

Instead of following the highway to the Rolling R, Mike detoured into Red Rock.

"Where are we going?" Rose asked, wariness creeping into her voice.

"I want to show you my condo."

She'd thought as much and gave an inward sigh. "I'm not staying the night, Mike."

Mike braked for a red light. He turned, his expression solemn in the light's pale glow. "I know. We won't even go inside. I just want you to see where it is."

She gulped in a breath. "W-why?"

"I want you to get to know me again. I bought the place last year. You've never seen it, even from the outside." He slid his fingers down her arm.

A shudder ran through her. She didn't dare look his way, lest their gazes meet and she'd agree to more than just looking at his place. "All right," she murmured.

Mike's condo was in the newer section of town. The three-story, white stucco building occupied half the block. A gated opening led to a parking garage underneath, while the street level housed a florist, a realtor, and an espresso bar, where customers perched on stools at high tables and jazz music streamed out the open door.

"This is pretty fancy for Red Rock," Rose said.

"Yep, I suppose it is. My apartment is on the top floor. It's roomy and modern, and with a view of the mountains." He took her hand and rubbed his thumb over the back.

Warmth zinged along her arm aiming straight for her heart. Another touch, another temptation. Each physical connection they made, however brief, however slight, made her want more. Rose cleared her throat and eased her hand away. "It's getting late."

He tipped up her chin and gazed into her eyes. "Sure you don't want to stay the night? I could give Jackson and Sara a call. They'd understand."

Breath tight in her throat, Rose lowered her eyelids and whispered, "No, Mike. Really. I—I'm sorry."

The seconds crept by. A car pulled into the driveway leading to the underground garage. With a soft whirr, the iron gate lifted, and the car disappeared into the garage.

Finally, Mike eased away his hand. "I'm sorry, too."

Out on the highway, a cloud had covered the moon. Without the moon's silver glow, the landscape turned dark and cold. Rose's stomach churned. Had she made a mistake refusing Mike's offer to stay the night? What harm would there have been in lying in each other's arms? Jackson and Sara wouldn't think ill of her. Most likely, they'd applaud her decision.

But no, she wasn't ready for intimacy.

At last, they arrived at the Rolling R. Mike parked in the ranch house's driveway, and then shifted to face Rose. "I had a great time today."

"Me, too. Thanks for taking me to the game." She spoke the truth. Despite the uncomfortable moments, she had enjoyed the outing.

"My pleasure."

For a few moments, the only sound was the chirping of crickets and the hoot of an owl. Finally, Rose said, "I should go in..."

"Uh uh, not until we say a proper goodnight." Leaning close, he took her face in both hands and closed his mouth over hers.

Wrapping her arms around his neck, Rose gave herself up to the kiss. Heat pooled in the pit of her stomach and spread along her limbs. Time slowed then stood still. The surroundings faded as she floated on a mile-high cloud. As far as she was concerned, the kiss could have gone on forever.

At last, Mike eased away and whispered, "Nice."

His husky tone sent a shiver down her spine.

"Cold?" he asked, drawing her close again.

She laid a hand on his chest to carve some distance between them. "No, I'm fine." Fingering a button on his jacket, she added, "And I *do* have to go in the house now."

Instead of the protest she expected, he laughed lightly.

"Okay, three strikes, and I'm out. Glad our team did better tonight than I did." He gave her cheek a lingering caress, and then sat back. "C'mon, we'll get you into the house."

A few minutes later, crutches securely under her arms, she stood at the living room window until the SUV's taillights disappeared down the road. She ran her tongue over her lips. With only a little imagination, she could experience once again his delicious mouth on hers.

Again, she wondered if she should have seized the opportunities he'd offered for spending the night together. She closed her eyes and shook her head. No. She'd only be sorry afterward. Their relationship couldn't go any farther than it had tonight.

Trouble was, she didn't know if she was strong enough to keep that vow.

Chapter Six

Half an hour after leaving the Rolling R, Mike sat in a booth at Red Rock's Roundup Restaurant nursing a cup of coffee he really didn't need. But, as late as the hour was, he didn't relish going home, either. Sure, as he'd told Rose earlier, he liked his condo. The trouble was he lived there *alone.* After spending most of the day and evening with Rose, being by himself for the rest of the night held little appeal.

Stopping in the restaurant hadn't done much to ease his loneliness. The place was full of people talking and laughing, enjoying one another's company.

He sipped his coffee and turned his thoughts to today's outing. Things had gone well, except for those few awkward moments in the Coors suite when the talk turned to abandoned children. His hackles rose, as they always did when the subject came up. Rose, too, had a strong reaction, curling up as though she were in pain. She said her leg bothered her, but he sensed her distress was more than that. And yet why wouldn't the idea of suffering babies upset her? She was a sensitive, caring person.

Holding her in his arms all night would've been great. He didn't blame her for refusing, but you couldn't blame a guy for trying, either. He was rushing their relationship, but he couldn't help it. They'd already lost two years since their breakup. He clenched his fist, angry at himself for letting so much time go by without contacting her. Not one of the women he'd dated in the interim could compare to Rose.

Tonight she'd kissed him and nestled in his arms as though she belonged there. Which, of course, she did. She was the one. No doubt about that.

If only he could convince her. He would, he vowed, setting his jaw. This time, he wouldn't let her go. Okay, so he still hadn't discovered the real reason she broke up with him before.

Sooner or later, he'd find out, and then he'd help her to heal. He was a healer, after all. He couldn't imagine her problem would affect how he felt about her. His love was strong. Nothing would destroy his love for Rose.

"How 'bout a warm up?"

He glanced up at the twenty-something waitress holding a steaming glass carafe of coffee. Her white blouse, red-fringed felt vest, and red miniskirt hung on her the way they would on a scarecrow. Mike suspected she might be anorexic.

"Sure, Tina, why not?" He slid his empty mug in her direction.

Her brow furrowed in concentration, Tina aimed a stream of coffee into his mug.

"How do you like your job here?" he asked, taking the cup back and warming his hands around it. He'd learned from Tina's talkative mother, who was a patient at the clinic, that Tina and her two small children had left an abusive husband in a neighboring town and moved into the family home.

She heaved a sigh and pushed a wayward strand of stringy brown hair behind her ear. "It's okay. Better 'n what I was doin' before."

He didn't want to ask what that was.

"Soon's I save up enough money, I'll be on my own again. But savin' is hard, with the kids and all." She lowered her eyelids.

"I'm sure it is." Mike lifted the mug to his lips and took a sip. "But you're smart to save as much as you can."

According to Tina's mother, Tina had become pregnant before she married the guy who turned out to be rotten. So, as far as Mike was concerned, part of her problem was her own fault. Tina's children had his sympathy, though. Kids such as Tina's were the main reason the new children's hospital wing was so important.

Shaking his head at his straying thoughts, he said, "Are your kids doing okay?"

She reached up and rubbed her forehead, as if she might have a headache. "Pretty good. Jared's got a cough, though."

"Bring him in to the clinic and we'll see what's going on."

She shook her head. "I don't have much money. I'm only workin' here part-time."

"Don't let that stop you. We'll work something out. Give my nurse, Lucy Alvarez, a call. Make appointments for all of you." Then maybe he could work on Tina's weight problem, too. He reached into an inner jacket pocket, removed one of the clinic's cards, and handed it to her.

She took the card, and a smile lit her thin face. "Thanks. I will."

Mike finished his coffee and decided to call it a night. On the way to the cash register, he spotted a blond-haired teen sitting in a corner booth. He paused to give a second look. Yep. Glenna Jordan. A boy about her age sat across from her. The guy's cloud of black hair hid most of his features. Mike guessed he was the father of Glenna's child and they were discussing the situation. Not too happily, either, judging from the slump of Glenna's shoulders and the bleak look in her eyes.

Gripping his check, Mike fought the urge to go

over and talk some sense into the couple, to help them make the best choices for their unborn child. But, of course, he couldn't. Maintaining boundaries was a downside of his profession. He could go only so far when it came to the decisions his patients made. Much easier to reach people after the fact, as he'd done a few minutes ago with Tina.

Glenna glanced up and spotted him. Her cheeks reddened and she lowered her eyelids.

The boyfriend must've caught her distraction because he jerked his head around. His gaze landed on Mike. As Glenna whispered in his ear, his thick brows furrowed and his lips twisted.

Mike fought the urge to mirror the guy's scowl. Instead, he gave a curt nod and continued on his way.

The next time he saw Glenna in his office, the only place where he *might* have power, he'd try again to convince her to tell her parents about her baby.

****

Rose made another cross-stitch in the kitten's paw, and then held the embroidery hoop at arm's length. Darn, the stitch was crooked. And, was she supposed to use black thread, as she had? Or yellow? She leaned forward to consult the instructions spread on her propped up cast. Neither. The correct color was brown.

She stabbed the needle into the cotton fabric and tossed the hoop onto the table beside her chair. Embroidery wasn't her thing. Never was and never would be. She should have been honest when Anna Gabraldi offered her the dishtowel embroidery kit, but she hadn't wanted to hurt the housekeeper's feelings, knowing she'd only wanted to help Rose pass the time.

A throb pulsed in her calf, and she shifted to a more comfortable position. If she didn't get out of this cast soon, she would explode. She felt even more confined today here in the family room than she did at her usual post on the porch, but a rainstorm prevented her from sitting outside. She raised her gaze to the window. Dark clouds covered the sky, matching her mood. She sighed, and as she settled back against the cushions, her gaze fell on the coffee table, where her old photo album still sat, a grim reminder of the origin of all her troubles.

No, she didn't want to look at the photos again. She'd be better off watching TV or reading. And yet, as if controlled by a force outside herself, she leaned forward and picked up the album. Dragging it onto her lap, she let it fall open and found herself at the very place she'd left off when she'd looked at the book a few days ago. She ran her finger around the jagged hole where she'd torn out the photo of her and Kurt Fuller.

She hadn't destroyed all his photos, though. On the next page were pictures of a graduation party they'd attended at the home of one of his friends. The shots of partygoers clowning around in the swimming pool made her smile. How excited she'd been to go on their first real date. Not even Kurt's former girlfriend, Samantha's, presence spoiled Rose's enjoyment. Sam and Kurt ignored each other, and Rose figured their relationship was over.

Yes, the party was fun. What happened afterward wasn't. What happened then had changed her life forever. Thankfully, no photos recorded the event, but Rose didn't need them. She could close her eyes and with no effort at all play back those hours in living, breathing color...

"Try it, Rose. Don't be such a chicken." Kurt had held out the joint between his thumb and forefinger.

The sweet smell of marijuana filled Rose's nostrils, and she jerked away her head. "No, Kurt, I don't want to, and I wish you wouldn't either. Let's go home."

They sat in the back seat of his car atop the bluff overlooking Red Rock. The setting sun cast a pale pink glow over the landscape. One by one, lights in town twinkled on.

"What's the hurry?" he drawled. "I thought your curfew was midnight?" He took a drag from the joint then blew out a circle of smoke.

"It is, but my folks know the party must be over by now."

"So? Tell 'em we went for a ride afterward. That's the truth, isn't it?"

Guilt pulled at her conscience. "I wouldn't exactly call this riding."

Kurt tossed back his head and laughed. "You are so funny!" Then he sobered and poked the joint between her lips. "Come on, Rosie, time to bite the bullet. Ha ha."

Tired of arguing and admittedly curious, Rose closed her lips around the cigarette and sucked in a breath. Smoke flooded her mouth, burning the back of her throat. She choked and coughed it out. "Yuk!"

"Let the smoke go down your throat," Kurt said. "Come on, try again."

Rose inhaled, and this time she let the smoke glide over her tongue and down her throat.

"Now blow it out," Kurt instructed.

A thin stream of smoke floated out her mouth and into the air.

"There ya go! I knew you could do it."

Pleased at his compliment, she leaned back against the seat and grinned. "That wasn't so hard."

"Told ya."

Paper rustled as he dug into a sack on the floor and pulled out a bottle of beer. He twisted off the cap and tossed it out the window. Raising the bottle to his lips, he leaned his head back and took several swallows.

He handed the beer to her. "Bet you haven't had booze before."

"Yes, I have," she said, jutting her jaw. "Lots of times." She spoke the truth. Sometimes when her parents poured themselves a drink and then turned their backs, she sneaked a sip.

She grasped the bottle, still wet with condensation, and drank. She was thirsty and it tasted good. After a few sips, she handed the bottle back to Kurt and wiped her hand on her jeans. She gazed at his profile while he drank. He was so handsome. High forehead, strong nose, full lips in a perpetual, sexy pout, kind of like Elvis on her parents' old record albums.

Was she in love with Kurt? She'd never been in love before, but now she had such a wonderful, light feeling. With no effort at all, she could float right out the car window and off into the twilight sky. What else could such a feeling be but love?

Kurt passed her the joint.

Without hesitation, she poked it in her mouth and took a drag. Smoking was fun, after all.

"Good combo, huh?" Kurt said.

"Yeah, it is."

Leaning over the front seat, he switched on the ignition, then the radio. They sat there listening to rock music and smoking and drinking.

Rose lost count of how many drags she had on the joint, or how many sips from the bottle. She gazed out the window. The sky was very mellow now, all soft pinks and yellows and shades of rose. Rose, like her name, and mellow, like she felt inside. She turned to Kurt and reach for the joint.

He clamped his hand over hers. "Uh uh. Too much puts you outta commission. We don't want that."

He tossed the joint stub out the window, followed by the empty beer bottle. The bottle hit the ground with a dull clunk. Grabbing her shoulders, he pulled her to him and kissed her hard on the mouth.

And when he wanted to go farther, she let him...

Still, when the act was over and she'd managed to pull her jeans back on, her head was so muddled she wondered if what she'd thought happened really had. Maybe she'd been dreaming, and all they'd actually done was sit there in the back seat of the car smoking and drinking and listening to music.

When Kurt dropped her off at home, she'd returned to her senses enough to worry about Mom and Dad finding out what she'd been doing. Her clothes reeked of the joint and the beer, and, she was sure, of the sex, as well.

Hoping to escape undetected to her room upstairs, she crept into the house. However, as she passed the open door of the den, her father, sitting in his favorite chair reading a golfing magazine, glanced up.

"Hi, honey," he said cheerily. "Glad you're home. I've been lonely. Mom's at bridge club and Jackson's at basketball practice."

Rose mumbled something, and then fled, stumbling up the stairs and down the dark hallway to her room. She slammed the door shut and fell onto the bed, her stomach churning with nausea. She had made her way to the bathroom just in time to throw up in the toilet...

Rose's eyelids fluttered open. Her surroundings gradually sharpened into focus. No, she wasn't in her old room in her parents' house, but sitting in Jackson's living room at the Rolling R. She clutched her stomach, experiencing the same nausea she'd had that night so long ago.

Her cell phone rang. Welcoming the interruption, she shoved the album onto the coffee table and grabbed the phone lying nearby. Mike's number flashed on the caller ID.

After they exchanged greetings, he said, "I had a break between patients and wanted to check in, see how're you're doing."

"I'm resting a lot, like the doctor ordered."

"Good for you. How's the leg?"

She absently picked at a piece of lint on the cast. "Still attached."

He laughed. "I'm glad you've kept your sense of humor about this."

Rose stifled a sob. If he only knew how close to tears she was. She waited, knowing there was more to this call than a simple "how're you doing?"

"How about dinner Saturday night?"

Dinner. Saturday. She ran a hand over her forehead, struggling to focus. "Ah, sorry, I have book club that night." Her gaze fell on the historical novel lying next to the album. She still had a few chapters left to read. Why hadn't she been reading instead of looking at the album? Then she would've saved herself a lot of grief.

"I know. You told me a couple weeks ago your club would be meeting soon. When Jackson and I were discussing our upcoming basketball game on Saturday night, he mentioned he'd be bringing you into town for your meeting. But I'll come get you at the ranch instead and we'll have dinner first. Does four-thirty work for you?"

"Wait a minute," she said, her head spinning. "I haven't said yes."

His laughter rang in her ear. "Go ahead, then. I'm listening."

She couldn't help matching his laugh. "Mike, Mike, I don't know what I'm going to do with you."

"I can think of several things..." His voice dropped a notch.

Hearing the playful leer in his voice, she blurted out, "Never mind! You win. I'll see you on Saturday."

After they ended the call, Rose replaced her cell phone on the coffee table. Emotionally exhausted, she sagged against the cushions. Mike went to great lengths to provide opportunities for them to spend time together. Refusing him was difficult.

Not that she wanted to refuse. Even though they'd spent most of yesterday together—and not without some tense moments—she ached to see him again. Since her broken leg had brought them together, she'd become accustomed to his calls, his presence. With a sigh, she pressed her fingers against her lips. And, yes, his kisses, too. When the time came for them part—and it *would* come, when her transfer came through, if for no other reason— she'd have to again say good-bye.

Telling him about her past was still out of the question. He'd surely reject her, and, besides, she'd promised her mother she'd keep the secret forever.

Guilt lumped in her stomach. To keep seeing Mike wasn't fair to either of them. And yet, when she heard his voice, or saw him, *or kissed him*, all her reasoning fled.

****

"Dominic's isn't the fanciest restaurant I could take you to tonight." Mike gestured to the establishment's front door. "But it has great historic importance."

Rose gazed at Dominic's, tucked between Jake's Barber Shop and Henson's Office Supplies. If you weren't looking for it, you might miss the place. The Greek fare was excellent, though, and the eatery never lacked customers. She'd been there countless times, with Mike, and other friends. Still, she had no idea what Mike was talking about tonight.

Wrinkling her brow, she turned. "I'm sorry, you'll have to tell me why it's so important."

The light faded from his eyes. "You really don't remember?"

She shrugged and shifted her weight on her crutches. "I know we used to come here a lot."

"You're on the right track." Mike stepped aside to let a noisy group pass by. "This is where we had our first date. Our first *official* date, where I formally asked you out and you accepted."

The memory surfaced, and Rose smiled. "Oh, yes, I remember now. We had dinner here and then went to see a movie."

He patted her arm. "Right. I knew you'd remember." Opening the door, he waved her inside.

While his sentimentality warmed her heart, Rose wondered if a trip down memory lane was a good idea. Bringing up the past usually caused trouble.

Determined that would not be the case tonight, she lifted her chin and aimed her crutches for the open doorway.

Inside, the restaurant's owner, Dominic Spanos, stepped from behind the reception counter. His round face lit up with a smile. "Ah, Dr. Mike." His gaze moved to Rose. "And Rose—what's this?" He nodded at her cast.

Rose explained her injury, while Dom solemnly shook his head and "tsk-tsked."

"Got a nice, quiet table for us?" Mike asked, keeping his hand on Rose's elbow.

Dom's black mustache curved upward as he broke into a grin. "You bet, Dr. Mike."

He grabbed a couple menus and swept them past several potted plants to a row of green vinyl booths against one wall. From the kitchen came the clatter of plates, the sizzle of a grill, and voices speaking in Greek—not a word of which Rose understood. She breathed in the delicious smells floating on the air—saffron and turmeric, and beef and lamb, and of course, the ever-pervasive olive oil.

Dominic seated them underneath a colorful

mural of Greek goddesses feeding purple grapes to a bearded Greek god, probably Zeus himself, judging by his golden crown.

As Dom handed them the menus, he looked from Mike to Rose. "Nice to see you two again. Enjoy your meals." He made a slight bow, and then left.

Rose's gaze followed Dom for a couple seconds then she turned to Mike. "Does everyone know our history?"

Mike arched an eyebrow. "My coming here without you was pretty obvious."

She cast him a skeptical glance over her menu. "Don't tell me you were always alone?"

"Well...I may have had company a time or two. But no one who lasted. No one who could compare to you." He pinned her with his gaze.

Rose squirmed in her seat. "Maybe you don't know the real me," she blurted, and then wished she could take back the words. What on earth had possessed her?

"Oh, yes, I do know you," he said in a husky voice.

Clearing her throat, she focused on the menu. "I wonder what tonight's special is?"

A discussion of what to order eased Rose's tension. They finally settled on *dolmades* for appetizers and *moussaka* for the entree.

"Find any good Greek restaurants on your travels?" Mike asked when the waiter had taken their order.

Rose nodded, relieved the conversation was off to a safe topic. "Several in New York City, as one might expect—but none any better than this one."

"Good to know. The more there is to keep you here the better."

"Red Rock is my home. Leaving will—*would*—be sad." Her correction came too late. Once again, she'd opened a door to a subject she didn't want to discuss.

Alarm flared in his eyes, and he leaned forward. "Leaving? What's that all about?"

Rose bit her lip. Should she tell him she'd asked for a transfer? But why, when it wasn't yet a reality? And, even if a new position were offered now, she couldn't accept it, not with her leg in a cast. She shrugged, as though the matter were of little importance. "In my line of work, transfers are sometimes called for."

A frown knit his brow. "You can always turn them down."

"Let's not worry tonight about my leaving," she said with a dismissive wave. "I'm not going anywhere soon, that's for sure." She nodded at her leg, sticking out from under the table at an awkward angle. "And, you're the one who said getting together while my leg heals didn't mean we needed to plan the rest of our lives."

Mike hunched his shoulders and ducked, as though to dodge something she'd thrown his way. "Ouch. Thanks for the reminder. I tend to get impatient sometimes about something I want."

The *dolmades* arrived. The rice was fragrant and spicy, the grape leaf wrappings tender and succulent. They dug into them, while Greek zither music played in the background. They talked about the Rockies' latest game, the upcoming city council election, the highway repairs that had traffic in turmoil.

An hour later, Rose drained the last drop of strong Greek coffee from her *demitasse* cup. She leaned back and patted her full stomach. "Everything was wonderful."

"Including the company?" Mike's lips twitched with teasing.

"Of course. I always have a good time with you."

He picked up the check and reached in his back pocket for his wallet. "Then what was the problem?"

His sudden change of tone put her on alert. "The problem?"

"With us. Two years ago."

Rose stiffened. Just when she'd relaxed, he threw her a curve. She should know better than to let her guard down. But, the delicious food, the cozy atmosphere, and the casual talk had wrapped around her like a warm, safe cocoon. She must remember there was no safety, ever, when she was with Mike.

She carefully folded her napkin and laid it by her plate. With a sideways glance, she said, "I was too young to get engaged?"

He leveled her a frown. "Okay, funny girl. You're off the hook this time, because we need to go. But, sooner or later, you're going to tell me the real reason. You owe it to me."

Later, as they drove through the downtown streets, Mike's words, "You owe it to me," echoed in Rose's mind.

He was right; she did owe him a better explanation than the one she'd given him at the time, which was something vague about "not being ready for commitment."

With all her heart, she wished she could tell him the truth. But even imagining his rejection made her insides quake. Wasn't keeping quiet the best course of action? As soon as her cast came off and she returned to her job, she'd be able to escape again.

Chapter Seven

"So glad you could make the meeting tonight!" Silhouetted in the doorway of her Aspen Hills home, Ellie Jordan greeted Rose.

Rose carefully set her crutches on the stone doorsill and lifted herself up. "I'm glad, too. I've been looking forward to seeing everyone again."

Ellie stood on tiptoes to peer over Rose's shoulder. "Is that Dr. Mike?"

"Sure is." Mike stepped from the shadows into the light cast by the round globes on either side of the door. "Hi, Ellie."

"I thought Jackson was bringing you." Ellie stood aside to let them enter the house.

"Mike's been taking his doctor's duties *really* seriously," Rose said.

"I see." Ellie raised her eyebrows. "Lucky you."

Mike handed Rose's yellow vinyl tote to Ellie. "Yep, gotta make sure my patient gets good care."

As soon as Mike left, Ellie turned to Rose, her eyes sparkling. "Are you two, um, back together?"

Rose hesitated then said, "We're just friends." Although Ellie had been her confidant on some matters, Rose was not ready to discuss her and Mike's current situation with anyone.

Ellie's pink mouth turned down. "Too bad. I always thought you were a perfect match."

Ellie, who was a size five, and who lived in this exclusive neighborhood, and whose husband's salary was in six figures, always made Rose think of the saying, "You can never be too rich or too thin."

And yet she liked the woman. During the two

years the book club had met, they'd become fast friends. When Rose was in town, they'd sometimes meet for lunch or coffee. Rose had attended several of the Jordans' dinner parties, as well.

Ellie led Rose through a living room furnished in beiges and off-whites to the dining room. "Since you're the first to arrive, you get first choice of seats."

Rose surveyed the rectangular table covered with a white cloth and set with silverware, napkins, and Delft pottery dessert plates. "I'll take the end one. Then I can keep my cast out of everyone's way."

"Good idea." Ellie hung Rose's tote over the back of her chair.

Rose gazed around. "Where's Glenna?"

"In her room." Ellie shook her head. "Didn't even want to help me bake the carrot cake for tonight. Normally, she loves to bake."

"I know she does." She'd often seen Glenna in the kitchen whipping up a batch of cookies or a cake. "I hope she's not sick."

Ellie wrinkled her forehead. "Not that I know of. I can't get much out of her, but I think she might be having boyfriend trouble. I never thought Tony was right for her. I wish she'd break up with him." Her chest heaved in an exaggerated sigh. "But who am I to tell her what to do? I'm only her mother." She held out her hands. "Here, let me have your crutches."

Rose eased into her chair and handed over her crutches.

Ellie propped them against the wall. "Can I get you a cup of coffee?" She gestured to a teakwood sideboard where Delftware cups, a silver urn, and a sugar and creamer were on display.

"Sounds good."

"Maybe you can talk to Glenna?" Ellie held a cup under the urn's spigot and the smell of the fresh brew filled the air. "She likes you. Sometimes, I think you'd make a better mother to her than me."

Rose winced. "Ellie, no!" Taking a deep breath, she added in a calmer tone, "You're a good mother."

Ellie set the coffee in front of Rose. "I try to be a good parent. So does Len. But since he made partner in the law firm, he works longer hours than ever. He's under a lot of stress, too. Which doesn't help his temper any."

The doorbell chimed.

"Excuse me," Ellie said and hurried from the room.

Talk and laughter floated in from the living room, and then the three remaining members of their group swept into the dining room. They all leaned down to give Rose hugs and cheery greetings. Rose smiled up at them with delight. Although they'd exchanged phone calls since the train accident, she'd missed these women friends.

After a few minutes of settling in with coffee and catch-up conversation, they turned to discussing the book. Although Rose entered in with vigor, worry about Glenna hovered at the back of her mind. When the discussion was finally over, the last bite of carrot cake eaten, and the book for their next meeting chosen, the women said their good-byes and left.

"I guess you're stuck with me until Mike gets here," Rose told Ellie. "Sorry I can't be much help cleaning up tonight."

Ellie loaded the plates, cups, and silverware onto a wooden tray. "Not to worry. I'm glad to have your company. Tonight's Len's poker night, and he won't be home until midnight." She paused to slide Rose a glance. "Why don't you peek in on Glenna? I'm sure she'd like to see you."

Rose smiled to herself. Just the opening she'd hoped for. "I'd like to do that. I'll miss doing dishes with her tonight."

"I admit I *am* worried about her. I plan to set up

an appointment with Dr. Mike. Maybe he can figure out what's going on. Maybe she's anemic or something."

Fearing even the slightest response might give away what she knew, Rose kept her mouth closed and her gaze averted. Obviously, Glenna hadn't told her mother she'd already seen Mike. That sounded ominous. A niggling suspicion crept into Rose's mind. "I'll go say 'hi' to her," she said.

Ellie handed Rose her crutches, and she hobbled off down the hallway. The door to Glenna's room was closed. Rose hesitated. Did she really want to bother the girl? Perhaps she was sleeping. No, having come this far, she'd make an effort to at least say "hello."

She tapped her knuckles on the door. "Glenna. It's me, Rose."

Glenna opened the door. "Oh, Rose! I heard you coming down the hall and hoped you were coming to see me."

Rose stifled a gasp. Glenna looked even worse than when Rose had seen her at Mike's office. Her eyes were red-rimmed, and her cheeks, usually pink and healthy, were sunken, throwing her cheekbones into prominence.

"Your mom said you weren't feeling well, but I wanted to at least say 'hi.'"

Glenna peered around her down the hallway. "Mom isn't with you, is she?"

"No, she's cleaning up."

"Come in, then." Glenna opened the door wider.

After stepping a few feet into the room, Rose turned to face Glenna. "Is something wrong? I'm worried about you. So is your mom."

Closing the door and leaning against it, Glenna steadily eyed Rose. "If I tell you, you have to promise not to tell Mom. Or anyone."

Rose tightened her grip on her crutches. She'd been expecting the caveat. "Sorry, I can't make that promise."

"Why not? I thought you were my friend."

Glenna's stricken look tugged at Rose's resolve. Keeping her tone gentle, she said, "I am. But what you tell me might be dangerous to you or to others. If I kept your secret and something bad happened, I'd be responsible. Wouldn't I?" She waited, wondering if adult logic would sway Glenna or only alienate her.

Crossing to the unmade bed, Glenna pushed the bedclothes aside and slumped down. She put her head in her hands and began to cry.

Rose's heart wrenched. She hobbled to the bed. Careful to keep her balance, she took a hand from her crutch and patted Glenna's trembling shoulder. "Are you pregnant, Glenna?"

Glenna stiffened.

Rose feared she'd ruined the trust and friendship the two shared. But then Glenna went limp again and the tears flowed even harder than before.

Rose's crutches clattered to the floor as she dropped them and sank down beside Glenna. Putting her arms around her, she rubbed her back and made soothing noises. Minutes passed. Not having been in Glenna's room before, Rose gazed idly around. Posters of rock stars, a Red Rock High pennant, and a make-up set on the dresser reflected a typical teen. Yet, a doll collection, various stuffed animals, and a stack of picture books indicated that, at least some of the time, the room's occupant was still a child.

At last, Glenna shifted on the bed and raised her tear-stained face. "Yes, I am pregnant. But I can't tell my parents. I just can't. Especially not Dad. He'd kill me. Do you understand, Rose?"

Her heart heavy, Rose squeezed Glenna's shoulder. "I do. Believe me, I do." *More than you know, more than I dare admit.* "What about Tony? He's the father, isn't he? Does he know about the baby?"

"Yes, I finally told him. Dr. Mike thinks I should tell Mom and Dad. What do you think?"

Rose's chest tightened. How could she, of all people, give advice to a pregnant teen? "Parents are generally the best ones to help at a time like this," she hedged, then cringed, knowing how lame her answer must sound.

"Not my parents!" Shaking her head, Glenna balled her hands into fists. "They'll be sooo angry. Mom'll say how embarrassed she'll be when all her friends find out. She'll throw up her hands and tell Dad, 'You handle this.' And he'll yell at me. He has an awful temper." Fresh tears rolled down her cheeks.

Rose grabbed a tissue from a box on the nightstand and handed it to Glenna. "Maybe they'll surprise you and be supportive. Even your dad might handle it better than you think."

Glenna took the tissue and swiped at her wet cheeks. "I'm going to run away."

Run away. Rose closed her eyes against the memories flooding her mind. "No, no! Don't do that. Talk to someone."

"I am talking to someone—you."

"I mean, someone professional. What about the counselor in Dr. Mike's office?"

Glenna crumpled the tissue in her hands. "Yeah. Ms. Eagle. I saw her, once. She's nice, but she just said to tell my parents."

"That might be the best advice you'll get from anyone. But what do you want to do about your baby?" Rose brushed strands of hair from Glenna's cheek.

"Oh, Rose, I want to keep it!" Glenna's eyes shone through her tears.

Instinctively, Rose knew that would be the teen's answer. "But how can you take care of a baby?"

"I'll figure out some way."

The urge to tell Glenna her own story gripped Rose. Dare she? Would knowing what had happened to a young girl fifteen years ago in a similar situation help Glenna?

She'd never told anyone, not a soul. Maybe now the time had come...

Rose's heart thudded. "Glenna—"

Footsteps sounded along the hallway. A knock on the door. "Rose?" Ellie called. "Mike's here."

Rose whooshed out a breath. No time to tell Glenna now, even if she wanted to.

"I'll be right there, Ellie!" She turned to Glenna. "Please, promise me you won't do anything rash— like running away—until you give your situation some more thought."

Glenna scowled, but she said, "Well...okay. You won't tell my parents, though, will you?"

Rose hesitated, her conscience telling her that, despite their response, Glenna's parents should know about their daughter's condition. But she didn't want to destroy Glenna's trust in her, either. She finally said, "No, I won't. That's for you to do. But keep on seeing Dr. Mike and Ms. Eagle, too. Taking care of yourself and your baby is important."

"I will."

"We can talk again whenever you want. I'll give you my cell number."

Her scowl eased into a smile. "Really? That'd be cool."

Crossing to her desk, Glenna dug out her cell phone from under a pile of books and papers. She added Rose's number to her speed dial then wrote her own number on a slip of paper and gave it to Rose.

Rose tucked the paper into her slacks' pocket. She stood and gave Glenna a hug. "'Bye now, sweetie. And remember, I'm just a call away."

****

"Good discussion?" Mike asked when they were on their way home, the moon beaming down from a blue-black sky.

Her mind full of her visit with Glenna, Rose took a moment to focus on Mike's question. "Yeah, it was great to be with the group again."

"Did you see Glenna?"

"Not until after the meeting when I went to her room. We talked for a while."

He shot her a glance. "She tell you what's going on?"

"Not at first. But when I asked her if she was pregnant, she admitted she was. That's why she was in your office, isn't it?"

Mike accelerated up the freeway entrance ramp, sliding into place behind a car merging from the adjacent lane. "You know I can't violate a patient's privacy. But, since that's what she told you, I hope you urged her to confide in her parents."

She bristled at his authoritative tone, his assuming she would handle the situation the same way he would. "I said I thought they were probably the best source of hclp at a time like this. Mostly, I listened and sympathized."

"Sympathized? Isn't that the same as condoning?"

"Not necessarily."

"So what did you tell her? Or am I violating a confidence?"

"If you must know," Rose began, irritation edging her voice, "I advised her to keep seeing you, and Betty Eagle, and to think about telling her parents."

"Think about!" He slapped a palm against the

steering wheel. "Of course, she should tell them. Tonight when I picked you up, and Ellie said she wanted to make an appointment for Glenna, I had a heckuva time not admitting I'd already seen Glenna. Keeping doctor-patient confidentiality in a situation like this is rough."

"I'm sure it must be," she murmured, wishing they'd never started this conversation. Shifting away, she gazed out the window at the landscape rushing by. They were in the country now. Except for an occasional light from a distant farmhouse and the swath of silver moonlight, darkness spread over the land like a soft blanket.

After five minutes elapsed without another word from either of them, she considered the subject closed. Taking a deep breath, she laid her head back against the seat.

"So how'd you leave it with Glenna?"

His sharp tone grated. "We exchanged cell numbers and I told her to call me if she needed to talk. Does that suit you?"

"If it's the best you can do."

Rose bit back a retort and stared out the window again.

At last, they exited onto the road leading to the Rolling R. When they reached the ranch house, Mike pulled to a stop. Rose welcomed the lights glowing from the porch and from the rooms inside. They promised warmth and safety—and escape.

He cut the engine and turned, his eyes bleak. "I'm sorry I jumped on you, Rose. But you know this kind of situation really pushes my buttons."

Mine, too, she almost said, but swallowed the words in time. "I know," she said instead.

"I thought you could help Glenna." He softened his tone. "In so many ways, my hands are tied."

Her irritation melted away. He cared about Glenna and her unborn child just as he cared about all his patients. He couldn't know Rose was the wrong person to help Glenna.

Then you should tell him.

And, for the second time that evening, the urge to break her long-held silence goaded Rose. And, yes, Mike would reject her when he knew the truth. But she'd be free of the burden she'd carried all these years. Swallowing hard, she began, "Mike, I—"

He laid a forefinger against her lips. "Hey, no more about Glenna. The last thing I want to do is ruin what's going on between you and me." Grasping her hand, he buried his lips in her palm.

Rose struggled against the warm tingles his touch ignited. "This isn't about—"

He raised his head and tipped up her chin. "Rose, the past few weeks have been great. I've been happier than I've been in a long time. You've been happy, too. Haven't you?"

"We've had some good times," she hedged, gritting her teeth to keep from blurting out her true feelings.

"But not good enough to—oh, hell, I don't want to push you."

"Yes, you do." The words finally rushed out. "You're always pushing me, trying to make me into someone I'm not. Someone I can't be."

"Rose, honey, no. I know what you are. You are as perfect as any woman can be." He leaned forward and brushed his lips across her cheek, and then settled his mouth over hers.

Her muscles stiffened, but soon the warmth of his kiss spread like liquid fire through her veins, and she went limp in his arms. He drew her closer and deepened the kiss. Unable to resist, she opened her mouth and their breaths mingled, their tongues danced. For long moments, she was lost to time and place, conscious only of Mike, his nearness, his kiss.

At last, he drew away and pressed his forehead

to hers.

"Oh, Mike, what—"

He slid a finger over her lips. "You don't have to say anything. I know what I know. I told you before, Rose, and I'll tell you again. We belong together."

****

Long after she was in bed, Rose lay awake thinking about her and Mike's unpleasant disagreement over Glenna. Of course, she cared about the teen and what happened to her, as much as Mike did. They just differed in their opinions of how to help.

Mike was convinced Glenna should tell her parents, and perhaps she should. But Rose hadn't been able to back Mike as solidly as he would have liked. She recalled another teen in trouble who'd sought her parents' help with tragic results. With little effort, she could turn back the clock and be that scared girl in trouble...

"Kurt Fuller did this to you?" Hands on her hips, her face mottled with anger, Rose's mother loomed over her.

Rose scrunched her shoulders and shrank back against the bedpost. "He didn't do it *to me*, Mom. We did it together."

"That's ridiculous. You're underage. We should have him arrested."

"Oh, no, Mom, please!"

"Don't worry, I'm not going to do that. Then everyone would know. But you're sure?"

"I'm sure." Rose twisted both hands together in her lap. "I took two of those pregnancy tests. They both showed positive."

"You haven't told Kurt, have you?"

Rose lowered her eyelids under her mother's fierce glare. "N-no, I haven't told him. He went back to his girlfriend, Samantha. And now he's at football camp. In the fall, he's attending a college in

California that gave him a scholarship." She glanced up. "But, Mom, I want to have my baby anyway."

"Oh, you'll have it." Her mother crossed both arms over her chest and lifted her chin. "Abortion is against our beliefs."

Rose's shoulders sagged with relief. She'd known that, but, under the circumstances, she feared her mother might've changed her mind.

"I want to keep it, too," she said, amazed at her boldness in the face of her mother's anger.

"Absolutely not!"

Her mother's shrill voice hurt Rose's ears. Good thing no one else was home to hear. Her dad was at work. So was Jackson, at his part-time job at a local fast food restaurant.

Steeling herself for an argument, Rose straightened her spine. "Lots of girls keep their babies. Mary Ellen Thompson even came back to school afterward. So did Heather Gardner. Nobody thinks they're bad."

"I didn't say you were bad, Rose. Just incredibly stupid. The Thompsons and the Gardners don't have the position in this community that your father and I have." She shook her head, and the lines between her brows deepened. "Why, I could never face my friends if they knew you were having a baby. What were you thinking to throw away your future like this?"

Rose twisted her hands in her lap. *I was thinking I loved him.*

Of course, she couldn't say that to her mother. Her parents rarely spoke of love. She often wondered if they loved each other. They never hugged or kissed, the way her friends' parents did.

Her mother paced the floor, her high heels clicking against the hard wood. "There has to be a way out of this."

"But why can't I—"

"Hush, will you! I'm thinking!" Her mother stopped to glare at her, then resumed her pacing.

Rose reached over to the pillows, grabbed her plush white bunny, Rags, and clutched him to her chest. She'd had Rags since she was five. Always before, he'd been a comfort. But today, hugging him was an empty gesture. Today she was different. She was no longer a child.

Finally, her mother stopped and snapped her fingers. "I've got it figured out. You're going to your Aunt Nelda's in Boston. You'll have your baby there and put it up for adoption. Aunt Nelda will home school you so that you can earn a diploma. She home schooled her twins, you know. They're in Europe for a year before they begin college, so they won't be around. We'll tell everyone you've received a scholarship to Swinton."

Rose's eyes widened. "What's that?"

"An exclusive private school in Boston. In the meantime, you're not to tell anyone about this, you understand? Not Daddy, not Jackson, and not your friends. You haven't told anyone yet, have you?"

"No," Rose said, her voice muffled against Rags' soft head.

"Well, don't! You must never tell anyone about this, Rose. You'll carry the secret to your grave. Promise me."

Helpless in a situation where she had no power, Rose had to agree. "I promise..."

"I promise." Barely moving her lips, Rose repeated the vow she'd made all those years ago. She opened her eyes and blinked as the past faded away and her surroundings came into focus. She wasn't in her old room at home after all, but in Jackson and Sara's guest room at the Rolling R. Pale moonlight seeped under the blinds, casting a white glow over the darkened walls. An owl's soft hoot, followed by the distant call of a train's whistle, pierced the stillness.

Searching for a more comfortable position, she shifted under the covers. Both her mother and Aunt Nelda were gone now, and she assumed the secret died with them. Rose's heart had never stopped aching for her lost child. Other women who'd given up their babies had put the matter behind them, had married and born other children.

But Rose was stuck in the past.

Whenever she considered telling someone, she heard her mother's command—"You must keep this a secret forever, Rose!"

Tonight, she'd come close to breaking her promise, first when she'd wanted to confide in Glenna, and then when she'd started to tell Mike. But then he'd kissed her and made her forget everything except the thrill of being in his arms and tasting his lips.

What if she had told him? Imagining first his shock—perhaps disbelief—then, as the truth sank in, his disgust and revulsion, made her tremble. No, she could never tell him.

Her mother may have taken charge of Rose's life and of her baby's destiny, but Rose hadn't given up. She'd made one, last-ditch effort to be in control. That, above all, was the reason she could never tell Mike her secret.

Hot tears pushed against Rose's eyelids. Gripping the quilt, she rolled over and sobbed into the pillow.

Chapter Eight

"Did you have a good time last night, Rose?" Sitting on the living room sofa, Jackson bounced Ryan on his knee.

Rose looked up from her magazine. "Do you mean at the book club or with Mike?"

Jackson shrugged. "Either. Both."

From her seat at the roll-top desk in the corner, Sara slit open an envelope from the day's mail. "Cut to the chase and tell us about Mike. Are you two getting back together?"

"They are if Mike has anything to say about it," Jackson said, keeping his gaze focused on the baby.

Rose leaned forward in her recliner and tapped her elevated cast. "Hey, I'd date a gorilla, if he'd get me and this cast out of here for a while."

Sara pushed her lips into a pout. "Are we that bad?"

"You're okay. And the kid's cute. But he's another matter." She pointed to Jackson. "I had to put up with him while we were growing up."

"We had some good times, didn't we?" Jackson picked up a basketball-shaped rattle and handed it to Ryan.

The baby grasped the handle and shook the rattle. "Da, da."

"Oh, and speaking of growing up," Jackson continued, did you take a look at the photo album Sara found in some of Mom's old stuff?"

Rose turned down her mouth at the mention of the troublesome keepsake. "Yeah, I saw it. I'll, uh, be sure to take it with me when I leave. And that's only

108

a few weeks away, folks."

"Hey, Sis, you'll be out of your cast in time to see Buck in the Glennbrook rodeo."

Recalling the tense scene at the dinner table a few weeks ago, Rose asked, "So Molly's gonna let Buck ride?"

"She doesn't want him to." Sara put down the letter she'd been perusing and turned to face Rose. "But there's nothing she can do."

Her attention thoroughly captured, Rose closed her magazine. "I thought you didn't want him to ride, either."

"Molly's my good friend and I do support her. But, as my loving husband pointed out"—Sara paused to give Jackson an affectionate look—"the matter is between her and Buck."

"I understand how you and Molly must feel," Jackson said. "But I'm backing him on his decision. He'll do fine."

"I hope so." Sara turned her gaze on Rose again. "Will you join us at the rodeo?"

"I will. I want to be there to support Molly, if nothing else."

And yet, she wondered if Buck and Molly really had come to an agreement. Molly was a stubborn woman with strong convictions. To suddenly change her mind about Buck's rodeo riding would be out of character.

But, as Sara said, the matter was between him and Molly. Right now, Rose had her own worries, not the least of which was getting rid of her cast.

****

The day Rose had circled on her calendar finally arrived. At ten a.m., she lay on the exam table in Mike's office listening to the whir of his circular saw cutting away her cast. She stared up at the photo of a sunset pasted on the ceiling, but it did little to calm her. What would happen? Would removing the cast hurt? Mike had reassured her it wouldn't, despite the ominous-looking saw. Still, tension crawled along her skin when he began his work.

The seconds and then minutes, ticked by, and all she experienced was a tingling sensation traveling up and down her leg, as though the limb had gone to sleep. She raised her head enough to study his profile as he bent over her. His set jaw and furrowed brow signaled deep thought and concentration. Admiration brought a smile to her lips. How lucky she was to be under his skillful care. She'd never known a doctor more dedicated to his profession than Mike.

Easing back down on the pillow, she folded her arms across her chest and took a deep breath. No need to worry—she was in good hands.

At last, Mike turned off the saw and set it aside. He pulled the two cast sections away from her leg then began removing the bandaging underneath. When the air hit her exposed skin, Rose shivered.

Mike gently tugged off the last piece of bandage. "There. You're free."

"Yay!" She rose up on her elbows and studied her leg. Her cheer died away. The skin where the cast had been was pale and scaly, and a bit hairy, too. What would Mike think? She cast a covert glance his way, but he was busy brushing bandage lint from the exam table. *Relax*, she told herself. *He's seen the effects of a leg cast many times before.*

Finished with his task, he turned his attention to her leg and, sure enough, his face registered neither disgust nor horror. He was all business as he said, "Okay, let's see how everything works. First, wiggle your toes."

Rose arched her foot and wiggled her toes. "They're stiff, but they still work."

"Good. Now stand up and we'll see how you do on your feet."

He grasped her arms and helped her to sit up. She scooted off the edge of the table and rested her feet, one shod, one bare, on the carpeted floor. Placing her weight first on her "good" leg, she then gingerly transferred pressure to the newly healed leg. She exhaled a relieved breath. "So far, so good."

"Take a few steps," he said, holding on to her elbow.

Rose took a few tentative steps. "Being on both feet feels strange, like I'm learning to walk all over again."

"That's not unusual. Your leg will be stiff for a while, and you might have some pain now and then, too. But eventually, you'll be as good as new. The physical therapy at Valley General will help speed your recovery."

Fighting to keep the excitement from her voice, she asked, "I can go back to work, though, right?"

He frowned. "Yes, you can go back to work. Take it easy, though. Hang around the office for at least a couple weeks, before you start traveling again."

"No problem. My boss, Stan, has some desk work all ready for me."

"Okay, then. Sit on the table again until Lucy gets your leg cleaned up and your shoe on, and then you'll be set to go." Keeping a secure grip on her elbow, he guided her to the exam table. "I saw Sara in the waiting room. I'm glad she's here to drive you home. You're still staying at the ranch?"

Rose scooted onto the table, glad to rest her leg. "Yes, for a few more days. Then I'm moving back to my apartment. I can hardly wait."

"I'm sure that will be a red-letter day for you." He gave her a long look, and then strode to the door.

A sinking feeling invaded her stomach. Their doctor-patient relationship was almost over. Even though she'd sometimes given him a bad time, she had the feeling she'd miss his doctoring.

"Mike?"

With one foot in the doorway, he stopped and turned. "Questions?"

"Thanks for taking such good care of me."

A grin broke through the doctor's mask. "You're welcome. But I'm not through yet, you know. This is only the beginning. More about that later." He wiggled his eyebrows then ducked into the hallway, closing the door behind him.

Rose chuckled. He'd finally let his professional demeanor slip—if only a little—and alluded to their personal relationship. Then she sobered. What would happen after she resumed traveling? How would they manage to see each other then?

Well, she'd worry about that later. Right now, having both feet on the ground again felt wonderful.

****

"Good-bye, Sara! Jackson! Thanks for all your help! Talk to you soon." Rose shut the door on her brother and sister-in-law and leaned against it, breathing a sigh of relief. At last, she was back in her Red Rock apartment. Sara and Jackson had brought her home and helped unload her belongings. They'd volunteered to stay and help her unpack, but Rose wanted to savor her homecoming alone. She shooed them off, promising to call if she needed anything.

She gazed around her living room, her eyes lighting on familiar possessions with the delight of a treasure hunter discovering a cache of gold. Her antique maple rocking chair, a garage sale find she'd slavishly refinished. The crocheted pink throw won at a church raffle, perfect for curling up under when she watched TV. Shelves loaded with books, her stereo system and speakers, and racks of CDs. All waiting for her, just as she'd left them.

Crossing to the wrought iron plant stand where her geraniums grew, she fingered the silky blossoms.

Thanks to her next-door neighbor, Nancy Reese, the flowers were perky and well-watered. She'd have to think of an appropriate gift of appreciation for her neighbor.

After opening a couple windows to air out the place, she went into the kitchen, limping a little as she favored her left leg. As Mike had warned, her leg was stiff and occasionally it ached. Overall, though, she was doing quite well.

Finished stowing away the groceries, she moved to the bedroom and, humming "Home Sweet Home" under her breath, opened her suitcase. Nightgowns lay on top. When she pulled them out and saw the suede-covered photo album underneath, the song died on her lips. She pressed a hand to her cheek. Sara must have tucked the album in when Rose wasn't looking. Although she'd told Sara she wanted the album, she'd intended to "forget" it when she packed, and leave the troublesome reminder of her past at the ranch.

Rose rubbed her forehead, trying to decide what to do with the album. She didn't want it here in her apartment. She could burn the album in the fireplace, or rip it up and toss the pieces into the apartment trash bin. Either would take care of the thing, once and for all.

For some unexplained reason, she couldn't destroy the album. Not yet. With a sigh, she lifted it from the suitcase and carried it to the dresser. Opening a bottom drawer, she pushed aside a stack of scarves and socks, and slid in the album. She shoved it all the way to the back, where it would be out of sight, and, she hoped, out of mind.

The phone on the nightstand jingled. Her heart skipped a beat. Mike, calling to see how she was? Rose held her breath as she picked up the cordless receiver.

"Y'all are home," Nancy Reese said in her lilting

Southern accent.

Rose exhaled a little sigh of disappointment then said in a bright tone, "I am, and, boy, does it feel good! Thanks so much for taking care of my place while I was gone. I'll treat you to lunch soon."

Nancy brought Rose up-to-date on her job as a cosmetics company representative. "Ah just got back from a conference in Denver, and guess what? I met a really hot guy."

"Why am I not surprised?" Rose stuffed down a giggle while she plucked a pair of pink slippers from her suitcase. Nancy was always meeting a "hot guy," only to become disillusioned and dump him after a few dates.

"We're going out Friday night," Nancy continued. "And, guess what?"

"He has a friend." That, too, was a familiar scenario.

"Right. They're both software designers for the same firm. Can we make it a double date?"

Rose carried the slippers to the closet and stuck them on the metal shoe-rack. "I appreciate your thinking of me, Nancy, but I'll have to say no."

"Not feeling well enough? We could make it next weekend."

Nancy's cajoling tone often swayed Rose, but not today. "'Fraid not, Nancy. But thanks, anyway."

"No problem, but can you come to the makeover party I'm giving Wednesday night? The company has some great new products."

Rose met that invitation with enthusiasm. She'd attended Nancy's makeover parties before and always had a good time. "I'd love to."

"Great. Come at seven."

Rose hung up, pleased about the party invitation but experiencing doubts about turning down the chance to meet someone new. Although none of Nancy's arranged dates had turned into a relationship, the outings had been fun and entertaining. Today, the refusal popped from her mouth before she'd given the invitation any real thought.

Was Mike the reason? Rose heaved a sigh and resumed her unpacking. When dinnertime arrived, she heated the roasted chicken dinner she'd bought at the deli. Afterward, she went into the living room, switched on the TV, and settled onto the sofa to watch the news. Ah, this was nice, she thought, as she plumped up the cushion behind her head. And yet, as the evening passed, Rose grew restless. After channel surfing for a while, she turned off the TV and picked up the newspaper, but her mind kept skipping to what Sara, Jackson, and Ryan might be doing. She hated to admit she missed them, but she did.

Most of all, she missed Mike. Why hadn't he called to see how she was doing? He promised he would.

Her gaze kept straying to the phone, willing it to ring. The phone remained stubbornly silent.

At eleven o'clock, she finally gave up waiting and went to bed. She tossed and turned, unable to get comfortable and fall asleep. She'd looked forward to this day. Now that it had arrived, instead of being happy, she was, yes, she'd admit it, disappointed. And, okay, lonely, too. What was the matter with her?

****

Shortly after eleven p.m., Mike entered his condo and switched on the hall light. The hospital board meeting lasted longer than he'd expected. Gripping his briefcase in one hand, he tossed his keys into a copper bowl on the hall table with the other. He continued on through the living room to his office. Propping the briefcase on his desk, he snapped it open and took out the architectural drawing of the new children's wing.

Although he'd studied the plans at the meeting, he wanted to look at them again. He traced a forefinger along the lines showing the facilities for single moms, including rooms for classes on parenting and counseling. Excitement kicked up his pulse rate. He could hardly wait for the two-dimensional rendition to become a reality. If he could save one child from the fate he'd suffered, all the work he'd put into spearheading this project would be worth it.

Carrying the drawing to his bulletin board, he pinned it up to remind him of his goal.

As he turned away, his gaze fell on the bookshelf and a framed photo of him and his adoptive parents, Bev and Lloyd Mahoney. Some of his joy faded and sadness trickled in as he focused on their smiling faces. He wished they were still alive to see his accomplishment, but Dad Mahoney passed away from pancreatic cancer while Mike was in med school. A year later, Mom succumbed to Parkinson's disease. Not a day went by that he didn't miss them. As long as he lived, he'd be grateful for all they'd done.

A second photo sat on the shelf, a shot of him and Rose taken at a New Year's Eve party. One of his favorites, he'd kept it on display even though they were no longer together.

Rose! He snapped his fingers. She'd moved back to her apartment today, and he'd promised to call her. Was it too late to phone now?

He glanced at his wristwatch. Eleven thirty. She was probably in bed asleep. Better not disturb her. He'd call her first chance he had tomorrow.

The thought of her lying in bed, wearing one of her thin-as-a-whisper nightgowns, her skin all warm and soft, sent his temperature soaring. He shook his head. *Don't go there, you'll only torture yourself with wanting.*

Taking a last look at the image of her lovely face, he switched out the light and left his office.

Yet, as he prepared for bed, his thoughts lingered on Rose. Although he was glad she was back in Red Rock, now that her leg had healed, he wouldn't be her doctor much longer. Once she started traveling again, she'd be gone sometimes a month or more at a time. He feared long separations would put a strain on their renewed relationship. Plus, the transfer she'd hinted about posed another, more serious, problem. He gritted his teeth. If only he could get a commitment from her.

He'd better work fast. Now that her cast was off, there were more things they could do together. When he talked to her tomorrow, he'd make arrangements for a date.

****

The following morning, after finishing his rounds at Valley General, Mike stepped into the staff lounge. Bypassing the coffee pot and tables where colleagues sat talking and reading the newspaper, he crossed to a small desk near a window overlooking the parking lot. He sat, pulled out his cell phone, and selected Rose's number on the phone's contacts list.

"Sorry I didn't call you last night," he told her when she came on the line.

"That's okay. I went to bed early, anyway."

Her voice sounded disappointed, and he hurried to explain about last night's meeting. "I didn't get home until eleven and figured you'd be asleep. But I said I'd call, and I felt bad about not keeping my word. Don't want you to think I'm unreliable."

"You're a doctor. You're busy."

"Not too busy for you, Rose." Dropping his voice to a deeper level, he added, "Ever." He waited for a response, but the silence on the other end loomed like a deep, dark hole. He tried a different tact. "You get settled in your apartment okay?"

"Almost. I'm going to finish unpacking today."

Spying a notepad and pen on the desktop, he pulled them near. He picked up the pen and idly drew a row of circles. "Holler if you need some help. How's the leg?"

"Pretty good. It ached last night after being on my feet so much, but I rested, like you told me to do."

"That's the ticket. When's your next therapy session?" He added stick arms and legs to one of the circles.

"Next Tuesday morning. I'll be back to work then. But, like I told you, Stan said I can work my schedule around the therapy."

"Your boss is a nice guy. Hey, Jackson reminded me about the rodeo this Saturday in Glennbrook. Buck's going to be in it, after all." Behind him, laughter erupted from one of the groups, and he clamped the phone closer to his ear.

"He's bronc busting. Sara said Molly's accepted his decision."

Mike drew a baseball cap on one of his stick figures, and scribbled curly hair on another. "Must be tough having someone you love keep putting themselves in harm's way."

"Yeah. He sees it differently, though. I doubt he considers rodeo dangerous. To him, riding is an adventure."

"Kind of like the way you think of your job— when you're traveling."

"Kind of. Wish I were traveling now."

Hearing a wistful note in her voice, he winced. "You'll be back at it soon enough," he said, keeping his voice light. "In the meantime, we need to get together. How does dinner tomorrow evening sound?"

Her sigh trickled over the phone. "Sorry, I can't. My next-door neighbor, Nancy, is having a makeover party. The cosmetic company she works for has some new products she wants to share. I promised her I'd come."

"Hmmm. Thursday I'm playing basketball. Friday?"

"That's my Current Events Club meeting at the library." She added in a low voice, "I think we're too busy for each other."

Exactly what he didn't want to hear. He sat up straighter. "No way. What about Saturday's rodeo?" He'd have to share her with others, but afterward they'd squeeze in some time by themselves.

"That would work. I had planned to go."

Yes! Mike linked a small stick figure to the two larger ones. "I'll pick you up about eleven," he said, before she could think of a reason to change her mind.

"All right. I'll be ready."

Mike disconnected the call and slipped the phone into its case attached to his belt. Although he'd made a date and would be seeing her soon, he still felt she was slipping away. His chest ached with the fear of losing her again.

As he rose to leave, he glanced at his doodles. The figure with the baseball cap was a man, the one with curly hair a woman. And in between, linking hands with them, a child. They were a family. How telling that he would create this particular drawing while talking to Rose. Would he ever convince her they could make a family together?

Chapter Nine

"There they are." Mike pointed up into the Glennbrook fairgrounds' grandstand. "I see Jackson's white Stetson."

Rose followed the line of Mike's finger and spotted her brother. Sitting on either side of him were Sara and Molly. Their cowboy hats bobbed as they leaned together talking.

A warm feeling spread through Rose. She'd looked forward to being with her family again. "Looks like they saved us places."

Sliding an arm around her waist, Mike grumbled, "Yeah, I suppose I have to share you today, at least for a while."

She laughed and gestured at the rapidly filling stands. "If not with them, with hundreds of others."

He shook his head. "Heavy competition. Don't know if I can take it."

"Oh, I think you can hold your own. C'mon, let's join the others."

One eyebrow peaked as he nodded at her left leg. "Sure you want to climb? We can take the elevator."

Rose laid a reassuring hand on his arm. "I'll be fine. I've been climbing the practice steps at therapy with no trouble."

After a short hike up the center aisle, they reached the others.

Jackson grinned from under his Stetson. "Hello, you two. 'Bout time you got here."

Eyes twinkling with mischief, Sara added, "We were beginning to think you'd found something else to do today."

"I'm beginning to wish *I* had." Molly clutched her abdomen. "This is giving me a stomachache already."

Jackson patted her hand. "Buck is gonna be okay. Don't worry."

Rose sat next to Molly, with Mike on her other side. He put an arm around her shoulders, and when he leaned across her to speak to the others, the familiar scent of his aftershave tickled her nose. She smiled to herself, reminded of all the times in the past when they'd enjoyed an outing in the company of friends and family.

They'd barely settled in when Buck made his way down the aisle toward them. Underneath his cowboy hat, his eyes shone and his grin reached ear-to-ear. Rose could tell he was in his glory.

Stopping beside Sara, Buck tipped his hat. "Ladies...gentlemen. Thanks for comin'."

"Wouldn't miss it." Mike reached up to shake Buck's outstretched hand.

"You're gonna do us proud," Jackson added, landing a soft punch on Buck's shoulder.

Rose darted a glance at Molly. Her smile looked forced, but when Buck sidled over to her, saying, "Gotta get my good luck kiss from my honey," she raised her arms and gave him a hug as well as a sound kiss on the lips.

"We'll be rootin' for you." Jackson shaded his eyes with one hand as he gazed up at Buck. "Hope you draw a good one."

"I'd better!"

"But not too wild." Molly wagged a finger at her husband.

Buck propped hands on his hips and stuck out his chin. "Aw, honey, the wilder the better. I need to win. I'm gonna, I feel it in my bones."

Familiar with the rules of the sport, Rose knew

Buck had no control over which horse he rode, either today in Glennbrook or in any other rodeo. He had to take the luck of the draw. He wanted a wild mount because part of his score was based on how the horse performed. The more the animal resisted, the more points for Buck—provided he remained in the saddle the requisite eight seconds.

They chatted about Buck's competition for a few minutes then Buck said, "Gotta go. Time for the grand entry." After planting a kiss on Molly's cheek and nodding to the others, he headed back down the aisle.

Excitement humming along her veins, Rose settled back into the curve of Mike's arm, ready for the show to begin. Today was the rodeo's second day. Yesterday featured calf roping and steer wrestling. Today highlighted the rough stock events, saddle and bareback bronco riding, and bull riding.

Her gaze skimmed the stands across the arena, filled near to capacity. The weather was perfect, the sky a cloudless blue and a slight breeze tempering the hot sun. The smell of hot dogs and popcorn from roving vendors mingled with the earthier aromas of leather and dust and horses.

Rose had grown up attending rodeos and fairs, but since she'd been working for the railroad and traveling frequently, her attendance had dropped off. Today's outing made her realize how much she'd missed these events.

Mike leaned close to her ear. "How're you doing? Leg okay?"

She patted his knee. "I'm fine, thanks."

"We'll have you on the dance floor next." Taking her hand, he ran a thumb over her fingers.

They turned toward each other. His eyelids lowered, his lips parted.

Rose's breath caught. He was going to kiss her, right here in public. But, oh, she wanted him to.

Why couldn't they sneak a little kiss before the show started? Closing her eyes, she waited, heart racing, nerves tingling, for the sweet touch of his lips.

Just then, the opening strains of "Stars and Stripes Forever" swept through the arena.

Rose opened her eyes and jerked upright. "Here comes the parade," she said, with a nervous giggle. "We'd better pay attention."

"Until later, then." Mike traced his finger over her lips before he drew away.

His husky drawl sent a shiver skittering along Rose's spine. With a reluctant sigh, she turned her attention to the arena. Switching mental gears took effort, and a few moments slid by before she could fully concentrate on the scene below.

Two women astride elegant white horses led the parade. Their red-sequined costumes glittered in the sun, and the United States flags they held fluttered in the breeze. More horses and riders followed. The rodeo queen, a brunette dressed in white, waved and blew kisses. Local dignitaries nodded and tipped their hats. Jackson and Mike kept up a running commentary on who was who.

With a fanfare from the band, the performers trotted into the arena. Rose leaned forward, eager to catch a glimpse of Buck.

Sara was the first to spot him. "Oh, look, there's Buck!" she cried, pointing toward the middle of the line of mounted riders.

Following the direction of Sara's gesture, Rose located Buck. He sat tall and straight in the saddle, just as she knew he would.

He saluted the crowd then tipped his hat as he circled the arena. When he passed their section, he reined his horse to do a little prance, while he grinned up at them.

Rose chuckled at his display of showmanship and turned to Molly. "Aren't you proud?"

"I guess so." Molly sighed and brushed strands of flyaway hair from her eyes. "He's like a big kid, isn't he? This is like playing a game to him."

Mike leaned across Rose to ask, "Speaking of kids, where are Ryan and Karli today?"

Sara spoke up. "Anna's minding them. They'll join us when we have dinner later."

Mention of the children prompted Rose to ask Molly, "Has Karli ever seen Buck in a rodeo?"

Molly nodded, fingering the fringe on her denim vest. "I let her come once, but she couldn't handle it. She was okay when he rode in the parade. But, later, when he flew out of the chute on the horse, she started to cry. Watching the horse thrash him around terrified her."

"Maybe when she's older..." Rose began.

Molly's green eyes flashed. "He'd better come to his senses before then."

Rose clamped her jaw shut. So much for Molly and Buck having come to terms about his rodeo riding.

A red pickup truck full of clowns rumbled into view, drawing Rose's attention away from Molly. The clowns waved to the crowd and tooted miniature trumpets. One, who wore enormous yellow shoes, kept climbing onto the back of the truck and tumbling off, much to the faked disgust of the others. Whenever he took a pratfall, his companions cheered and tooted their horns.

When the clowns finally roared off, the master of ceremonies led the recitation of the Pledge of Allegiance, and a soprano sang "America the Beautiful." Then the crowd settled for the main event.

"When is Buck's turn?" Rose peered over Mike's shoulder at his program.

Mike ran a finger down the page, stopping halfway. "Here he is. Should be in about half an hour. Barebacks are after the saddle broncs."

Rose's eyes widened. "Buck's riding bareback? I thought he rode saddle?"

"He used to." Disgust laced Molly's voice. "But that wasn't challenging enough."

"Be glad he's not riding the bulls," Sara said, rolling her eyes.

Molly reached up to steady her hat against a sudden gust of wind. "I am glad, but I'm afraid that's next."

A voice over the loudspeaker announced the beginning of the first competition. Pushing aside her concern about Buck's change from saddle broncs to bareback, which of course carried new risks, Rose focused on the chute.

The wooden gate sprang open and, like a ball from a cannon, a cowboy on a sleek brown horse shot out. The animal bucked and reared and whinnied. Clouds of dust swirled around the rider, his mouth set in a tight, grim line.

Mike squeezed Rose's hand. "He's good."

Jackson leaned around Molly to add, "Yeah, but the horse is wimpy."

"If that's wimpy, I'd hate to see wild." Rose held her breath, expecting the rider to be dumped any moment.

A buzzer sounded. The rider's eight seconds were up. Relieved the rider hadn't been spilled, Rose sagged against Mike's shoulder.

Two "pickup men," cowboys on horses who'd been waiting near the fence, trotted over. One of them held out a gloved hand to the rider. The rider grabbed it, swung his leg over the saddle, and slipped to the ground. With spurs no longer piercing its sides, the animal settled down to aimless prancing. The second pickup man easily lassoed the horse and led him away.

Along with the rest of the crowd, Rose clapped

and cheered.

Several more saddle riders followed, then the bareback bronc riders. Finally, Buck's turn came. Rose glued her gaze to the chute, waiting for him to appear.

The gates opened, and Buck and the horse flew out. Buck's jaw was tightly set, and his left hand gripped the rope cinched around the bronc's belly, his only means of holding on.

His hat hid his eyes, but Rose imagined the fiery determination burning in their depths.

The horse galloped a few paces then bucked so high it almost flipped backward.

Rose put a hand to her chest where her heart beat a fast tattoo against her ribcage.

"Close one." Gripping his program, Mike half rose from his seat.

Jackson cupped both hands around his mouth and yelled, "Go, Buck!"

Rose shot Molly a quick glance. Her eyes were shut and her mouth was twisted into a grimace. So, that was how she coped. She didn't watch. Rose gave Molly's hand a squeeze.

Molly squeezed back, but didn't open her eyes.

The scene below was so hair-raising that Rose herself was having trouble watching. She bit her lip and forced herself to focus on Buck and his struggle.

Now he was stretching his legs to draw his spurs across the horse. The animal whinnied and reared. Dust bloomed, swirled, cleared. The crowd roared their approval. The horse had time for a couple more suntails, neither of which unseated Buck, before the buzzer blared. Buck slipped off the horse while the pickup men were still *en route*. "Ye haw!" he yelled, lifting his hat to the cheering crowd.

Molly sagged against Rose's shoulder. "Whew!" she said, wiping her eyes with a handkerchief. "Those are the longest eight seconds I've ever lived through."

"I agree." Rose struggled to provide a strong shoulder for Molly when she herself was limp. "But they're over now, and Buck did great!"

"Let's hope the judges think so." Mike settled down again and put his arm around Rose.

Gazing up at the judging booth, Rose glimpsed the judges huddled together while they discussed Buck's score. Finally, they broke apart. The announcer raised his microphone to his lips and boomed, "Here's Buck Henson's score, ladies and gentlemen, eighty-two points!"

"Wow!" Jackson pumped the air with his fist. "That puts him ahead in overall points for this year."

Mike and Jackson high-fived, while Sara stood and hollered, "Yay, Buck!"

Rose threw her arm around Molly's shoulder. "He did it!"

Molly nodded, yet her eyes were bleak, and Rose sensed that for her, Buck's win meant more sorrow than joy.

****

Mike scooted closer to Rose and slid his arm along the back of her chair. The rodeo was over, and their group had adjourned to The Wagon Wheel, a popular Glennbrook restaurant. Much of the rodeo crowd had had the same destination, but they'd managed to snag a table. They'd been served a round of drinks and a plate of buffalo wings in preparation for the barbecue buffet. Not surprisingly, everyone's attention focused on Buck.

"I'm in the lead now." Buck's eyes glowed in the light from the wagon wheel chandeliers. "And there's some big prize money waiting at the end of this rainbow."

While they listened to Buck talk about his win, Mike glanced at Rose. Her cheeks were pink, her eyes bright. Satisfaction spread through his veins.

The outing had been good for her, for them. He still wanted some alone time with her, though. He'd considered spiriting her away for a cozy dinner for two, but in the end had decided to make the best of the group situation.

Mike looked up to see Anna Gabraldi, with Ryan and Karli in tow, weaving her way toward them.

"Daddy! Daddy!" Copper curls bouncing underneath her cowgirl hat, Karli let go Anna's hand and made straight for Buck.

Buck leaned over and swept his daughter into his arms. "Here's my little pumpkin! How 'bout a kiss?"

While Karli planted a smooch on Buck's cheek, Anna transferred Ryan to Sara's waiting arms.

"Hello, little guy." Sara tipped up his cowboy hat to peer into his face. "Were you a good boy?" She turned to Anna for confirmation.

Anna nodded and tucked a wisp of gray hair behind her ear. "You bet. They both were little lambs the whole time."

Glancing at Rose again, Mike noticed her expression had turned wistful as she focused on Sara and Ryan. A dull ache settled in his chest. He and Rose should be joining in the fun with their own children. He'd always dreamed of them having babies together. She'd make a wonderful mother.

"Stay and eat with us, Anna." Jackson motioned to the chair they'd saved.

Anna held up a hand. "Oh, no, thank you. My husband's cooking his famous beef stew tonight."

"You don't want to miss that!" Sara said.

After Anna left, a group of teenagers breezed into the restaurant. Laughing, talking, and punching one another, they followed the hostess to a table. As they passed by, one of the boys pointed a forefinger at Buck. "Hey, you were in the rodeo today."

"Right." Buck set down his beer and gave them his full attention.

"Cool," a girl with a silver nose ring said. "Can we have your autograph?"

"Why, shore," Buck drawled as the kids crowded around him. He took a pen from his shirt pocket and began signing.

When they finally wandered off, Mike hoped they'd be left alone, but more kids came in and soon learned a celebrity was present. They beat a path to their table, shoving napkins, rodeo programs, and scraps of newspaper under Buck's nose for him to autograph.

"Don't let all this go to your head," Sara teased during a lull in the activity.

Buck shoved his pen into his shirt pocket. "Don't worry, my darling wife will help me keep my head. Won't you, honey?" He cocked an eyebrow at Molly.

"You go right ahead and enjoy yourself, dear," Molly said with a toss of her red curls.

Mike winced at the sarcasm dripping from her words. Buck must have heard it too, for a shadow crossed his face and his mouth tightened.

Then someone shouted, "Hey, Buck!" and his grin returned as he greeted the newcomer.

At last, dinner was over, good-byes were said, and Mike and Rose were in his SUV on their way to Red Rock. He glanced at her. The freeway lights outlined her pert nose and rounded chin, her dark hair curling around her cheek and along the collar of her denim jacket. Pleasure trickled down his spine. He relished having her beside him. This was where she belonged.

"We had a good day, didn't we?" he asked, breaking the silence.

"We did. Everyone had fun—except Molly." Her voice dropped a notch. "I worry about her and Buck. His rodeo riding is driving them apart."

"Right now's a tough time for them."

"I suppose you're going to take his side, like Jackson does."

He bristled at her edgy tone. "Not necessarily. Why do you say that?"

"Because guys always stick together."

"Well, women do, too. I notice you and Sara rallying around Molly."

She huffed a breath. "We're trying to help her through this. Hopefully, he'll get the rodeo out of his blood and they can go back to being a close family again."

With both arms crossed over her chest and her chin jutted, she appeared ready for battle. Alarm flickered through him as he saw their day ending on a sour note. Not what he'd planned.

"I wish them well," he said, careful to keep his voice calm and even. "But, hey, I don't want to talk about them anymore. And no way do I want to argue."

She sighed, and then lightly touched his arm. "I'm sorry I got carried away. I don't want to argue, either. And I really did have a good time tonight."

The remainder of the drive passed with more pleasant conversation, and soon they reached her apartment. He pulled to the curb and checked the dashboard clock. Only eight, still plenty early. He cleared his throat. "Anything else you'd like to do tonight?"

He knew what he wanted to do—take her in his arms and kiss her senseless, show her how much he cared.

She hesitated a moment then said, "Would you like to come up for a while?"

Would he? "Sure. I'd like to see your place." *I'd like to see you. Anywhere.*

She cast him a warning look from under her lashes. "I'm not the world's best housekeeper."

He held up both hands. "I won't even notice. And if I do, I promise I won't complain."

"All right, then. Drive around back and park in my extra parking space."

Excitement surging through him, Mike swung the car into the driveway. The moment he'd been waiting for had finally arrived. At last, he and Rose would be alone.

Chapter Ten

Mike gazed around Rose's cozy living room. Her apartment wasn't as large as his condo, but she made use of every inch of space. Her décor was like a free-for-all, with quilts, pillows, plants, wicker, and wrought iron all thrown together, yet managing to look coordinated. The smell of a spicy potpourri drifted through the doorway to the kitchen.

He took a step farther into the room. "Nice place."

Shutting the door, she leaned against it for a moment, and then came to stand beside him. "Thanks, I like it."

"You've lived here for two years?"

"Right. I moved in shortly after we, ah, stopped seeing each other. I stayed with Jackson for a while. He was so lonely, you know, after Catherine passed away."

"That was a tough time for him." Mike felt a hitch in his chest at the thought of losing Rose.

"But then he met Sara. And I took the job with TransAmerica. Moving back to Red Rock made a shorter commute to the Denver office than if I'd stayed on the ranch. But, here, let me take your jacket." She extended a hand.

He shed his denim jacket and held it out. As she grasped it, their fingers brushed. He was tempted to capture her hand and pull her into his arms. Instead, he sucked in a breath and cautioned himself to be patient.

Crossing to a closet, she slipped his jacket onto a hanger then gestured toward the sofa. "Why don't you relax while I make coffee?"

"I'll tag along. Maybe I can make myself useful." He didn't want to let her out of his sight, even for the short time it took to brew coffee.

In the bright yellow kitchen, she directed him to the cupboard where the dishes were kept. He took out a couple of mugs, while she prepared the coffee maker. Covertly, he traced her travels from sink to counter. She moved smoothly, as though her broken leg were all but forgotten. And, for a moment, he wanted the other Rose back, the one held prisoner by the fiberglass cast, the one who had to rely on him to take her somewhere.

A hot wave of guilt brought him to his senses. Of course, he wanted Rose to be strong and independent. Those were admirable qualities, and he wouldn't wish weakness and dependency on anyone. Trouble was, her strength and independence could also work against him.

When the coffee was done, the aroma mixing pleasantly with the spicy potpourri, they carried their mugs back to the living room and settled on the sofa. He sat as close as he dared, forcing himself to wait until the time was right to make his move and take her into his arms. He trusted he would know when that was.

They talked about the rodeo, changes in Red Rock, people they knew. When she asked about his practice, he mentioned the children's wing at the hospital. "We're having an auction to raise money."

Rose adjusted the cushions at her back. "Sounds like a good idea."

"I hope so. We've rented the ballroom at The Commodore. You know, where we went with the Stones after the baseball game?"

"Oh, right. A very nice place."

He reached out and ran a finger along her arm. The touch of her soft, warm skin left him aching for more. "I'd like you to go with me. Besides the auction, there'll be dinner and dancing."

When she kept her gaze averted and didn't answer, his stomach tensed. Was she going to turn him down?

"When is it?" she finally asked.

"Two weeks from tonight."

Pulling her arm away, she picked up her cup and cradled it in both hands. "I'll be back on my regular job then. I might be traveling."

Deep down, he'd been afraid of that. Unwilling to give up, he sucked in a breath and asked, "Can't you arrange to be here?"

Rose stiffened. "I'm not in control. Others besides me are involved."

With every ounce of sincerity he could muster, he said, "Rose, I really want you to come with me."

"I'll try, but I can't promise." She shook her head. "Don't count on me. Maybe you should ask someone else."

"There is no one else. I don't want anyone else. I want you." He took her cup from her hands and placed it on the tray. "And you want me."

Now was the time. He put his arms around her, and when she didn't resist, he pulled her close. The warmth of her body seeped into him. Ah, so good, so good. Why had they taken so long getting to this moment?

He savored their closeness for a while then drew back. Cupping her face in both hands, he gently brushed his lips across hers. The barest contact was enough to set him on fire. When he deepened the kiss, she wound her arms around his neck and molded her body to his. And when she twined her fingers in his hair, the way she always used to do, the years of separation faded away, and happiness filled him.

"Oh, Rose," he whispered, "I want you so

much..." He kissed her again then trailed kisses down the smooth and graceful curve of her neck.

"I want you, too, but—"

"But what?" he murmured.

Placing her hands on his chest, she eased away. "I can't be what you want me to be, Mike. I am what I am."

He frowned. What was she talking about? "What you are is fine with me."

She hugged her upper arms and shook her head. "I don't think so. Mike, I have to talk to you about—"

When she didn't continue, he let a few seconds roll by, and then said, "About what happened two years ago?"

She moved a few inches away and gave him a blank look. "Two years ago?"

"Yeah. When we broke up. When you broke up with me."

"Oh. Well, no. Not that."

"Then what?"

"I, um, do you really think we should keep seeing each other?"

Startled by the unexpected question, he sat back. "Of course! We haven't given us that second chance yet." In a low voice, he added, "But that isn't what you meant, is it? You do want to talk about two years ago."

With a sigh, she ran a hand over her forehead. "I don't know...I'm all mixed up."

The pain in her eyes alarmed him. He sat there, indecision knotting his stomach. He sensed that with just a little more patient probing he'd finally learn why she left the relationship. And wasn't that what he wanted?

Yes, but not tonight. All day, he'd dreamed only of holding her in his arms and making love to her. The past would always be there. The past could wait.

He tipped up her chin. "Whatever's bothering

you will keep until another time. Right now, just let me be here and hold you in my arms."

"You're sure?" Her voice was the barest whisper.

"Very sure."

Again he pulled her into his arms. With a soft sigh, she nestled against his chest. He stroked her hair, whispering, "Everything will be all right, honey. Everything will be all right."

****

The timer dinged, signaling the apple crumb cake was done. Rose put down her book, jumped off the sofa, and hurried to the kitchen.

When she'd come home from work, the sudden urge to do something domestic seized her. She'd dug out the recipe her neighbor, Nancy, had shared at her makeover party a couple weeks ago, just a few days before she and Mike had gone to the rodeo. Tonight, with time on her hands, Rose decided to give the recipe a try.

Grabbing an oven mitt, she opened the oven and removed the cake. The edges were slightly pulled away from the pan, the crumb topping toasty brown and glistening with melted butter. Yes, the cake was done. She set the pan on the counter and picked up the empty coffeepot. While a fresh pot brewed, the cake would cool enough to sample.

As she flipped the Brewmaster's On switch, the phone rang. She hurried to the living room to answer it.

"Rose? This is Glenna."

Rose's pulse jumped. "Glenna! I've been thinking about you. How've you been? How're things going?"

"N-not very well."

Rose clutched the cordless phone. She'd been afraid Glenna had not solved her problem. The last time Rose had spoken to Ellie, she was still worried about her daughter. "Oh, I'm sorry. Is there anything I can do?"

"I d-don't know."

In the background, car horns honked and engines revved. "Where are you, honey?"

"Downtown."

"Have you been shopping?"

"No, I was at the library. But I didn't want to stay, and...I don't want to go home, either."

The distress in Glenna's voice alarmed Rose. She crossed to the window and gazed out. Pale blue twilight had settled over the town, but the evening was still young.

"Why don't you come up to my place?" she said. "I just took a cake out of the oven. I'd love to share it with you."

In the long silence that followed, Rose braced herself for a refusal.

But then Glenna said, in a barely audible voice, "Okay. For a while."

Rose gave Glenna her address and directions. Ten minutes later, Glenna arrived. As Rose had feared, the teen's appearance and demeanor hadn't improved since the last time Rose had seen her. If anything, she appeared even more troubled. A recent crying binge left her eyes bloodshot and her cheeks puffy. Her shoulders drooped under the weight of her canvas backpack and her steps were slow as she shuffled into the apartment.

"Come in and sit down," Rose said, leading her into the living room.

Glenna stood in the center of the room, twisting her hands together. "I shouldn't have come."

Rose slanted her a questioning look. "Why do you say that?"

"'Cause I'm bothering you. You're busy."

"Not at all. And the cake I baked is waiting to be sampled. How about a slice?" Rose offered a smile she hoped would put Glenna at ease.

Glenna's shoulders shifted as she heaved a sigh.

"Okay."

"That backpack looks like it weighs a ton. Take it off and sit down while I get us some cake."

Rose waited until Glenna set the backpack on the floor and had settled herself on the sofa then she went into the kitchen. Her stomach churned with worry about Glenna and how she might help her. She dished up a couple slices of cake, adding a glass of milk for Glenna and a cup of coffee for herself. Arranging everything on a tray, she carried it to the living room.

Perched on the edge of the sofa, hands clasped in her lap, Glenna stared into space.

"Here we are!" Rose announced. She slid the tray onto the coffee table, handed Glenna her cake, and put the milk down where she could reach it.

Seconds passed while Glenna sat as still as a stone.

Rose opened her mouth to offer more encouragement.

But before she could speak, Glenna finally reached for the plate. She picked up her fork and took a small bite. "This is good," she mumbled.

"Thanks." Rose rambled on about the recipe and where she'd obtained it, and then asked, "What were you looking up at the library?"

Glenna took a sip of milk. "The books on a summer reading list one of my teachers gave us. But it was a waste of time, because I'm not going to school anymore."

Rose raised her eyebrows, but kept her voice calm as she said, "You've made a decision then."

Glenna's eyes filled with tears. "Not exactly. I know you said I should tell my parents, but whenever I start to, the words stick in my throat. Do you know what I mean?"

"I do." Only two nights ago, she'd worked up the courage to tell Mike her secret. Or thought she had.

Then when the moment came, she too had frozen.

Setting her plate on the coffee table, Rose stood and went to sit beside Glenna. "Would it help if I were with you while you tell them?"

"No, I don't think so. My dad'll throw a fit no matter who's there." Glenna took another couple bites of cake then set her plate next to Rose's. "I'm sorry. I'm not very hungry. I'd better go home. I told my parents I'd be back by eight."

"Would you like a piece of cake to take home for later?"

"No, thanks."

Not wanting Glenna to leave while in such distress, Rose said, "Why don't I drive you? That'll be faster than taking the bus."

Glenna shifted in her seat. "I'm not taking the bus. Tony's picking me up. He's probably out front waiting now. After I talked to you, he called my cell. I told him I was coming here and gave him the address. I hope you don't mind."

"No, that's fine, Glenna. But, what does he think you should do about your pregnancy?"

"He doesn't want me to tell my parents, because they'd tell his parents, and he'd be in big trouble."

"How old is Tony?" Rose realized how little she knew about the other half of Glenna's dilemma.

"Sixteen. A year older than me." Glenna stood and picked up her backpack. "Thanks for letting me come. And for the cake. It was real good."

Rose stood, too, and placed a hand on Glenna's shoulder. "I don't think I've helped you very much."

Glenna shrugged. "No one can."

After Glenna left, Rose slumped into a chair and heaved a deep, troubled sigh. Glenna had come to her for help, and she'd let her down. She didn't know what to do in her own situation, and she didn't know what to do in Glenna's, either. What a mess everything was.

****

A week later, Rose left her St. Louis hotel room and stepped outside into the muggy July evening. Behind her, the Gateway Arch, the city's famed landmark, rose into the twilight sky. The restaurant where she was to meet her friends was only a few blocks away. Rather than take a taxi, she'd decided to walk. Her leg rarely bothered her anymore, and after a day of indoor meetings, the exercise would do her good. She started off with her chin high and a spring in her step. This promised to be a fun evening.

The trip to St. Louis was her first since the accident. She'd feared being on the train again might make her apprehensive, but she experienced only one bad moment. Once when she was on her way down an aisle, she caught sight of the crosses marking the accident site. Suddenly faint, she slid into the nearest empty seat, leaned her head back, and squeezed her eyes shut until they were well past. Then she'd managed to focus on her tasks again and the remainder of the trip went smoothly.

After walking a couple blocks, while she waited for a red traffic light, her gaze wandered to a nearby antique store window. Illuminated in the store's nightlight was an elaborate bronze sculpture of a cowboy roping a calf. She stepped closer and studied it. She'd planned to get Sara and Jackson a thank-you gift for caring for her at the ranch while her leg healed, and this piece would be perfect. She made a mental note of the store's location, so she could stop by tomorrow and make the purchase.

At the restaurant, amid plaster statues and burbling fountains and urns of fake ivy, the maitre d' led Rose to the semi-circular booth where Teri and Roger Decker waited. Teri was a dietician for TransAmerica, and Roger a partner in a local law firm. With them were three other people unknown to

Rose—two women journalists and a male colleague of Roger's.

They ordered their food, and soon *antipasto*, *ravioli*, *gnocc*i, and garlic bread filled the table. At first, Rose joined in the lively conversation, but after awhile, for some reason, her enthusiasm faded and she lapsed into silence.

Teri peered at Rose through her black-framed glasses. "You're awfully quiet tonight, Rose."

Rose touched her napkin to her lips. "I guess my first trip back on the job tired me more than I thought."

"Maybe you need more time to recover," the lawyer, whose name was Jess, suggested. He told a story about a friend who'd also dealt with a broken leg.

The others chimed in with more tales of broken bones, which carried them through the meal. When their checks arrived, one of the women suggested they adjourn to the lounge where a jazz combo performed. Rose loved jazz, but, despite her earlier enthusiasm, she suddenly found herself with no desire to extend the evening. She made her apologies and asked to be excused. Jess offered to accompany her to her hotel, but she declined. "The hotel is only a few blocks away," she said. "I'll be fine."

Once on her way, a cold loneliness settled over Rose. Maybe she should have let her would-be escort come along. He was pleasant and nice-looking and about her age. Then she finally realized why her spirits had taken a dive this evening.

She missed Mike.

He'd haunted the corners of her mind the entire trip. At home, they had frequent phone conversations, but she hadn't heard from him since she'd left Red Rock. He'd said he wouldn't bother her while she was away, and he'd been true to his word. Even though she'd told herself taking a break from each other was for the best, still, she ached to hear his voice.

Finally, she reached her hotel and crossed the lobby to the bank of elevators, where an empty car swept her up to the fifth floor. The minute she shut the door to her room, her gaze flew to the phone. No blinking red light to signal a message.

Pulling her cell phone from her purse, she checked for missed calls or voice mail messages. None. Her shoulders sagged and she sank onto the bed.

She could call him. Her thumb hovered over the cell phone's buttons.

Do it.

No, better not.

Leaving the phone on, she placed it on the bedside table within easy reach.

Her wristwatch showed nine o'clock. Too early to go to bed. Giving herself a mental shake, she vowed to prove to herself she could enjoy this trip, just as she had enjoyed all the trips she'd taken for the railroad.

She shrugged out of her navy blazer, tossed it over a chair, and kicked off her navy pumps. Taking a book from her suitcase, she curled up on the bed and began to read. No more than five minutes passed before she gave up and tossed aside the book. Grabbing her briefcase, she pulled out the agenda for tomorrow's meeting. That didn't hold her interest any better than the book had. Disgusted, she shoved the papers back into the briefcase.

She gazed around the room as if seeing her accommodations for the first time. Although attractively furnished in blues and greens, the room offered none of the comfort or warmth of her bedroom at home. Why had she ever thought she liked traveling and staying in strange places?

Of course, she knew the answer—her job offered

escape from the past, a way to forget all the troublesome memories.

The awful truth hit her with the force of an earthquake and made her heart pound. She sat up and put her head in her hands. Her job no longer worked as an escape. Now that she and Mike were seeing each other again, she wanted to be with him.

Yet, as always, like a boulder on the path, the past blocked her way.

You can't change what happened. What's done is done.

Rose lay back on the pillows. What to do now? Work up the courage to tell Mike her secret? Or keep the past buried and enjoy what they had?

Chapter Eleven

Three days later, Rose stepped from the train onto the Red Rock station's platform. She stopped and gazed around. There was the red brick station house, with people passing in and out the automatic doors. Next to the station sat a large warehouse with a blue slate roof. Beyond that was a parking lot where aspen trees planted in circular oases of greenery waved in the breeze. All familiar sights she'd seen dozens of times upon returning from dozens of trips.

Familiar...and yet different.

Or was she different?

That was it. She had changed, because coming home today filled her with warm pleasure instead of cold distress. She looked forward to settling in her apartment and, come Monday, returning to the office.

Most of all, she looked forward to seeing Mike again. She wished she could see him now.

Pulling her suitcase on wheels, she headed toward the station house. Someone called her name. She stopped and turned.

Mike hurried toward her. "Rose, wait!"

Rose's eyes widened. Her fairy godmother must really be on the job today. "Mike! What are you doing here?"

"Meeting you. I phoned your office and they told me this was your train. I've missed you. Couldn't wait any longer, so here I am, your welcoming committee of one." He grinned and held out his arms.

Nothing had ever looked so good. Rose dropped her suitcase and closed the gap between them. He folded his strong arms around her and pulled her close. His warm embrace was exactly what she needed. Unmindful of passersby, she put her arms around him and nestled against his chest. Drank in his warmth, his scent. She was truly home now.

He drew away and lowered his mouth to hers. Familiar heat surged along her veins as she parted her lips to receive his kiss. The world around her spun until her surroundings blurred and faded away.

When the kiss was over, he drew back and gazed deeply into her eyes. "Miss me?"

His husky voice sent a shiver of excitement down her spine. "I did." *More than you know. More than I want to admit.*

"Good. How was the trip?"

She sighed and blew out a breath. "Long." *And lonely.*

"You can tell me all about it over dinner." His eyebrows rose. "Or have you already eaten?"

She reached up to smooth away strands of hair blowing across her eyes. "No, and all I have at home are frozen dinners."

"I was counting on that." Gazing around, he added, "Where's your car? I didn't see it in the overnight lot."

Rose lifted one shoulder. "At home. My neighbor, Nancy, brought me to the station. I was going to call a cab for a ride home."

"Your cab is here, madam." He grabbed her suitcase and offered her his arm.

Grasping his elbow, she fell into step beside him. "Can't say I've ever had such a handsome driver."

"How about the Woodhouse Grill for dinner?" he asked as they headed toward the parking lot.

"Perfect. I love their spinach salad."

"I remembered that from before."

She slowly shook her head. "Is there anything you don't remember from before?"

He chuckled and patted her hand tucked into his elbow. "Very little. Every moment with you is etched in my brain."

"Ouch," she said, hunching her shoulders. "That sounds painful."

"Uh, uh. The only pain was the day you said good-bye."

Rose tensed and missed a step in her stride. She hoped he didn't want to discuss the past. That would surely spoil her happy homecoming.

But then he made a joke that had them both laughing, and her tension eased.

Later, as they sat in a cozy booth at the restaurant, Rose dug into her spinach salad brimming with egg and bacon, while Mike tackled a juicy grilled steak. How different this was from the evening she'd spent with her friends in St. Louis. Then, as good as the food was, she'd only picked at her meal.

That night, she'd been hard-pressed to make conversation, too. Today she and Mike had talked nonstop. So much to say, so much to catch up on. Mike's basketball team was ahead in the league. After the last game, he and Jackson and the others celebrated at the Pizza Palace. When she told him about the sculpture she'd bought for Jackson and Sara, he mentioned a new sculpture exhibit in a local gallery. They should go see it.

"We should," she agreed.

"There's something else we can do together."

"What's that?"

He leaned forward. "The auction to raise money for the children's wing is coming up next weekend. I've reserved a table for eight. Jackson and Sara,

Patricia and Carl Stone, from the Rockies game, my partner, David, and his wife, Sorvina. And me. All the seats are filled except the one I saved for you. Will you come?"

Several weeks ago, when he'd first mentioned the auction, she'd used her traveling as an excuse to avoid commitment. But tonight, eager to spend more time with him, she said without hesitation, "I'd love to."

He sat back and gave her a wide-eyed look. "Hey, that was fast. I must be making progress."

She wrinkled her nose. "Oh, oh, I really wrecked my playing-hard-to-get image, didn't I?"

"Never mind." He made a dismissive wave. "That's one image I wouldn't mind you losing."

Their banter continued through dinner. Afterward, on the way home, while they were stopped for a red light, he asked, "Mind if we take a detour? There's something I want to show you."

"Your condo?" she said in a dry tone. "Been there, done that. Remember?"

"You haven't seen the inside yet." He wiggled his eyebrows. "But I'm biding my time on that. No, there's something else I want you to see."

The eagerness in his voice piqued her curiosity. "All right, I'm game."

They left the business district and entered a residential area with older, frame homes and tree-shaded streets. Rays from the setting sun shone through the leaves, casting mottled shadows on the pavement.

Gazing out her window, Rose spotted a familiar, wooded area up ahead. "Isn't this the way to Valley General?"

Mike slowed down to complete a turn. "It is. Hard to make a mystery out of a place we've both been so often."

The hospital's blue neon sign appeared, followed

by the driveway leading to the five-story stucco building. Bypassing the front entrance, Mike continued on to the back of the building, where he pulled into a parking space.

He cut the engine and faced her. "Figured out what I'm up to yet?"

His sly smile made her nerve endings tingle. "Something to do with the children's wing?"

"Right again. I want to show you where it'll be built. We need to get out and walk, though."

Rose bit her lip. "This project is really important to you, isn't it?"

His eyes shone, and he gripped her hand. "You bet it is. Next to you, this is the most important thing in my life. If our facility can prevent even one baby from being abandoned like I was, I'll consider my mission accomplished."

A lump filled Rose's throat. While sharing his vision made her feel close to him, it also reminded her that his crusade was deeply rooted to the very problem keeping them apart.

"Isn't it kind of late?" She pointed to the dashboard clock.

"This'll only take a few minutes." He peered at her. "What? I thought you'd be interested."

"I am..." Swallowing down her distress, she scooted toward the door and grasped the handle. She might as well go through with the rest of his plan. Besides, by agreeing to attend the auction, she'd already become involved.

Once they both were out of the car, Mike grabbed her hand and drew her to one side of the building. "The wing comes out here," he said, leading them across an expanse of grass, "and extends all the way to those trees over there." He nodded toward woods rimming the parking lot.

Rose followed along and listened and wished with all her heart she could share his enthusiasm.

But all she could manage were a few polite comments. When at last they returned to his SUV, she sank onto the seat with a relieved sigh.

"You're quiet all of a sudden," he said after they'd been on the road awhile.

Rose studied her hands folded in her lap. "Guess I'm talked out. Today has been a long one."

"We'll get you home, then."

When they reached her apartment building, he parked at the curb. He wheeled her suitcase to the front door and stood gazing at her, as though uncertain what came next.

"You're welcome to come up for a while," she said, part of her hoping he would, part hoping he wouldn't. She'd been so happy to see him, so ready to do anything; but now, like nasty little imps, doubts had crept into her mind, telling her she was foolish to think she and Mike had a future.

He stepped closer and ran a knuckle along her cheek. "There's nothing I'd like more, but you need your sleep, and I do, too. I've an early day at the clinic tomorrow. Rain check?"

Savoring the warmth of his touch, yet at the same time, relieved, she said, "I'd like that."

"I'm glad we saw each other for a while tonight, anyway."

"Me, too. Your meeting me was a nice surprise."

"I hoped it would be." Placing his hands on her shoulders, he gave her a quick kiss on the lips, and then turned and headed back to his car.

As she watched him drive away, melancholy filled Rose. No matter how good a time they had together, each occasion included a painful reminder of what kept them apart. Tonight, the trip to see the future children's wing was the spoiler.

Each time, the urge to pour out her story gripped her. And, each time, she stuffed the past back down inside, as she'd always done. Rose opened the door to the building and with slow, heavy steps, went inside. How much longer could she keep up the charade?

****

"Another trip to the buffet table, or are you ready for dessert?" Mike nodded to the other end of The Commodore Hotel's ballroom, where waiters wheeled dessert-laden carts from the kitchen.

Rose laid her knife and fork across her empty plate and leaned back in her chair. "Dessert sounds good."

He gave her a wink. "Look for the ice cream cake you like. I made sure it was included."

"You are so thoughtful," she said, patting his arm.

He caught her hand and squeezed it. "Like I've told you, I'm always looking for ways to get on your good side." He leaned nearer. "Glad you came?"

Rose took a moment to scan their tablemates— Carl and Patricia Stone; Mike's clinic partner, David Genoa, and his wife, Sorvina; and Sara and Jackson—then widened her gaze to include the room full of people gathered to raise money for the new children's wing. An orchestra seated at one end of the room played soft dinner music, while colorful balloons and streamers lent a gala touch to the occasion. She turned back to Mike and favored him with a smile. "Yes, I am."

"I thought you would be."

Sitting next to Mike, David Genoa leaned forward and said, "The evening's going well, don't you think?"

Mike picked up his water glass and took a sip. "The attendance is more than we expected. But the real test will be how generous people are when the bidding starts."

"There's some good stuff up for grabs." Carl Stone nodded toward the far wall where tables

150

displayed the auction items.

Patricia laid a hand on her husband's arm. "Carl, did you see the Super Bowl package? We've never been, and I've always wanted to go."

Carl chuckled. "How could I miss it when you paraded us by three times?"

"Just a little hint." Patricia's grin showed off the dimple in her cheek.

"I'm ready." Jackson picked up his bid card by the stick handle and waved it. "A fancy pair of boots caught my eye." He turned to Sara. "How 'bout you?"

Sara touched her chin with her forefinger. "Hmmm, I can't decide."

Rolling his eyes, Jackson said, "Good thing I brought my checkbook. This gal loves to shop."

Rose joined in with the laughter rippling around the table. Jackson spoke the truth. A native New Yorker, Sara grew up in a privileged environment with a father who gave her a generous allowance. But Rose also knew Sara could be frugal when she needed to be.

David Genoa's Russian-born wife, Sorvina, spoke up. "My favorite is hot tub," she said in her accented voice. "I'm wanting one of those for long time. You will bid on it, David?" She fluttered her thick eyelashes in her husband's direction.

"Sure, honcy." David patted her hand and gave her a loving smile. Then he turned to Rose. "What tickles your fancy, Rose?"

Rose had spent considerable time during cocktail hour perusing the auction tables, and her choices rolled readily off her tongue. "The weekend at the Denver spa, and the gift certificate from Lily's Boutique."

Carl nodded at Mike. "That leaves you, buddy."

"I've got something in mind," Mike said, shooting Rose a glance.

Rose jerked her head around. When she'd made

her choices, he'd been vague about his. "What is it?" she asked.

"You'll see," he replied with an air of mystery.

Rose's stomach tensed. Was he keeping his bid choice a secret because he wasn't sure she'd approve, or because he genuinely wanted to surprise her?

A waiter wheeled a dessert tray to their table.

"Ah, here we are." Mike surveyed the offerings then told the server, "The lady will have the ice cream cake and I'll try the apple pie."

As Rose enjoyed the light-as-a-feather white cake layered with vanilla, chocolate, and strawberry ice cream, her tense stomach began to relax. As she'd told Mike, she was glad she'd come and especially surprised to find she enjoyed being a part of this group of couples. Although the conversation often turned to children, or the problems of owning a home, or the roles of husbands and wives, still, she felt as though she belonged.

"Too bad Buck and Molly couldn't be here tonight." Sara's voice broke into her thoughts.

Rose sat back while a waiter refilled her coffee cup then said, "Don't tell me Buck's riding in another rodeo?"

"Yep. He's off to Woodlawn this time."

"I bet Molly's having a fit."

Sara took a bite of her chocolate mousse. "There's not much she can do. We told Molly that Anna would stay with the kids while she came with us tonight, but she refused. Said without Buck, she'd feel out of place." Her brow wrinkled. "I worry about her. She's on her way to becoming a rodeo widow. From what I've heard, that's a frustrating and lonely life."

Scooping up her last bit of cake, Rose asked, "Will Jackson keep Buck on the job, even though he's away a lot?"

"Oh, yes. Those two are like brothers." Sara

paused. "But what about you? Bet you're glad to be traveling again."

Visions of her loneliness in St. Louis flitted through Rose's mind. She pursed her lips then said, "I, ah, guess so."

Sara leaned closer. "Do I hear hesitancy in your voice? Is home finally looking better than all the other places you visit?"

"Good evening, ladies and gentlemen!" boomed a voice over the public address system.

No time now to answer Sara's question. With a sigh of relief, Rose settled back in her chair and shifted her attention to the master of ceremonies, a distinguished-looking man in his sixties with thick, white hair.

The gentleman introduced the dignitaries, warmed up the crowd with a few jokes, and then turned the microphone over to the auctioneer.

A lanky man with a long, narrow face stepped forward, and the auction began. The lively bidding left no doubt the crowd intended to do their best to raise money for the hospital wing. Although she lost out on the boutique gift certificate, Rose managed to outbid an opponent across the room for the spa weekend.

"Good job," Mike whispered after the auctioneer declared Rose the winner.

David ended up with the hot tub Sorvina coveted. Jackson won the boots, plus a learning package for children that included books, toys, and games. "That'll keep Ryan and Karli busy," he remarked, showing Sara a list of the kit's contents.

Sara claimed a pair of ruby earrings, while Carl and Patricia managed to snag the Super Bowl package. When they all had oohed and aahed over that, Carl pointed a finger at Mike. "Okay, buddy, I haven't seen your hand go up yet this evening."

"My choice is coming up soon." Mike picked up

his bid card.

Recalling his earlier secrecy, Rose asked, "Why can't you tell us what it is?"

His animated gaze met hers. "I want to surprise you."

Rose's nerves thrummed. As she'd suspected—and feared—the prize he sought had to do with her. More likely, with them.

Several more items came up for bid, all of which Mike ignored.

"Here's our last prize," the auctioneer announced, holding up a colorful pamphlet. "And it's a beauty. An all-expense paid trip for two to Jamaica!" He read the particulars of the package and opened the bidding.

Rose sneaked a glance at Mike just as he held up his card for the first bid.

Sara whispered in Rose's ear, "Jamaica is a great place for a honeymoon, don't you think?"

"Sara!" Rose twisted around and stared at her sister-in-law.

A light laugh escaped Sara's lips. "Oh, come on, Rose, you know what Mike has in mind for you two. Everyone knows."

Rose gazed around the table. The other couples were nodding and exchanging knowing looks with one another. Her cheeks felt hot, and she wished she could shrink down in her seat and become invisible. Instead, she forced herself to sit up straight and paste a smile on her face.

The spirited bidding continued until one by one the contenders dropped out and only Mike and one other bidder remained. Knowing how determined Mike could be when he wanted something, Rose had no doubt he would win. She was right—a couple minutes later, Mike's opponent shook his head and put down his bid card. Still, Rose held her breath through the auctioneer's "going once, going twice," and, finally, "sold, to number seventy-seven."

Their tablemates cheered and applauded.

Mike leaned over and planted a quick kiss on Rose's lips. "We'll have a great time on this trip."

So he was purchasing the trip for the two of them. But it didn't have to be a honeymoon...could be just a vacation. Somehow, though, Rose thought she was only kidding herself to consider the trip a casual one.

"You haven't asked me to go with you yet," she said, hoping a joke would cover the butterflies crowding her stomach.

"Oh, Rose." His voice dropped a notch. "There's a lot I haven't asked you yet."

Rose's heart flip-flopped. She grabbed her wine glass and gulped the couple of swallows remaining.

"Don't worry." He laughed and clasped her free hand. "All I'm asking for tonight is a dance." He gestured to the bandstand, where the musicians had returned and picked up their instruments.

"Yes," she said, carefully setting down her glass, "let's dance."

On the dance floor, Rose wanted to savor being in Mike's arms, but concern about the trip to Jamaica kept her nerves on edge. If, as Sara speculated, the prize were to be for Rose and Mike's honeymoon, then he'd have to propose. If she said yes, there would be a wedding. Just the thought of marriage made her tremble inside.

Why couldn't they stay the way they were? They were happy now, weren't they? Why did their relationship have to progress to something more permanent?

But of course she knew the answer. Mike wanted a home and family. He would never be content with an affair. And, when she searched her heart, she knew an affair wouldn't be right for her, either.

His love seemed so strong, so true. Hers was, too, she realized with a jolt. She loved him with all her heart. Surely a love as strong as theirs could withstand the truth. The truth would only strengthen their bond. But, did she really want to put her reasoning to the test?

Chapter Twelve

Mike rounded the end of Red Rock High School's outdoor track and started on the home stretch of his third lap. He belonged to a health club with an indoor track, but he preferred to run outdoors. Nothing like fresh air and sunshine to rev one's engine.

Not that he needed the boost today. He'd awakened still on a high from last night's auction and winning the trip to Jamaica. The prize would be a perfect honeymoon for him and Rose. Visions of the two of them strolling the white-sand beaches and swimming in warm turquoise waters, not to say making love, popped into his mind. His lips curved into a smile of eager anticipation.

The more time he and Rose spent together, the more certain he was that she would accept his marriage proposal. He hadn't decided exactly when he would propose, but he didn't want to wait much longer. They'd already wasted the past two years, time during which they'd have been enjoying married life, and starting a family.

Voices behind him signaled the arrival of other runners. He shot a glance over his shoulder. A group of a dozen or so teenage boys dressed in T-shirts and blue trunks were quickly gaining on him. All husky guys, they probably were football players getting in shape for the coming season. Grinning and waving, they sprinted by.

One of them was the shaggy-haired kid he'd seen with Glenna Jordan in the café. The kid recognized Mike, too, because when their gazes met, his grin faded and a stricken look crossed his face. Mike wanted to catch up and reassure him he wouldn't tell anyone about his and Glenna's dilemma, that he wanted only to help. But of course, that was out of the question.

As the boys headed around the track, Mike loped along in their wake, wondering if Glenna would keep her next appointment at the clinic. A wave of sadness rolled over him, chasing away his earlier happy thoughts about Rose. He wanted to help people—that was why he'd gone into the profession—but he could do only so much. He hoped Glenna would make the right choices for herself and her unborn child.

****

"Rose, this is Kyra VanWinkle. Remember me from high school? I was Kyra Sergeant then."

Gripping the phone receiver, Rose sank onto the sofa. She'd been on her way out of her apartment to run errands and had been tempted to let voice mail pick up the call. Hearing her old friend's voice made her glad she'd answered it.

"Kyra? Of course, I remember you! Good to hear from you. Are you in town?"

"I sure am. I brought the kids for a month's stay with the folks. Randy'll be joining me later."

"I don't even know where you live now." Kyra had married soon after graduation. Since Rose hadn't lived in Red Rock then, she'd missed the wedding.

"Minneapolis. Yeah, we've got a lot of catch-up. Let's do lunch soon. But of course we'll see each other at the All Class Reunion. That'll be so fun."

The excitement of talking to Kyra faded, and Rose's shoulders sagged. "I'm not going to the reunion."

"Not going? Why ever not?"

Kyra's indignant tone indicated Rose's absence

would be a personal affront. "In case you've forgotten, I didn't graduate from Red Rock High." The flimsy excuse hadn't worked with Sara, but maybe it would with Kyra. "I, ah, got a scholarship to a school in Boston for my senior year."

"Yes, I remember. We all thought your going away for your senior year was strange, even if it was to a fancy private school."

Rose swallowed hard. "My parents were set on my going." Eager to steer the conversation away from the dangerous topic, she rushed on, "Anyway, that lets me out of the reunion."

"No, it doesn't." Kyra laughed. "Graduation from Red Rock is not a requirement. The party's for anyone who went there at any time. Rose, you have to go. Jolene's coming. She lives in Tucson now." She named other mutual friends who would be there.

"You must have kept in touch with everyone to know all this," Rose said, feeling guilty she'd let so many friendships lapse. But, then, she had an excuse. Keeping up friendships would invite questions about the year she'd spent away from Red Rock.

"No, I haven't," Kyra admitted. "Except for Jolene. We get together at least once a year."

"Then how do you know so much about who's coming to the reunion?"

"There's a list on the website."

"There's a website?" She'd no idea the reunion of a small town high school would be such a big deal.

"Rose, where have you been? Didn't you read the invitation? The website's listed at the bottom."

Knowing she wouldn't be attending, Rose had only skimmed the invitation. "I missed that part."

"The list is pretty impressive. I hope you'll change your mind and decide to go. In the meantime, how about lunch with me and Jolene?"

They made a date for Wednesday. When Rose

hung up, she sat with her chin propped in her hand thinking about the reunion. Although she'd told Mike she didn't want to go, he'd not given up. Neither had Sara and Jackson, who wanted to make the occasion a foursome. No one accepted her excuse that she couldn't go because she hadn't graduated from Red Rock High. Still, she'd managed to keep putting them off.

Of course, Rose hadn't told them the real reason she didn't want to go was because she couldn't risk running into Kurt Fuller. No way did she want to lay eyes on him ever again.

She chewed absently on a fingernail while her mind spun a new scenario. What if he wasn't coming? Then she could go, couldn't she? Nothing else she could think of stopped her. Seeing her old friends would be fun. She'd enjoyed high school— until she'd made the mistake of becoming involved with Kurt.

Her errands forgotten, she went in her office and rummaged in a desk drawer until she found the invitation to the reunion. Sure enough, at the bottom of the page was the event's website address.

Rose sat at her computer, turned it on, and keyed in the site's URL. When the page came up, she easily located the "Who Will Be There?" link and clicked on it. Holding her breath, she scanned the alphabetical list, slowing when she reached the "F's." Faller, Fenton, Franklin, Furston... No Fuller. To make sure, she studied the list again. No, Kurt Fuller's name was not among those attending the reunion.

Blowing out her indrawn breath, she sat back and crossed both arms over her chest. If Kurt wouldn't be there, then she was free to go. Visions of attending the party with Mike stirred her emotions. He'd be so pleased. So would Sara and Jackson. They'd have fun. She'd reconnect with her old friends.

A sudden thought jerked her upright. Kurt could still be coming. Maybe he just hadn't made his reservation yet. Leaning forward and scanning the page, she saw the deadline was two days away. Should she take the chance? She switched off her computer, still puzzling what to do.

When Mike brought up the subject in a phone call that evening, she made her decision on the spot. "Yes, I'll go." For a moment, only silence flowed from the other end of the line, and then he said, "Great, Rose."

"You sound unsure now."

He cleared his throat. "No, of course not. I just wondered what made you change your mind."

Sticking as closely to the truth as she dared, she told him about the phone call from Kyra. "She mentioned a few other non-graduates who were coming, so I figured I wouldn't be out of place."

"You wouldn't be, anyway. You weren't a dropout; you transferred to another school."

Her stomach knotted. *Let's not go there.* "Whatever, I'd like to attend. Still want to take me?"

"Of course! I'll make the reservations right away."

****

Sitting in his living room, Mike hung up his call to Rose, happy she'd finally agreed to attend the reunion. And yet, like an annoying itch, something nagged him. He still couldn't understand why Rose's friend Kyra had convinced her, when he, Jackson, and Sara could not. Mulling that over, he stood and went to the window overlooking the town.

A couple birds circled the flagpole atop the Post Office, and then soared out of sight. Farther in the distance, purple clouds over the mountains signaled an approaching storm.

Finding no answer to his question about Rose's

sudden change of mind, he shrugged off the worry. Bottom line was Rose was coming to the party. With him. They'd have a great time. He rubbed his hands together in eager anticipation.

An idea popped into his mind, and he snapped his fingers. There was a way to make the evening truly memorable.

He hurried to his bedroom and entered a walk-in closet. Sliding aside a wall panel, he uncovered a small safe. He keyed in the combination, opened the door, and removed a black metal box. The hinged lid creaked as it swung back to reveal a cache of glittering necklaces, bracelets, earrings, and finger rings. The jewelry had belonged to Bev Mahoney, his adoptive mother. "Keepsakes," she'd called them. She'd wanted him to pass them on to his children. And, he would. But tonight he was on a different mission.

He dug around until his fingers closed on the smooth surface of a blue ring box. Carrying the box to the bedroom window where the light was better, he flipped it open. Diamonds sparkled from their nest in the box. The muscles in his chest tightened and he sucked in a breath. He'd almost forgotten what a great wedding ring set this was. The two carat diamond in the engagement ring and the smaller, yet equally brilliant diamonds in the wedding band were perfect compliments to one another.

Lifting out the engagement ring, he studied its facets, recalling his excitement the night he'd planned to propose and give the ring to Rose. Before he could utter a word, she'd broken up with him, told him her plans for the future no longer included him. After that, he hadn't wanted to look at the rings, or even return them to the jeweler. Instead, he'd put the set in the metal box he kept in the safe.

Now, he was glad he'd kept the rings. The

dinner-dance would provide the perfect setting to propose. The grange hall had a pleasant garden with secluded walks where he could pop the question. She'd say yes, and they would announce their engagement before the evening ended. Perfect.

Mike tucked the engagement ring back into its slot, closed the box, and placed it in a dresser drawer. Squaring his shoulders, he turned out the light and left the room.

****

Each day, Rose checked the All Class Reunion website list of attendees and, not seeing Kurt's name, each day she relaxed a little more.

On Wednesday, she met Kyra and Jolene for lunch at The Roundup. Rose's heart warmed at the sight of her old friends. "Kyra, you haven't changed a bit," she said as she hugged the tall, thin redhead.

"Would you believe her?" Jolene thumbed in Kyra's direction. "Three kids and she hasn't gained a pound since we were on the swim team."

Rose turned to hug Jolene. Shorter in stature and plumper than either Rose or Kyra, she'd always worried about her weight. "Hey, you're looking good, Jo. We always envied you, you know, because you filled out your bathing suit so much better than we did."

They all laughed, and then the hostess came to show them to their table. They ordered and their meals arrived, and all the while they were having a good time reliving memories.

Then Kyra piped up, "Speaking of envy, Rose, we all were green after Samantha James dumped Kurt Fuller, and he picked you as his next girlfriend."

Rose's laughter over the last joke died, and she clamped her lips shut. "Nothing to be envious about," she finally said, struggling to keep her tone casual.

Jolene slapped the table and hooted. "Yeah, right. The coolest jock in school."

If they only knew...

"What broke you two up?" Kyra picked up her roll and daintily took a bite.

The prepared excuse, so often given over the past decade, rolled off Rose's lips. "Don't you remember? He graduated and went to college in California, and I went to Boston for my senior year."

"No long-distance romance for you two, huh?" Kyra exchanged a raised-eyebrow look with Jolene.

Jolene sipped her diet coke. "Here we are, married with kids, and you're still single. How did that happen?" She exhaled a wistful-sounding sigh.

Kyra cast a sly look in Rose's direction. "I hear you and Dr. Mike Mahoney are seeing each other."

The small town grapevine at work again. Rose didn't particularly want to talk about Mike, either, but at least then she wouldn't have to answer any more questions about Kurt. She finished a bite of her chicken salad and said, "He was my doctor when I broke my leg in the train wreck."

"But weren't you together a couple years ago?" Jolene's forehead bunched under her fringe of bangs. "I seem to recall my cousin telling me about you two."

"Ah, well..."

Kyra spread her hands. "We should back off, Jo. Maybe Rose doesn't want to talk about it."

"Sorry," Jolene said, ducking her head. "I guess because I'm an old married, I'm looking for some romance and was hoping you could throw us a bone or two."

Jolene's woeful tone made Rose giggle, easing her tension. "Not much to tell, I'm afraid. We're seeing each other, that's all. He's been a good friend of Jackson's since high school. He's practically family."

"And you're coming to the dinner-dance together?" Kyra leaned forward, her eyes bright.

"Yes, we'll be there," Rose said, infusing her voice with an eagerness that matched Kyra's.

"Great!" Jolene clapped her hands. "Can't wait to see everyone. It'll be so fun."

Later, as Rose drove home, the excitement generated at lunch began to wear off, and she wondered if she'd made the right decision to attend the reunion, after all. Even if Kurt weren't there in the flesh, he would be in spirit, as today's lunch had proved.

She'd looked forward to visiting with Kyra and Jolene, but she'd ended up dodging questions about Kurt—and about Mike, too. Was there no escape from the past, ever?

****

"Fun," Rose said to herself as she slipped on the yellow cotton dress she'd chosen to wear for the reunion dinner-dance. "Tonight is going to be fun."

Since her lunch with Kyra and Jolene, Rose had been pep-talking herself about the reunion, determined to have a good time at the various events.

Yesterday, she'd attended the reception and picnic lunch, held at the high school. Tonight's dinner-dance at the local grange hall was a bit more formal—but not much. Certainly not as formal as the auction she and Mike attended. That had been in Denver; this was Red Rock. Here, where everyone practically lived in their jeans, boots, and Stetsons, dressing up meant a fancier pair of boots, a hat without sweat stains, and maybe a bolo tie for the guys and a pretty scarf for the women.

She was glad she and Sara chose to wear dresses, though. Rose's dress had a straight, knee-length skirt, a fitted bodice, and spaghetti straps that showed off her shoulders. She finished zipping up the back, and then added an amber necklace and a pair of matching earrings.

Stepping to the full-length mirror, she twirled around, checking herself from all angles. She exchanged a smile of satisfaction with her mirror image. *Not bad for an old lady of thirty-two.*

A few minutes later, Mike arrived to pick her up. His eyes shone as his gaze traveled over her. "You look great."

"So do you," she said, admiring his denim suit worn over a light blue, Western-style shirt with pearl buttons.

When Mike and Rose reached the Rolling R, Jackson was ready but Sara was nowhere in sight. "She'll be a couple of minutes." Jackson motioned for them to take a seat in the living room while they waited.

Sara finally appeared, her blond hair a cascade of curls around her heart-shaped face. Her turquoise dress had a short, flared skirt that showed off her long legs.

Jackson let out a low whistle. "She wouldn't let me see her until she was ready," he said to the others. "You'd think this event was a wedding or something."

Sara gave him a playful punch on the arm. "Come on, big guy, quit teasing and let's go."

"Seriously, Sara, you are as beautiful as the day you became my bride."

"You say the nicest things." Sara blushed and lowered her eyelids.

Jackson caught her hand and pulled her against him. The two exchanged a lingering kiss.

Their display of affection brought a flush to Rose's cheeks. Wondering what Mike thought, she shot him a glance.

He met her gaze with a wink. "Think we can stand riding with those two?"

Picking up on his teasing tone, she propped her hands on her hips. "I don't know. Maybe we should go alone..."

"Oh, no, you don't!" Releasing Sara, Jackson grabbed his Stetson from the hat rack and settled it on his head. "We've been looking forward to this double date for a long time. You'll have to put up with us."

Anna came in with Ryan in tow, which prompted a round of good-byes, along with a few last-minute instructions for Anna. The housekeeper took them with a smile, and then made shooing motions. "Go, already! Ryan and I will be fine."

They finally got underway in Mike's SUV. The banter continued during the drive to the grange hall. Rose's spirits were high. This would be an enjoyable evening. Seeing old friends again would make up at least a little for all she'd missed the last year of high school.

At the grange hall, colorful paper lanterns swaying in the light breeze led the way up the stone walk. From the open double doors came the strains of lively western music. Once inside, there was a flurry of signing in, pinning on nametags, and greeting other attendees. Sara and Jackson disappeared into the crowd. Some basketball team buddies swept Mike away, while Kyra and Jolene joined Rose.

Over the next half hour, Rose reconnected with friends, some of whom she hadn't seen in over fifteen years. When the call for dinner came, she joined Mike, Sara, and Jackson in the buffet line. After loading their plates with broasted chicken, a variety of salads, and a fruit medley, they went outside to the garden, which the grange hall ladies had turned into a Grecian courtyard. Paved paths intertwined beds of roses and lovely shade trees, wrought iron benches, and stone statues of Greek gods and goddesses. For tonight's party, tables had been set up wherever space allowed. They found a table in a cozy corner next to a burbling fountain.

Jackson gave Sara a loving look. "This place is familiar. We made some great memories out here at another dance, didn't we?"

"We did." Sara unrolled her napkin-wrapped silverware. "You remember that night, don't you, Rose?" She turned to Mike. "And you were here, too, Mike. I wasn't going to come that night, but Rose insisted. I was glad I did."

"I do remember," Mike said, spreading his napkin on his lap. "It was shortly after we broke up, Rose. We had only one dance that night. Tonight we're going to have many more, and make our own memories."

Rose steadied her knife and fork as she cut a piece of chicken. Was he up to something? After his secrecy about the trip to Jamaica, she wasn't sure she trusted him not to spring any more surprises. Then, as others joined them, she pushed aside her worries and concentrated on enjoying her meal.

Later, Rose excused herself to go inside to the ladies' room. As she touched up her lipstick in the mirror, she encountered a few more friends she hadn't yet greeted.

"Great party, isn't it?" one of them said.

"It is!" Rose tucked her lipstick back into her purse. "I'm so glad I came."

Wrapped in her glow of happiness, Rose stepped into the hall's main room. While making her way to the garden exit, she heard someone call her name. She turned, ready with a smile to greet another acquaintance. When she saw who the person was, her smile faded and all the breath drained out of her lungs.

Kurt Fuller.

No, not him. Please, God, no.

Rose closed her eyes, hoping he would disappear. But when she opened them again, he was still shouldering through the crowd toward her. Desperate to escape, she whirled around. People were everywhere, laughing, talking, closing her in. The band's music blared. Her brain whirled like a kaleidoscope; her stomach churned.

Finally, she spied a break in the crowd. Like a mole seeking daylight, she tunneled toward the door.

Too late. Kurt caught up.

"Hey, Rose. Don't take off yet. I want to talk to you."

Chapter Thirteen

Rose met the gaze of the man who'd haunted her for the past fifteen years, the man she wished she'd never met, the man she'd tried so hard to forget.

The years had not been kind to Kurt Fuller, Red Rock High's star quarterback and every girl's secret crush. His blond hair, once thick and wavy, had thinned on top, and his blue eyes had lost their luster. Deep lines were etched around his eyes and from nose to mouth, and a potbelly strained the buttons of his tan shirt.

"You weren't supposed to be here!" she blurted.

Eyes narrowed, he peered at her face. "What do you mean?"

"I, uh, nothing." She didn't want to admit she'd been checking the website list, didn't want him to know his attendance was of the slightest interest. She was certain he knew nothing about her pregnancy, or that he was the father of her child. Her mother had made her promise not to tell anyone, ever, a promise she'd faithfully kept. Wouldn't her mother have kept the promise, too?

"How've you been?"

His serious tone made her think he might really care. But of course, that was only her imagination. Or a trick of the hall's acoustics. She lifted her chin. "Just fine. You?"

He shrugged. "I've had a few ups and downs. Look, Rose, I need to talk to you."

Alarm arrowed through her. "Why?"

"I just need to. It's important."

"Whatever you have to say, you can say right

here."

Hands on his hips, Kurt stuck out his jaw. "No, I can't. Come on, Rose, give me five minutes of your time. I'll come to your place tomorrow."

"No!" The refusal shot from her lips. If anyone saw them together, rumors would fly around town with the speed of a bullet. "Isn't your wife with you?" She craned her neck to see around him, but spotted no woman waiting in the background.

He shook his head. "I'm divorced. I wasn't gonna come tonight, but I'm between jobs and had the time. So, here I am."

"So that's why your name wasn't on the list," she said, half to herself.

"List? What list?"

"The one on the website. Oh, never mind." Impatience ran through her and she waved the air.

"No, I didn't sign up, if that's what you mean. I figured they couldn't turn me away, now, could they? And I was right. Why, the minute I walked in the door tonight, my old buds flocked around me like they used to when I'd made a touchdown." He flashed his crooked grin.

Once, she'd thought that grin charming. Tonight his smile—and everything else about him—left her cold. How could she ever have been attracted to him?

"Meet me for coffee somewhere," he said, shedding his grin and pressing his lips together. "That's all I ask."

As she opened her mouth to refuse again, a familiar voice behind her said, "Well, look who's here."

Mike.

Her entire body stilled before she turned. "Mike, you remember Kurt Fuller?" She was amazed at how calm she sounded, when her insides were crumbling into little pieces.

"Of course. Who could forget the guy who helped

us win the State Championship? Hey, Kurt." Mike stuck out his hand.

Puffing up his chest, Kurt shoved his hand into Mike's. "Mike Mahoney, right? Hey, I heard you're a doctor now."

"Yep. Family practice." Mike's gaze moved back and forth from Kurt to Rose. "You two catching up?"

"Just saying hello." Rose eyed Kurt. "G-good seeing you, Kurt." She choked on the blatant lie and prayed Kurt wouldn't repeat his request to get together. Not in front of Mike.

Kurt pointed a finger and began, "Ah, Rose—"

Before she could speak, Mike grasped her elbow. "Ready to hit the dessert table, Rose?"

She blinked with relief, and then, with a forced brightness, said, "Yes, let's."

"Excuse us." Mike nodded to Kurt.

Certain Kurt's gaze was boring into her back, Rose followed Mike through the crowd to the buffet table. She stared at the array of pies, cakes, and cookies. How could she eat when her stomach churned like a cement mixer?

Vaguely, she heard Mike speaking, but the words were all jumbled together.

"Rose?" he said, louder.

"W-what did you say?"

"I said the blueberry pie looks good."

She took a deep breath and focused. "Yes, it does."

He picked up two plates of blueberry pie, and turned to peer at her. "Are you okay?"

"I'm f-fine."

"I don't think so." His brows bunched together. "What did Kurt say that upset you?"

She stepped aside as the person next to her reached for a piece of carrot cake. "Nothing. We'd barely said 'hi' when you came. I'm okay." She pasted a smile on her lips. "Let's go eat our pie."

Settled again at their table in the garden, although every bite stuck in her throat, Rose managed to eat the blueberry pie. And, through sheer determination, she managed to survive the rest of the evening. A couple times when she and Mike were dancing, she caught sight of Kurt watching from across the room. Her stomach churned with the fear he would approach and cut in, and she'd have to dance with him. Thankfully, he kept his distance.

The evening over at last, they headed home. While Sara and Jackson carried on an animated discussion in the back seat, Rose and Mike spoke little. Mike focused on his driving, while Rose gazed out the window at the passing landscape. The hills were dark, the mountains darker still against a night sky sprinkled with stars.

She glanced at Mike. His mouth was set in a grim line. Was he angry? Worried? She couldn't tell. She was certain, though, that the evening had not met his expectations. All her fault. She shouldn't have come. Maybe she should have stuck with her first decision to stay away. When would she ever learn? Wherever she turned, the past leaped out and grabbed her by the throat.

When they finally reached the Rolling R, Sara leaned forward and said, "Coming in for a nightcap, you two?"

"It's late," Rose mumbled, knowing she sounded lame.

"Thanks, anyway." Mike gave a curt nod.

Once they were underway again, Rose wished they had taken up Sara on her invitation. Silence as thick as smoke filled the SUV. The twenty-minute ride to Red Rock seemed more like an hour. Keeping her back rigid against the seat, Rose longed to be home.

At last, Mike pulled up in front of her

apartment. He cut the engine, and then rested an arm on the steering wheel as he turned. "Okay, what's going on, Rose?"

Wilting under his intense gaze, Rose pressed a hand against her stomach. "N-nothing. I had a good time tonight."

"Yeah, until you saw Kurt Fuller." He paused, and then added, "Is there something still between you two?"

The absurd question sent shock waves through her. "What? No, of course not! I haven't seen or spoken to him since...since—" Her throat closed, blocking any more words.

"Since when?"

Tears burned behind her eyes. Not sure she could hold them off much longer, she said, "Please, Mike, could we have this discussion another time?" *Like, never.*

The rigid lines around his mouth softened. "I never meant to upset you, but I'm worried about you. Something's not right."

"I'm fine." The words tasted bitter. "Please, don't worry."

He slowly shook his head. "Rose, Rose, when will you learn to trust me?"

"I do trust you..."

"Then what is wrong?" He laid a hand on her arm. "What happened between you and Kurt tonight?"

Rose licked her dry lips. If only she could tell him the truth. But, of course, that was out of the question. "Nothing."

He leaned back and crossed both arms over his chest. "So you're going to stand by your insistence that 'nothing' happened tonight between you and Kurt?"

Sick inside, keeping her gaze averted, she nodded. In the long silence that followed, Rose's nerves drew so taut she was ready to scream.

Finally, he said in clipped tones, "I'll see you to the door."

"No need." Rose flung open her door and jumped out. Her feet hit the sidewalk with a jolt. Barely maintaining her balance, she stumbled into the building. The corner of her eye captured his SUV still parked at the curb. Knowing what a stubborn man he could be, she half expected him to follow her. But he didn't.

Her heart ripped into shreds, she couldn't hold back the tears any longer. Crying in front of him would only require more explanations. Explanations she couldn't give.

As the elevator swept her up to the third floor, hot tears spilled down her face. Later, worry kept her tossing and turning long after she'd gone to bed. Kurt's sudden appearance tonight had shaken her to the core. What could he possibly want to talk to her about? She only hoped he'd leave town soon, and this time, stay away forever.

****

Once again, Mike found himself sitting alone in a booth in an all-night café, nursing a cup of coffee he didn't really want. Yet he couldn't face going home to his condo. His spirits, so high when he'd begun the evening, had now sunk lower than a coal miner's elevator.

He'd begun the evening full of hope, full of plans. On the way to pick up Rose, the engagement ring tucked safely in his jacket pocket, he'd rehearsed The Proposal. The grange garden, with its flowers, wrought iron benches, and Greek statues, would be a perfect place. He'd find a time for them to be alone, declare his love—as if she didn't already know he loved her—and ask her to marry him. She'd say yes. He'd place the ring on her finger, and they'd go inside and announce their engagement to the party attendees.

But he hadn't proposed, and, instead, they'd ended the evening on a sour note.

Absently stirring his coffee, he wondered what had gone wrong. They'd been having a fine time with Sara and Jackson and connecting with old friends. Rose was happy and enjoying herself—until Kurt Fuller showed up. Then she'd become sullen and withdrawn.

He slid his hand down to his jacket pocket where the ring box all but burned a hole in the fabric. No way could he propose after Kurt appeared.

She insisted nothing had happened between her and Kurt, but he wasn't buying it. A troublesome thought had hovered around the corners of his mind for some time now, but he'd managed to ignore it. Now, like a jack-in-the-box with an evil grin, the idea popped up to taunt him.

Rose still had feelings for Kurt Fuller. All these years, she'd been pining for the high school jock. That was the reason she'd broken off their relationship two years ago. She couldn't commit to him when she was still in love with Kurt.

Shaking his head, Mike shifted on the booth's hard seat. Rose still in love with Kurt? Ridiculous. She was a teenager when she'd dated Kurt. He recalled Jackson and her parents weren't too thrilled about Kurt. They thought he was wild—and from what Mike had heard, their worries had substance.

Mike hadn't given Kurt much thought since high school. No reason to. He did hear that a steroid scandal had ruined Kurt's pro football career. After that, he'd dropped out of sight—until tonight.

After all these years, did Rose still fancy herself in love with Kurt?

Mike fisted his hand and pounded the table, rattling his coffee cup and spoon against the saucer. No, not possible. She loved him, not Kurt. He could tell by the look in her eyes when their gazes met. He could tell by the way she melted in his arms when he kissed her.

Then why had she shut down tonight after meeting Kurt? When she'd dodged his questions, he'd let the matter go. The hour was late; they both were tired. Not the best circumstances for a talk.

He wasn't going to let it go for long, though. He'd give her space over the weekend. Then, come Monday, he'd expect answers.

****

Monday morning, Rose headed down the hall at TransAmerica when her boss, Stan Doyle, stuck his head out his office door.

"Rose, I need to see you. Got a minute?"

"Sure, Stan." She stepped into his office and sat in the chair he indicated. "What's up?"

Stan crossed both arms over his narrow chest and leaned a hip against his desk. "I'll cut to the chase. Are you still interested in a transfer?"

A gasp escaped and Rose's eyes widened. "A transfer? I'd about given up. Tell me about it."

"Okay, here's the deal. Joyce Mayburn, from the St. Louis office, called awhile ago. Her quality control manager, who's been on maternity leave, has decided to make it permanent. I know you have friends in St. Louis, so you wouldn't be a stranger." He paused to study her, eyes owlish behind round-framed glasses. "But I thought maybe your situation might have changed since you requested the transfer."

Rose idly gazed out Stan's window at Denver's skyline. Puffy gray clouds drifted across the sky, indicating a rainstorm in the offing. "Yes, my life's different now. A lot has happened since I broke my leg."

"Couldn't have to do with a certain doctor, could it?"

His teasing didn't offend her. She and Stan were friends as well as boss and employee. Many times, she'd been a guest at his and his wife, Grace's, home for dinner or a party. Still, she'd rather keep the details of her relationship with Mike private. "My decision depends on a lot of things. Can I think it over and get back to you?"

Stan straightened and ran a hand over his balding head. "Okay. But don't take too long making up your mind. Others are interested, too."

In her office, Rose sat at her desk mulling over Stan's news. Before Mike had come back into her life, a transfer was her goal. How did she feel now? Although she realized she still loved him, nothing had changed. Certain he would reject her, she still couldn't tell him about her past.

Seeing Kurt at the reunion was a strong reminder that her past still haunted her. Like a leech, the past sucked away her energy—and her courage.

Rose idly fingered a stray paperclip and dropped it into its plastic container. Perhaps a transfer was the best course of action. Still, moving out of the area was a huge decision, and she needed to be sure that was what she wanted.

Her desk phone rang. Glad for the interruption, she snatched up the receiver. "Rose Phillips."

"Rose, hey. How ya doin' this morning?"

Her stomach clenched. "Kurt?"

"Ya, it's me, Kurt."

Indignation bubbled up. "Why are you calling me at work?"

"I don't have your home number, so this is the only way I can get a hold of you."

"And you need to get hold of me because—?" Her grip tightened.

"Like I told you at the party, I need to talk to you."

Rose gritted her teeth. Why wouldn't the man take "no" for an answer? "And I thought I made it clear I don't want to talk to you."

"Five minutes, Rose. That's all I ask. Please."

"Can't you say whatever it is over the phone?"

"No, I can't. It's gotta be in person."

Rose glanced at the paperwork on her desk then at her computer, where an unfinished report needed her attention. Work certainly provided a justifiable excuse to deny his request.

And yet, the desperation in Kurt's voice made her hesitate. Maybe he was in trouble. Would it put her out too much to listen to whatever he had to say? She chewed her lip, considering. "Oh, all right," she grumbled. "But not here in my office, and not at my apartment. Somewhere out of town."

"Don't want to be seen with me, huh? Quite a change from when we were in high school. Then you liked to show me off."

Rose raised her voice a couple decibels. "I did no such thing! Kurt, do you want to talk to me or not?"

"Yeah, I do. Okay, meet me at the Blue Sage Café, on the road to Forksville. Five-thirty today."

"Fine. I'll see you there." She slammed down the receiver.

She'd barely begun work on her report when the phone rang again. Hoping the caller wasn't Kurt again, she grabbed the receiver.

"Hello, Rose."

Mike.

Her heart thudded. She'd thought about him all weekend, had even picked up the phone more than once to call him. But, not knowing what to say, she'd let the troublesome matter go.

"We didn't finish our discussion the other night," he said.

"I know." She heaved a sigh. "I felt bad about the way we left things."

"Me, too. So, I thought tonight might be a good time to get together. We could have dinner, take a drive..."

"I, ah..." Rose fumbled, groping for an excuse. "I might have to...to work late tonight." No way could she tell him about her meeting with Kurt. Especially when she didn't know what Kurt wanted to talk to her about.

"How late?"

"I'm not sure. I have a report due tomorrow that I've barely started." That, at least, was true.

"What about tomorrow night? I don't want to put this off any longer, Rose. You understand."

His firm tone rang in her ear. She didn't blame him, yet the thought of more discussion about the class reunion tied knots in her stomach. "Yes, yes, I do understand. All right."

"Dinner somewhere, then?"

No, dinner out would be too much like a date. "Ah, let's make it after dinner. How about my place at seven?"

He hesitated so long in answering she feared he would hold out for a dinner date. But, at last, he said, "Okay. Your place, seven o'clock."

****

At five o'clock, Rose shut down her computer and tidied her desktop. Guilt dragged at her because she still hadn't finished her report. Since Kurt's and Mike's phone calls, she'd bounced from one task to another like a ping-pong ball.

Out on the highway, headed to Forksville, the fresh air from her open window cleared her head, made her question her decision to meet Kurt. What if someone she knew saw them and the word got back to Mike? Maybe she should turn around and go home. But around the next bend the Blue Sage Café came into view.

In the parking lot, Kurt climbed from his rental

car. A Cadillac.

Just the kind of car she'd expect him to have. Pulling into the lot, she chose a space several cars over from his. She stepped out, sucked in a deep breath, and headed toward him.

Kurt stood with feet apart, hands resting easily on his hips.

She marveled that he could appear so relaxed when her stomach was tied in knots.

"Hey, Rose, good to see you."

She almost said she wished she could say the same, but bit back the words. No point in adding sarcasm to the mix. She settled for a simple, "Hello, Kurt."

Inside the café, in case anyone she knew should come in, Rose headed for a booth tucked away in a corner. They both ordered coffee. When they'd been served, Rose let her mug sit untouched. She had no taste or desire for coffee or anything else. Wondering why Kurt wanted to talk to her kept her nerves thrumming.

He rambled on about his new job managing a car dealership in Chicago, and then asked, "So how do you like workin' for the railroad?"

"I like it." She leveled him a stern gaze. "But let me remind you this isn't a social visit. You have a specific reason for seeing me. What is it?"

He sobered and glanced down at his coffee mug. When he raised his gaze again, his eyes were pinched at the sides. "Unfinished business."

Alarms clanged in her brain yet she kept her voice steady. "What do you mean?"

"Unfinished business," he repeated in measured tones. "Between you and me."

Rose stiffened. "That's ridiculous. There's nothing between us. This has been a waste of time. I'm leaving." She scooted to the end of the booth.

Grasping her arm, he held her in place. "You've

181

come this far, hear me out."

Jerking her arm away, she muttered, "Oh, all right." Then she settled back onto the seat, but her heart hammered and her mouth was as dry as dust.

Kurt dipped his head. "Rose, I know about the kid."

Rose's blood turned cold. She sat there as though she'd been turned into a statue. Then, aware he waited for her response, she drew herself up. With feigned indignation, she said, "I don't know what you're talking about."

"Come off it, Rose. The kid. You. Me." He waggled his forefinger back and forth between the two of them.

He knew about the baby? No, not possible. She had told no one. Surely, her mother would have kept the promise, too.

Don't admit anything. She clamped her jaw shut and crossed both arms over her chest, locking up the secret tight inside.

"You wanta know how I know?" Without waiting for a reply, he went on, "I overheard my parents talking about it. Just last year. So I barged in and said, 'What the hell?' and they told me your mother came to them, accusing me of knocking you up—"

Rose winced at the crude term, thankful no one sat close enough to overhear. When the rest of his words sank in, shock waves rippled through her. Her mother had told Kurt's parents about her pregnancy? Then why had she made Rose promise to keep the secret, even to her dying day?

Grasping the tabletop, she steadied herself. She couldn't dwell on the promise now. She must listen to the rest of Kurt's story.

"Your mom wanted money," he was saying, "or else she'd make a big stink. I was eighteen and you were underage. Your mom had it all worked out— send you away, give the kid up for adoption, and you go to some posh private school for your senior year. The money was to pay all your expenses, and then some."

He paused and studied her.

"Go on," she croaked.

"So, yeah, my folks went along with it. They coulda insisted on the DNA thing after the kid was born, but they knew we'd been running around together and, well, they knew me. Ya know what I mean?" Sitting straighter, he puffed out his chest.

"I suppose I do."

"So your mom's way seemed better than risking scandal..."

Rose closed her eyes, still unable to believe her mother's underhanded scheming. Her heart pounded.

"...My folks wanted me to go to college and play football, like my dad did. Yeah, they had high hopes for me." His mouth tightened and he glanced away.

She guessed he was recalling the steroid scandal he'd been involved in when he was a pro. Realizing he'd had his own problems, she softened a little. "So, why are you telling me all this now?"

Keeping his gaze averted, he toyed with his coffee mug. "Ever since I found out, it's been bugging me. I wanted to tell you I'm sorry."

He was sorry? Rose's mouth fell open and shock rippled through her. This meeting was all about him being sorry?

And yet, when he finally looked up, and she saw the sincerity radiating from his eyes, she believed him.

Still, she wasn't ready to completely let him off the hook. Lifting her chin, she said, "So, Kurt, what would you have done if you'd known at the time?"

He sat back and gave a dry laugh. "Everything probably woulda gone down like it did. Hey, I confess, I was a jackass back then. But I like to think I've changed as I've gotten older."

She tilted her head. "Hence the being sorry?"

"Yeah. When I heard, I felt bad for what you went through."

"And telling me—"

"Makes me feel better," he admitted, dipping his head. "I hoped it might make you feel better, too. But from what I heard, your life's been good. You went to college, you got a good job traveling all over the country."

So, according to Kurt, she had a good life. Yeah, right. If only he knew...

"So, what'd we have?"

Hearing him call the two of them "we" was like a stab in the gut. She raised her eyebrows. "What?"

He swept a hand across the table. "What'd we have? Boy? Girl?"

"Oh. A...a..." Her throat clogged up. "A g-girl," she finally managed to say.

A smile touched his lips. "A girl. Well, ain't that fine. I got three boys, two with wife number one, and one with wife number two."

He'd gone on with his life. He'd married and had children, while she'd been stuck in the past. Anger knotted in her chest.

"Do you know where the kid is now?

"I have no idea," she said in a carefully controlled voice.

"Don't you ever wonder?"

Rose held up a hand. "Was there anything else you wanted to say today?"

"Just that I'm sorry." He shrugged.

She spread her palms flat on the table. "Well. I appreciate your thoughts."

A grin tugged at his lips. "We had some good times, didn't we, Rose? Except for that one thing. And that was my fault. Shoulda used a condom."

"I take responsibility for my part in what

happened, Kurt."

Brows furrowed, he leaned over the table. "You sure the kid's mine?"

The bold question chased away some of her sympathy toward him, and she ground out her response. "I never had sex with anyone but you during that time period."

"Ah." His frown changed to a smile.

Neither spoke. At the counter, a waitress called an order to the cook. The front door opened and new customers, talking and laughing, entered. The teenagers in a booth across the room clattered silverware against plates.

Rose focused on the door, her entire body itching to bolt.

"Everything worked out for the best, didn't it?" Kurt finally said. "The kid got a home. We went on with our lives."

Fingers clenched in her lap, Rose gritted her teeth. Everything for the best? Hardly. Not when she had desperately wanted to keep her baby—for in her mind, the child was hers, and not Kurt's. No, not ever his. And not when desperation led her to ignore her mother's plans and devise one of her own, one that led to disaster. But, then, Kurt didn't know that part of the story.

Nor would he ever.

"Wasn't it, Rose?"

His voice jerked her back to the present. "What?"

"For the best. The way it all turned out."

"Right, for the best," she said, choking on the words.

Chapter Fourteen

"Dr. Mike, you're the best," Mary Morris said from the doorway of her mother, Violet's, bedroom. "Whoever heard of a doctor making a house call these days?"

Sitting on the edge of Violet's quilt-covered bed, Mike wrapped up his pressure cuff and tucked it into his bag. "I was in the area. Stopping by to check on your mother was no trouble."

Mary was right, though. Doctor's house calls were a thing of the past. Still, when he had the chance, he stepped back in time and gave his patients a special visit.

He'd spoken the truth about being in the area. After Rose turned down his dinner invitation, he'd had a call from Jay Barlow, a pediatrician in Forksville, who wanted to join the Timber Ridge Clinic. They'd been trying to get together for a couple of weeks without success. Today, Jay had some free afternoon time, and so did Mike. Visiting Jay at his office would also give him a chance to see Violet, who was staying with her daughter while recovering from a mild stroke.

He reached over and patted Violet's blue-veined hand lying on top of the quilt. "You're doing fine, young lady."

Violet's lips curved into a crooked smile. "I never thought I'd live to see my great-grandchild be born, but, thanks to you, here I am."

Mike rose and picked up his bag. "You're most welcome. But we'll also give credit to the medicine that regulates your high blood pressure. That plus your diet changes, and you'll be up and around in no time."

A few minutes later, Mary walked him to the front door. "Thank you again, Dr. Mike."

"My pleasure, Mary. Let my office know if Violet has any problems. Otherwise, I'll see the two of you in a couple of weeks."

On the road again, Mike thought about Violet and how far she'd come since she'd had her stroke. She was one gritty lady with a strong will to live. She'd do fine.

The meeting with Jay Barlow had gone well, too. He'd make a good addition to the clinic. Satisfaction settled a smile on Mike's lips as he left Violet's neighborhood and turned onto Forksville's main road. Then he thought of Rose. His smile faded and his chest tightened. As usual, his professional life sailed along on smooth seas, while his personal life battled storm after storm. Just when their relationship had seemed solid, and he'd been about to propose, she'd withdrawn again.

He fought against thinking Kurt Fuller's sudden appearance at the class reunion had anything to do with Rose's behavior. But deep down, he knew it did. He just didn't know what. Tomorrow's meeting had better clear up all his doubts and uncertainties. He didn't like being in limbo. He wanted to get on with his life—with their life.

Reaching the outskirts of Forksville, he headed for the freeway. An intersection loomed and traffic slowed. He braked for the light. As he waited, his gaze wandered. A gas station, a grocery store, a funky little café painted blue. The Blue Sage Café. He'd been there a time or two when passing through town.

His gaze caught two people exiting the café, a tall blond guy and a shorter woman with dark hair. Mike stared. Kurt? Rose? Yes, that was exactly who they were. What the hell? He kept his gaze glued to the couple as they headed around the side of the building to the parking lot. Yep, there was Rose's car. When the pair reached the vehicle, Kurt leaned down and gave Rose a hug. Was she hugging him back? She raised her arms, hesitated, and then, yes, she clutched his back in a hug.

The sight of Kurt and Rose—his Rose—in an embrace sucker-punched Mike's stomach. She had lied to him. She wasn't working late; she'd had a date with Kurt. He continued to stare at the couple. Should he whip into the parking lot and confront them? Find out what this was all about?

The traffic light changed to green. He tapped the steering wheel, debating. Behind him, a horn honked.

Make up your mind, man!

Okay, he needed to think this through before butting in like a raging bull. Gripping the wheel and jamming his foot to the accelerator, he shot the car through the intersection. A glance in the rearview mirror showed Kurt opening Rose's car door for her while she climbed in. They weren't leaving together, anyway.

What was going on? His mind rocketed in all directions, but the conclusion he reached was always the same. As he'd suspected, Rose still had feelings for her old teenage crush. That was why she'd been unable to commit to him. Kurt had realized he too still cared for Rose and came looking for her at the reunion.

Now, they were picking up where they left off.

So where did that leave him?

Out in the cold. *Sayonara*, buddy. A sense of loss cut a hole inside him.

But what about the day in the E.R., that had jump-started this new chapter in his and Rose's relationship? On that day, she'd gazed up at him with a love in her eyes that seemed to come straight from her heart.

Speeding along the freeway, he thought about all the times they'd had together since then. The fun, the camaraderie. Only friendship? What about their hot kisses? Had she been wishing he were Kurt? His gut twisted.

Come on, man, you're way off base.

Or was he?

His mind churned all the way to his condo. Still unable to settle down, he paced the living room weighing his options. Should he call her now, demand she explain what the hell she was doing with Kurt Fuller? What if she were still with him? Maybe they were hooking up later this evening. So what? If that were the case, let her squirm.

He held off calling, hoping she might phone him. She didn't. More than once, he reached for the receiver, only to let his hand fall away. *Coward.*

In the end, he decided to wait until tomorrow night, as planned. Then he'd have the matter out with her, once and for all.

****

At five o'clock the following day, Mike set out for The Roundup Restaurant. He didn't feel much like eating, but figured he'd better have something in his stomach before his meeting with Rose. Head down, hands in his pockets, his thoughts miles away, he paid little attention to his surroundings.

"Hey, Mike Mahoney!"

Jerking his head around, he saw Kurt Fuller lumbering across the street toward him. Speak of the devil.

When Kurt caught up, he stuck out his hand. "Good to see ya again."

"Hello, Kurt." Mike stared at Kurt's proffered hand, bile rising in his throat. The last thing he wanted to do was shake hands with this man.

Civility required a response, though, and, grudgingly, he pushed his hand into Kurt's.

Kurt rocked forward, then backward on his heels. "Got time for a drink?"

Judging from the smell of alcohol on the man's breath and his unsteady balance, he'd already had at least one. Mike narrowed his eyes, suspicious of Kurt's motive. Did he want only a drinking buddy, or something else? They'd never been friends. Even though they'd both played sports in high school, they'd barely known each other. Maybe Kurt's invitation had something to do with Rose. If he accepted, maybe he could find out more about what he'd seen in Forksville yesterday.

He set his jaw. No, he shouldn't be pumping Kurt for information behind Rose's back. He'd planned to go directly to her for an explanation. His conscience told him he should stick to his original plan.

Kurt laid a hand on Mike's shoulder. "Come on, man. Don't make me drink alone."

The hell with his conscience. He needed to know what was going on. "I'm on my way to The Roundup," Mike said. "That suit you?"

"Long as they serve booze."

When they were seated on high stools in the restaurant's bar, Mike glanced at the short order menu, but his stomach churned too much now to eat anything. He ordered a cola.

Kurt frowned. "That all you're gonna have?"

"I'm seeing patients at the clinic tomorrow," Mike explained, which was true. "Gotta keep a clear head."

"If you say so."

Once Kurt's Scotch and water arrived, and he'd taken a few sips, he seemed to forget about Mike's abstaining. They shot the breeze awhile about high school, mostly Mike listening to Kurt's reliving his football triumphs. Mike let him ramble on hoping Kurt would eventually bring Rose into the conversation.

"So I hear you and Rose been hooking up," Kurt said, leaning his elbows on the bar.

"We've been seeing each other." Mike paused then aimed a tentative glance in Kurt's direction. "You two were dating back in high school, as I recall."

Kurt straightened and puffed up his chest. "Yep, she was crazy about me."

"Is that right?" Mike narrowed his eyes. "So how come you didn't make it permanent?"

"Aw, we was too young." Kurt tossed back another swallow of Scotch. "I had to go to college and play football. My dad wanted me to, ya know. But, considering what happened, Rose 'n' me shoulda made it right."

Mike leaned forward, wondering what this guy was talking about. "Made it right?"

Kurt swept a hand across the bar, drawing the attention of the couple sitting a few stools away. "Well, ya know, when you have a kid together, you oughta raise it together, don't you think?"

A kid! Shock rippled through Mike. Had he heard right? Have a child together? Kurt and Rose? No, that couldn't be true. "What are you saying, man?"

"Didn't she tell ya about the baby? Oops." Eyebrows arched, he slapped a hand over his mouth.

Mike's hand shook as he reached for his glass. He carefully brought the glass to his lips and managed to take a drink, as if he hadn't a care. He shrugged. "I could hear your side of it."

"My side? Hah, I didn't even know about it until a year ago. Overheard my parents talking about how her mom stormed over to my house with the news that Rose was pregnant. By me."

"And were you the father?" Mike said through gritted teeth.

"Yeah. Rose said she didn't have sex with anyone but me, and I believe her. She's one straight arrow about telling the truth, isn't she?"

Mike itched to wipe the smug grin off Kurt's face. Instead, he grabbed his glass and took another drink. "So what happened? Fill me in, why don't you?"

Although Kurt tended to ramble, Mike managed to piece together the story. The more he learned the more his outrage grew. He clenched his fists under the table to keep from grabbing Kurt and punching him out. "So what happened to the child?"

Head bent over his glass, Kurt shrugged. "Adopted out, I guess."

"You guess?"

"That's what my folks paid for. That and Rose's year at that private school."

"So now you've come to make it right?" Mike shook his head in disbelief.

"No, man. I've got a woman waiting for me in Chicago, where my new job is. Doubt we'll get married, though. I already pay alimony to two exes and child support for three kids."

Mike's disgust for the man sitting beside him grew moment by moment. Yet, he was relieved to hear Kurt had no further designs on Rose.

Then why had they been together at The Blue Sage? Maybe Rose still had feelings for Kurt. He was, after all, the father of her child, even if the child had been given up.

In Mike's ideal world, conceiving a child together created the ultimate bond between a man and a woman. He'd always thought he and Rose would have that experience. Now, to learn she and Kurt had formed that bond threw him into a state of confusion. He ran a hand over the bunched muscles on the back of his neck.

"Gotta go now," Kurt mumbled, teetering on his stool.

Mike wanted nothing more than to have Kurt out of his sight. Personally, he didn't care that Kurt was drunk, either. Let him fall flat on his face. Let him crawl out the door and stumble into the gutter. Let him lie there all night. His fingers tightened on his glass.

But Dr. Mike had responsibilities, and so it was Dr. Mike who laid a hand on Kurt's arm and said, "Whoa, where you off to?"

"My m-motel." Kurt gripped the brass bar rail for support.

All the motels were on the outskirts of town, at least three miles away. "Kinda far to walk, isn't it?"

"I c'n make it. I'm in as good a shape as I ever was. 'Member the touchdown I made that cinched the championship?"

"I do. But I still don't think you should walk to your motel tonight."

Kurt slid off the stool, stumbling as he put his feet on the floor. "I walked here, didn't I?"

Mike laid a steadying hand on Kurt's shoulder. "Maybe so, but you need a way back. Hang on a sec, and I'll call you a cab."

Mumbling but not protesting, Kurt slumped back on the bar stool and put his head in his hands.

Ten minutes later, holding on to Kurt's arm, Mike led him out of the restaurant to a cab waiting at the curb. He opened the back door and Kurt crawled in.

With jerking motions, Kurt managed to roll down the window. He gazed at Mike with bleary eyes. "Thanks, man. Good t' see you again. You 'n' Rose be happy."

Happy? Mike choked down a cynical laugh. Not likely. Not now.

He waited until the cab pulled away. Then, his steps heavy, he turned toward his condo. Was he still going to confront Rose tonight? He straightened his shoulders with new determination. Yes, now more than ever.

****

Twisting her hands together, Rose paced her living room. Mike was due any moment, and she'd made the decision once and for all to tell him about her baby. She'd be breaking her promise to her mother, but her mother violated the promise herself when she demanded money from Kurt's parents in exchange for her silence.

Although she'd rehearsed over and over what she would say to Mike, dread lumped in her stomach.

The phone call she expected this evening from Glenna added to Rose's stress. She'd been urging Glenna to tell her parents about her condition, reminding her that her changing body soon would announce the news, even if she didn't.

Then, yesterday, Glenna called to say she'd decided to break the news tonight, as soon as her father came home from work. She promised to call Rose later and tell her the outcome.

The doorbell rang.

Mike.

Rose swallowed hard and hurried to answer it.

She opened the door and there he stood, as handsome as ever, his hair tousled from the wind, a tan jacket stretched over broad shoulders, snug-fitting jeans outlining sturdy legs. Her pulse quickened.

Then she took another look at his grim eyes and tightly pressed mouth. He was angry. But why? He hadn't heard her story yet. An ominous chill washed over her.

"Hello, Rose," he said in a flat tone.

"Come in, Mike."

He strode in, leaving swirls of tension in his wake.

Her stomach churning, she led him into the living room. "Sit down." With a trembling hand, she gestured to the sofa.

He planted his feet apart and propped his hands on his hips. "No, thanks."

"All right." Hugging her arms, she stared at the floor, searching for the right words to begin.

"I've been with Kurt," he said in clipped tones.

Her head shot up and her mouth fell open. Was Kurt the reason for Mike's anger? Had Kurt told him her secret? "I, ah, didn't know you two were friends." She searched his expression for clues but found none.

"We're not. But it seems we have something in common—you."

Shoving down the cold dread spreading through her, Rose asked, "So what did Kurt have to say?"

"Quite a bit, as it turned out. Seems you and he have a past I didn't know about." His chin jutted out. "Seems you and he had a baby together."

On wobbly legs, Rose stumbled to a nearby chair and slumped into it. "Then there's nothing for me to say, is there?"

"Yes, there is." His voice inched up a notch. "Why didn't you tell me about you and Kurt? Why didn't you tell me you had a baby and gave it up for adoption?"

No matter how much she'd prepared for this moment, the reality was almost more than she could bear. Clutching the arms of the chair for support, she took a deep breath and began, "At first, I kept silent because my mother made me promise never to tell anyone about my baby. But then, when you and I got, um, serious, I decided I'd to tell you..." Biting her lower lip, she paused to glance at him.

"Go on."

"Before I could, you told me about being abandoned and how you felt about women who gave up their babies. I was afraid that if you knew my story you'd...you'd reject me," she finished, her voice quivering.

"So that's why you broke up with me."

"Yes."

His shoulders sagged and a pained look crossed his face.

A little flicker of hope sparked within Rose. Maybe this was going to turn out all right, after all.

Then he drew himself up and lifted his chin. "Okay, I admit to a certain bias toward women who abandon their babies, because that's what happened to me. But, according to Kurt, you gave up yours for adoption."

Yes, she'd let Kurt believe that. But Mike was another matter. Her lips trembled as she searched for the right words.

Hands propped on his hips, he strode over to stand in front of her. His stern gaze burned the air. "Rose? Isn't that the truth? Your baby was adopted?"

"I, uh—"

The phone rang. With a gasp, Rose jumped. "I need to answer that. It might be Glenna."

He raised his eyebrows. "Glenna Jordan?"

"Yes, she finally decided to tell her parents about her pregnancy. She said she'd call me afterward and tell me how it went."

Rose leaped to the phone and snatched up the receiver. A sobbing filled her ear. "Glenna, is that you?"

"Y-yeah, it's me."

"Did you tell your parents?"

"Yeah."

"So, ah, how'd they take it?" Rose's heartbeat quickened as she waited for Glenna's reply.

"My dad kicked me out! I'm going to run away, like I shoulda done in the first place."

"Oh, no!" Rose covered the receiver with her hand and repeated the news to Mike.

"Tell her not to go," he said, crossing the room to stand beside her. "We'll help her find somewhere to stay."

"Come over to my place," Rose said into the receiver. "Dr. Mike is here. He wants to help you. So do I."

"No, I'm going away. Then I'll be able to keep my baby."

"Glenna, wait! You may be making a big mistake."

"I can't wait. I'm at the train station now. I wanted to call you and say thank you for being my friend." Her voice dropped to a whisper. "I-I wish you were my mom."

Rose's heart squeezed. *Oh, I do, too, honey.* Maybe she could've done a good job parenting, after all.

"Don't get on the train, Glenna! Please!"

The line went dead. Rose slammed down the receiver. "She's at the train station." Consulting her wristwatch, she added, "There's a seven-fifty for Denver. If I leave now, maybe I can get there in time to talk her out of going."

"I'm coming with you."

Startled, she turned and stared. "Are you sure you want to?"

Mike's eyes flashed. "You bet I am. Our discussion will have to wait. We need to help Glenna."

Rose bit her lip, wondering what effect Mike's presence might have on Glenna. But she couldn't worry about that now. Time was of the essence.

"All right. I'll grab my purse and we're on our way."

****

After a tense drive across town, Mike pulled into a parking place at the train station with only minutes to spare before the train's scheduled departure. Rose jumped out and, with Mike close on her heels, zigzagged her way through the lot to the station platform.

Engine humming, silver cars gleaming under the bright station lights, the train sat poised to leave. A station hand Rose recognized was assisting an elderly woman to climb aboard. Waving her arms, Rose ran toward him. "Jake!"

Jake turned. A grin spread across his craggy face. "Hey, Rose. What's up?"

Rose skidded to a stop. "We...need to...board," she said between gasps for breath. "It's an...emergency."

"Why, uh, sure." Jake stepped aside and waved them aboard.

Taking the lead, Mike grabbed Rose's hand and helped her up the steps and onto the train. Struggling to keep up with him, she stumbled into the coach car, just as the train chugged away from the station.

A brown-uniformed conductor hurried down the aisle toward them. His eyebrows shot up as he peered at her over Mike's shoulder. "Rose?"

Rose placed a hand on her heaving chest and blew out a couple breaths before speaking. "No time for tickets, Max. Need to find a teenaged girl. Blond. A little on the heavy side. She's alone."

Max pressed his lips together and nodded. "Yep. I wondered about her. Acts like she don't feel so well. She's in the car ahead." He jerked his thumb over his shoulder.

"Thanks."

When Rose and Mike searched the next car, Rose spotted Glenna slumped in a window seat, staring out the window. Weak with relief, Rose sank into the empty seat beside her. "Hey, Glenna."

She turned. Her eyes, red from crying, widened. "Rose!" For a moment, her lips wobbled, as though she might smile, but then her mouth turned down. "Why are you here? I didn't ask you to come."

"Maybe not, but I came anyway. Dr. Mike, too." Rose motioned to Mike standing in the aisle.

"Dr. Mike?" Glenna squeaked, leaning forward and gazing up at him.

"We want to help you, Glenna."

Mike's eyes were solemn but Rose thought his smile conveyed reassurance.

Glenna pushed out her lower lip and folded her arms over her chest. "It's too late. I told you my dad kicked me out."

"That doesn't mean you have to run away," Rose said, keeping her voice calm. "Where are you headed?"

"To Matson. I'm going to stay with a friend."

Rose glanced out the window. They were nearing the city limits, and the train had picked up speed. "Will you stay long enough to have your baby?"

"Sure. Why not? Susie'll help me. I can take care of my baby. I'm old enough." Glenna's eyes glistened with tears. "Please, leave me alone. There's nothing you can do. I wish I hadn't called you. But you were my friend and I wanted to say good-bye." She pulled a tissue from her purse and dabbed at her cheeks.

Chewing on her lower lip, Rose debated. Perhaps she could change Glenna's mind, after all, but it would mean breaking her silence. But she'd been about to tell Mike the truth back at the apartment, hadn't she?

Her mother's shrill voice filled her mind. *Promise you'll never tell, Rose!*

Rose straightened her spine and lifted her chin

in grim determination. This time, she wouldn't listen to the voice. The time had come to tell the truth. All of it. She leaned toward Glenna. "Since we can't get off the train for a while, I want to tell you about another young woman who also wanted to keep her baby."

Glenna shook her head. "If you're trying to change my mind, forget it. I've had enough time to decide what to do. This is the best."

"You may be right, but you can listen to my story anyway."

"I don't think so." Glenna pushed out her lower lip.

Ignoring her refusal, Rose gazed around at the half-full car. A couple sat directly in front of them and behind were two businessmen. "We need someplace more private," she said to Mike. "I'll see if Max can help us."

Pleased with his silent agreement, she stood and allowed Mike to slide into the seat beside Glenna. Heading down the aisle, she finally found Max in the next car. She made her request. Yes, there was an empty sleeping compartment they could use.

When she returned to Glenna and Mike and told them they'd be moving to a more private location, Glenna reluctantly agreed. "Only because you're my friend," she said.

"If that's what it takes." Rose put an arm around the girl and led her down the aisle.

Yet, minutes later, as she opened the door to the vacant sleeping compartment and ushered Glenna inside, Rose's courage wavered. Would she be making a big mistake by telling Glenna—and Mike—what really happened to her baby?

Chapter Fifteen

In the cozy compartment, Rose steered Glenna to a table with upholstered bench seats on either side. She and Glenna sat on one side, while Mike took the bench opposite. Outside the window, the brown land and green fields blurred like watercolors running together. Underneath the train, the wheels clacked steadily along the rails.

Glenna turned to Rose, her eyes defiant. "Okay, so what do you want to tell me?"

Rose's mother's warning again drummed in her ear. *"You must never tell anyone what happened to you, Rose. Never!"* She clenched her fists. She had kept her promise, but now she realized what a great price she'd paid for her obedience. Still, did she have the courage to finally tell her secret?

Mike knew part, but not all, of what she would tell Glenna. Not the really awful part. And would her story have the hoped-for effect on the teen? Rose had no way of knowing. But she'd come this far. The door to the past stood wide open, waiting for her to step inside. Her heart thudded.

"Go ahead, Rose," Mike said. "Tell Glenna—and me—your story."

Rose uncurled her fists and nodded. "Yes, it's time." She turned to Glenna, took a deep breath, and began, "There was a young girl about your age, who also got pregnant. She didn't mean for it to happen, but it did. Like you, she was afraid to tell her parents. But, also like you, she finally did. As she'd feared, her mother, especially, was very angry."

She paused to give Glenna a chance to comment,

but the girl's eyes were downcast and her mouth a tight line.

Rose continued, "But her mother didn't kick out the girl. She arranged for her to leave town and live with an aunt in another state, and to give up her baby for adoption."

Glenna looked up, showing her first spark of interest. "Did the girl want to give it up? I don't see how she could do that."

Long-buried emotion bubbled up, clogging Rose's throat. "N-no, she didn't want to give up her baby. Like you, she wanted to keep it. But her mother insisted on adoption. She was afraid of what her friends would think, and, she wanted the girl to finish high school."

Glenna squirmed on the seat. "That's what my dad said. 'What will our friends think?'" She mimicked her father's deep voice. "But, what happened to the girl? Did she do what her mother wanted her to do?"

"No, she didn't." The corner of her eye caught Mike's raised eyebrows. The real story would surprise him, too. Kurt had spilled most of it, but not this part.

"What did she do?" Glenna prompted.

The steady rhythm of the train's wheels, a sound that usually soothed Rose, today seemed to chant, *"Don't tell, don't tell."*

She straightened her spine and gritted her teeth. Yes, she would tell. No more secrets. "She boarded the train, like you did tonight, Glenna. But she didn't go all the way to Boston, like she was supposed to. She got off at another stop."

"Was she going to stay all by herself?" Glenna leaned forward.

Encouraged by Glenna's response, Rose forged ahead. "No. Like you, she had a friend, an older girl who'd been her camp counselor. They'd kept in touch after the friend moved away. She said it was okay for the girl to stay with her while she had her baby."

"The friend was gonna help her have it?" Glenna's eyes widened.

"Yes, she said she could help. Isn't that what your friend promised?"

"I don't know." Glenna's brow wrinkled. "Susie said I could stay there. Her mom got divorced and when she married again, she didn't want Susie to live with them. So Susie got her own place. She still goes to school and all."

"Well, because this girl was desperate to keep her baby, she didn't think things through. She jumped at the chance to stay with the friend."

"What about her parents?" Mike spoke for the first time since Rose began her story. "What happened when she didn't show up at her aunt's?"

Rose forced herself to hold his gaze, pushing the words past a tight throat. "She didn't want her parents—or her aunt—out looking for her, so she called and told them what she'd done. But not where she was. Her mother was angry, of course, but in the end washed her hands of the whole thing. The girl was out of the house, out of town, and that was what really mattered most to the mother."

Mike shook his head. "Okay, go on."

Shifting to face Glenna again, Rose continued, "She stayed with her friend all through the cold winter. In early March, when the time came to have her baby, the friend called in a couple of her friends—one of them a nurse—and they helped."

"Wasn't the girl scared?" Glenna asked, hugging her arms.

Rose gave a harsh, humorless laugh. "You bet she was. But she and her helpers managed. The baby came and it was a girl." At the memory, her voice softened to a whisper. "A very sweet baby girl."

Glenna sank back against the seat. "So

everything turned out all right."

"No, it didn't," Rose said, her nerves knotting up again. "What was the girl going to do now? She could get a job, but who would take care of the baby? And, the baby cried a lot, and the friend decided she didn't want the girl to stay there anymore. She couldn't go home, and she didn't want to call her aunt for help, either. She was so ashamed and so guilty and, and..." Her voice broke.

"So what did she do?" Glenna jerked forward again, her eyes wary.

"She—" Rose choked, cleared her throat, and fell silent.

"Rose?" Mike prompted.

In a voice barely audible to her own ears, Rose spoke, "She took the baby and left her friend's apartment. She wandered around awhile, not knowing what to do or where to go. Finally, she came to a church and went in. No one was around, but in a hallway, she heard voices coming from inside one of the rooms. A box full of hymnals sat on the floor. She emptied out the box and...and put her baby in it..."

Pressing a hand to her mouth, Glenna smothered a gasp. "She—she left her baby there?"

Rose's chest tightened against the painful memory. "Yes, she left the baby by the closed door. She was so sick to her stomach, she almost couldn't do it. But she did. And then she crept away." She swallowed against the burning in her throat. "That was the last time she saw her baby."

Glenna was silent a moment, and then she narrowed her eyes and asked in a suspicious tone, "Is this a true story? Or are you making it up to get me to go home?"

Rose held up a shaky hand. "I swear to you, Glenna, it's the truth. I know it's true, because..." The rest of the sentence stuck in her throat. She gulped in a breath then finished in a whisper, "Because I was that girl."

"You?" Glenna stared.

Rose didn't dare to glance at Mike; but he surely had guessed all along whom she was talking about.

"Yes. And you—and Dr. Mike—are the first people ever to hear the story. My mother made me promise not to tell anyone what I did, and all these years I've kept her promise." She paused to lick her dry lips. "But the promise needs to be broken now. I'm telling you, Glenna, because I don't want the same thing to happen to you."

"My experience might be different," Glenna said, jutting out her chin.

Despite the gravity of the situation, Rose risked a tiny smile. Glenna was as stubborn as she'd been at that age. Perhaps that was why they'd hit it off so well.

"Yes, it might," she said, resting a hand on Glenna's arm. "But do you really want to take the risk? Have you made plans for what you will do after the baby comes?"

Glenna hung her head. "Well, not exactly. But my dad kicked me out. I can't go back home."

Mike clasped his hands on the tabletop and leaned forward. "There are other places you can go, where you'll be taken care of."

"And maybe your mother will help," Rose added. "Was she as angry as your dad?"

"I don't know. She just cried a lot."

Rose reached for her purse. "I could call her..."

"No!"

Glenna's vehement refusal jolted Rose, and she jerked her hand away from her purse. Hadn't she changed Glenna's mind, after all? She wasn't giving up, though. She straightened and, keeping her tone gentle yet firm, said, "Why don't you think about it for a while?"

"You're not gonna make me go back?" Glenna gave Rose a sideways glance.

"No. The decision is yours."

Glenna pressed her lips together.

"Think about your baby," Mike urged. "What would be best for your baby?"

Closing her eyes, Glenna laid her head back against the seat cushion. She pushed aside her jacket and molded both palms to her round belly.

The car shifted as the train swung a corner, drawing Rose's attention to the window. Darkness had fallen, but lights from houses and farms signaled they were approaching a town. She checked her wristwatch. Yes, by her calculations, they were ten minutes away from the next stop. She turned to Glenna. "Have you made a decision yet?"

Glenna's eyes brimmed with tears, but a small smile traced her lips. "I want you to help me do what's best for me and my baby."

"Oh, Glenna!" Relief flooding her body, Rose scooted over and gave the teen a joyful hug.

Mike reached out and patted Glenna's shoulder. "You've made the right choice, Glenna. I'm proud of you."

Rose finally drew away and reached for her purse. "Now, I am going to call your mother!" She completed the call, assuring a distraught Ellie that her daughter was safe.

"Tell her I want her to come home," Ellie said. "We'll work everything out somehow."

"I'll let you tell her yourself," Rose said, and handed the phone to Glenna.

****

Hours later, after leaving the train, renting a car, and driving back to Red Rock, Rose and Mike took Glenna home and turned her over to her mother. As Ellie and Glenna hugged and the tears flowed, Rose had the feeling Glenna's story would have a different, happier ending than her own.

When Rose and Mike returned to their rental car, and Mike opened the passenger's door for her, Rose hesitated. Now they were alone, a new kind of dread filled her.

She cast him a sideways glance. "I can call a cab, if you'd rather."

"Of course not. I'll take you home." He gestured for her to climb into the car.

His stiff tone did nothing to relieve her anxiety. Yet, she slid onto the seat and let him close the door. He came around to the driver's side, settled in, and started the engine, all without another word. Rose kept her back rigid and stared straight ahead. The silence dragged on, making the short journey across town seem endless.

At last, unable to bear the silence any longer, Rose said, "So now you know the whole story."

"Yeah, now I know."

When nothing followed that flat statement, she decided silence was a good thing. If he continued talking, she'd hear his disappointment and his ultimate rejection. She'd failed him, like she'd failed her mother, and her daughter, her own flesh and blood. Her chin trembled, her eyes burned with tears. She turned away and hugged her arms against the nausea bubbling up in her stomach.

At last he pulled up to the curb in front of her apartment building. After he'd switched off the ignition, she expected him to turn to her and say something, but instead he stared out the windshield. She studied his profile—furrowed brow, mouth set in a tight, angry line—wanting to break the silence, but unable to conquer the fear that closed her throat. So, she waited.

He finally faced her. For a moment, she thought sympathy glimmered in his eyes. Then the light vanished and he said in a dull voice, "What I heard tonight threw me for a loop, Rose. I don't know what to think, what to say. I'm in shock."

Sick inside, she nodded. "I understand. I tried so many times to tell you, but I didn't have the courage. Until tonight."

She glanced up at him from under her lashes, still harboring the hope that, somehow, they could mend their relationship. But he just shook his head and turned away to stare out the windshield again.

Her heart sank. Yet, what had she expected? She had disappointed him beyond understanding. Beyond forgiveness.

"What are you going to do now?" he asked after an awkward silence.

"I've been offered a transfer to St. Louis. I guess I'll take it." She hadn't known until that moment she'd made up her mind, but nothing was left for her now in Red Rock.

"Ah, your transfer. Just what you've been waiting for."

"Right. What will you do?" she ventured to ask.

He shrugged. "Keep on being Dr. Mike."

The seconds crawled by and neither spoke. Finally, she said, "I'd better go in now."

"Sure. I'll see you to the door."

"No need." She scooted toward the door and grasped the handle.

"Well...take care, Rose."

"Yeah, you, too."

Choking back a sob, she opened the door and slipped from the car. Her steps heavy, she headed for the apartment house's front door. When she didn't hear him driving away, hope sprouted anew, but just as she turned to see, his car's engine sprang to life, and he pulled away from the curb.

Head bowed, she entered the building. Closing the door behind her shut out the sound of his leaving, but not the pain in her heart.

****

Mike shook his head in confusion as he drove along the darkened streets of Red Rock. What had just happened? Glenna was back with her parents. She and her baby were safe. But in the process, he and Rose had ended their relationship. Again.

Her confession had stunned him. He still couldn't believe what he'd heard. According to Kurt, she'd given their baby up for adoption. To learn she'd abandoned her baby shocked him to the core.

Her story churned up his own painful history. His birth mother had left him in a department store restroom. What kind of a person would do that?

Through the years, he'd made up stories that would exonerate his mother. She'd been kicked out of her home, as Glenna had. She'd been mentally unstable, and therefore wasn't responsible for her actions. She'd been physically ill, which again had clouded her judgment.

In the end, none of those excuses worked. In the end, he came back to one conclusion, plain and simple—she hadn't wanted him. The pain was always there ready to spring to life at the slightest reminder.

Today's events brought back the pain in full force.

If he and Rose stayed together, whenever he looked at her he'd feel the pain.

He didn't want that. Mike gripped the steering wheel so hard his fingers ached.

A red light up ahead brought him to his senses. As he braked to a stop, he realized he was only a few blocks away from the entrance to Aspen Hills. Why had his wanderings brought him here? He didn't want to be reminded of the home he'd hoped to have in Aspen Hills with Rose. Not tonight.

He turned in the opposite direction. Then, on impulse, he swung back around and headed toward the subdivision, after all. Maybe visiting the lot would breathe life into his dream.

He drove the several blocks to the adobe pillars set with globe lanterns marking the entrance. Once again, he hesitated. Setting his jaw, he pressed the gas pedal and sped ahead. He wound through the lighted streets until he came to his property. Cutting the engine, he stared at the vacant land attempting to summon his vision of a home built there, the rooms lighted, filled with the sounds of talk and laughter.

Tonight the vision refused to appear, and all he saw was a vacant piece of land, as dry and empty as he was inside. He started the car's engine and drove to his condo.

The following day, he called the realtor and told him to put the lot up for sale. The day after that he sold the wedding ring set to a local jeweler. And the day after that, he was so busy at the clinic tending to his patients that he barely noticed his pain.

Or so he told himself.

****

A week later, sitting at her desk at TransAmerica, Rose stared at the paper Stan had just handed her. The official order to report to St. Louis.

He leaned over and peered at her. "Hey, I thought you'd be jumping up and down for joy."

"I am happy. And thanks for all your help bringing this about."

He straightened and rested his hands on his hips. "You're welcome. But you know I don't want you to go. We'll miss you, Rose."

She gazed up at her boss. Behind his round glasses, his gray eyes were solemn. "I'll miss you all, too, Stan. But, believe me, this is for the best."

That evening, Rose sat at her kitchen table making a to-do list for the move. Give notice on her apartment. Break the news to Jackson and Sara, and other friends. Notify her St. Louis friends, Teri and Roger Decker, that she would accept their offer to stay with them until she found her own place.

A few items later, satisfied she had enough to start with, she stopped writing and tucked the list away in a drawer. As she turned out the light and prepared for bed, her thoughts strayed to Mike. She wondered how he was doing. A week had passed since the day they'd rescued Glenna, and there'd been not one word from him, a silence as big and deep as the Grand Canyon.

Would she ever see or hear from him again? Probably not, especially after she'd moved to St. Louis. She'd told Stan accepting the transfer was the right decision. But was it, really? An unsettled feeling crept over Rose, one that kept her awake far into the night.

On Saturday, determined to forge ahead with her plans, Rose cleaned closets. By afternoon, she'd filled several boxes for the charity thrift shop and a few to take with her to St. Louis. The phone rang.

Mike? Her heart leaped. *You never stop hoping, do you?*

Not Mike, but Sara.

"Thank God you're there!" Her sister-in-law sounded frantic.

"Sara, what's wrong?"

"Buck had an accident at the Forksville rodeo. The bull he was riding attacked him after he fell off."

Shock rippled through Rose, and she gripped the receiver. "Oh, no! Was he badly hurt? How is he?"

"I'm not sure. Forksville has no hospital, so they're bringing him to Valley General. Jackson, Molly, and I are heading there now. I know Molly would appreciate it if you could come. She's pretty shook up. She wanted Mike to be there, too, but he's at a conference in Atlanta."

"I'll come right away."

"Good. We'll see you soon. And, please pray, Rose. Pray really hard."

Rose did. As she sped across town to the hospital, she prayed for Buck, and for Molly and Karli, too.

At the hospital, Rose spotted Sara and Molly seated in the E.R.'s waiting area. Jackson stood nearby, gazing out the window facing the driveway. She hurried to them. "I'm here!"

Sara glanced up, and her lips trembled into a faint smile. "Hey, Rose!"

Molly raised a tear-stained face. "Oh, Rose, thank you for coming."

"Of course, I'd come."

Both women stood and the three exchanged hugs. Jackson came over and put his arms around all of them. Emotion surged through Rose. Surrounded by her loved ones, she couldn't help thinking how much she'd miss them when she moved to St. Louis.

Buck was the immediate concern, though, and she broke away to ask, "Is he here yet?"

"He was brought in a few minutes ago," Jackson said, stepping back but keeping an arm around Molly's shoulder. "We're waiting for word."

Molly twisted her fingers together. "I want to be with him, but they won't let me."

Sara straightened the collar of Molly's blouse then patted her cheek. "You'll be with him soon, honey. The doctors know best."

Rose sat with Molly and Sara, while Jackson paced. Rose kept an eye on the door leading to the patients' rooms. People shuffled in and out with regularity, but no one came looking for Molly.

At last, a nurse dressed in the hospital's blue blouse and slacks appeared and spoke to the receptionist. She pointed to them, and the nurse strode over. "Mrs. Henson?" she asked, her eyes roving over the three women.

Molly jumped up. "I'm Mrs. Henson."

"Dr. Baker will see you now."

"My husband, is he gonna be okay?" Molly asked as she followed the nurse.

As soon as Molly and the nurse disappeared through the door, Sara, her brow wrinkled, turned to Rose and Jackson. "I have a bad feeling about this."

"Me, too." Jackson pressed his lips together.

"I hope you're both wrong," Rose said, as icy fear crawled along her spine.

Time dragged even more than before, if that were possible.

Rose wished Mike were there to help care for Buck. Not that the other doctors weren't capable, but having someone they knew in charge would provide added comfort.

Hearing he was attending a conference told her he was getting on with his life. Well, good for him. She was, too.

At last, the nurse who'd summoned Molly finally returned.

"Mrs. Henson would like you to join her now," she said, beckoning them to follow her.

Rose scanned the nurse's face hoping for a clue to Buck's condition. But the woman's impassive expression revealed nothing. Rose joined Sara and Jackson and they followed the nurse through the door and into the hallway.

The hospital's antiseptic smell was much stronger here than in the waiting room. Doors to some of the exam rooms stood ajar, offering glimpses of patients hooked up with monitors and IVs. Vague memories of being here when she'd broken her leg surfaced, and then quickly faded, as she focused on Molly and Buck.

The nurse ushered them into a waiting room

furnished with overstuffed chairs and sofas. Drawn draperies covered the single window and a solitary light from an end table threw a dull shadow across the blue tweed carpet.

A cold chill swept over Rose as she stepped into the room. An aura of sadness hung in the atmosphere. This was where you received bad news about a loved one. When she spotted Molly slumped on one of the sofas, her face tear-stained and drawn, Rose's last hope that this tragedy would have a happy ending vanished.

Molly looked up and said in a monotone, "He's dead."

Rose briefly closed her eyes. Now she'd heard what she'd expected, her mind rejected the awful news. Not Buck. He was invincible. This couldn't be happening.

"Damn!" Jackson made a fist and pounded his palm.

"Oh, honey, oh, Molly, I'm so, so sorry!" Sara rushed to sit beside Molly and put her arm around the woman's slumped shoulders.

"H-he w-was gone when they brought him in." Molly bowed her head again. "I heard someone say he was a—a D.O.A."

"I'm sure they did everything possible to save him." Rose sat on Molly's other side and stroked her back. Her muscles were tense under Rose's fingers.

"I know they tried, but it wasn't enough." Molly choked out a sob.

Striding over to them, Jackson hunkered down in front of Molly. He picked up her hand and squeezed it. "We're all here for you, Molly. Whatever you need, you've got it, okay?"

Sara murmured her agreement, and Rose chimed in, too.

Molly's eyes brimmed with fresh tears as she gazed at them. "Thanks, all of you. I—I don't know what I'd do without you."

Later, as Rose drove home, her heart ached for Molly and Karli and their tragic loss. How would they ever adjust to life without Buck?

Chapter Sixteen

On the day of Buck's funeral, his heart filled with sadness, Mike joined the other mourners at the Red Rock Community Church. Strains of organ music led him to the flower-filled chapel where the service was held. Sunlight streamed through stained glass windows, beaming down on the people sitting in the wooden pews.

While the ushers escorted others to their seats, Mike had a chance to survey the crowd. He recognized ranch hands from the Rolling R and neighboring spreads, Anna Gabraldi and her family, and many of Buck's rodeo buddies. Mike allowed himself a small smile. Buck would be pleased to know he had so many friends.

Craning his neck to see the front rows, he glimpsed Rose sitting next to Sara and Jackson. His stomach flip-flopped. He wished he could sit beside her and hold her hand while they said good-bye to Buck. Every day he thought of her and missed her terribly, but couldn't forget—or forgive—what she'd done. Going their separate ways was the best—and only—course of action.

An usher approached. Mike pointed to an empty space in the last pew. "I'll sit here," he told the man.

Settled in his seat, clutching the program the usher gave him, Mike's thoughts returned to Buck and how he had come to live at the Rolling R. Not long after Jackson bought the ranch, Buck answered his advertisement for a ranch hand. The two men immediately hit it off, and Jackson hired him on the spot. Buck brought along his new wife, Molly, who was a young nineteen at the time. A year or so later, Jackson promoted him to foreman.

Then came the arrival of Buck and Molly's daughter, Karli, whom Mike had delivered. He remembered Buck at Molly's bedside, holding their baby daughter in his arms and gazing down at her with a father's pride and love.

All too soon Buck's life ended in the rodeo at Forksville. Mike's fingers tightened on his program as he recalled reading the grisly details of the tragedy. Buck drew Poison, a bull with a violent reputation, and stayed on the creature for the required eight seconds. When he attempted to slide off, his hand caught in the rope tied around the bull, the rope that helped to keep him on the animal in the first place.

He finally freed himself and tumbled to the ground, the report stated. The clowns raced to distract the bull, but the animal paid them no attention, determined to attack his hapless rider instead. Witnesses told how the bull charged Buck, goring him and pushing him against the arena wall. By the time others were able to rescue him, he'd been fatally injured.

Now Molly was a widow, and Karli had lost the father she adored. Mike shook his head in disbelief, still struggling to accept the loss of a guy everyone had loved and who had so much to give.

The organ music swelled to a crescendo then faded away as Pastor Robinson, the church's young minister, stepped to the pulpit. "We're here to celebrate the life of Bradley Andrew Henson," he said. "Affectionately know as 'Buck.' Let us begin with a prayer."

Mike swiped moisture from his eyes. Then, along with the others, he bowed his head.

****

At the gathering in the church's social hall after

the service, Rose searched for Molly, wanting to make sure she was okay. The service had been a beautiful tribute to Buck, but hard on all of them, especially Molly. Rose spotted her across the room. Holding Karli's hand, she spoke with Pastor Robinson.

Satisfied she wasn't needed at the moment, Rose joined the line at the buffet table. Picking up a plate, she selected a mini-croissant ham sandwich and a helping of macaroni salad.

As she stepped away, Rose bumped into someone behind her. She turned and locked gazes with Mike. Stifling a gasp, she managed to say in a calm voice, "Hello, Mike."

"Rose." His head dipped in a solemn nod.

She licked her dry lips. "Sad times, huh?"

"Hard to believe Buck's gone." Mike shifted from one foot to the other.

"I feel so bad for Molly and Karli." She glanced in Molly's direction. Yes, she was still with the pastor.

"Being without Buck will be tough on both of them."

Other mourners milled around them, and a medley of hymns played in the background. Rose scrambled for something to say to keep the conversation going, although she wasn't sure why. What did they have to say to each other, once they'd shared their thoughts over Buck?

"I, ah, heard you were in Atlanta," she finally said, staring at her plate.

"Yeah. Conference." He cleared his throat. "All ready to move to St. Louis?"

"Only a couple weeks to go." She glanced at him in time to see a shadow flicker across his face. Regret? No, more likely, a trick of the overhead lights.

He raised the cup to his lips and took a sip then

gazed at her over the rim. "So, ah, nice seeing you again."

"Good to see you, too."

And then he turned away.

Rose's hand trembled as she picked up her sandwich. And when she took a bite, the food stuck in her throat.

Today's encounter reminded her of the chance meetings they had after their breakup two years ago. Conversations on those occasions were also brief, overly-polite, and full of tension.

When she moved to St. Louis, she would no longer have to endure the awkward and painful encounters.

Searching out Molly again, Rose saw her talking to one of the ranch hands and his wife. Her lips wore a sad smile and her eyes were bleak. Rose's heart twisted. She'd better stop worrying about her own situation and focus on Molly and Karli and how she might comfort them in their loss.

****

"Is my baby okay?" Glenna brushed her bangs from her eyes and shifted her position on the exam table.

Mike patted her shoulder. "Your baby is doing fine. But today we're going to run a few blood tests to make sure."

Glenna's lower lip pushed out. "That means your nurse has to stick a needle in my arm."

"'Fraid so."

"You've had blood tests before." From her seat near the window, Ellie Jordan spoke in a dry tone.

"I know, Mom, but that doesn't mean I have to like them."

Mike smiled to himself as he followed the exchange between mother and daughter. Today's appointment was the first he'd had with Glenna since she'd returned home after running away. Ellie

219

had come, too, and when she wanted to sit in on the exam, he'd welcomed her. With her support, Glenna's care would be much easier.

A few minutes later, Mike left Glenna and Ellie in the exam room so that Glenna could get dressed and prepare for her lab tests. He stood at the nurses' station checking on his next appointment when Ellie approached.

"While Glenna's getting dressed, can I talk to you for a few minutes alone?"

"Sure. Come on in my office."

Curious to know what was on Ellie's mind, Mike led her down the hall to his office. When they were seated, Mike behind his desk, Ellie across from him, he leaned forward, waiting for her to begin.

Ellie absently smoothed the lapel of her brown suede jacket then gazed at him with solemn eyes. "I can't tell you enough how grateful I am to you and Rose for bringing Glenna back home. Those hours she was gone were the worst I've ever experienced."

Mike grimaced. "That was a tense evening, all right. But I'm glad we could help. I'm also relieved to have her back under my care and to know that you and Len are on board."

"Oh, there are rough spots to iron out," Ellie said, twisting her fingers together. "Len's still angry. But I know he loves Glenna, and I have faith that, eventually, he'll get used to the idea of being a grandfather."

"Any contact with the baby's father?"

"Not yet. What role Tony will play in the baby's life is still uncertain, but I'm meeting with his mother later today."

Mike idly fingered a round glass paperweight anchoring a stack of notes on his desktop. "That sounds like a good start. And, you and Glenna seem to be on pretty good terms now."

A frown creased Ellie's brow. "I won't pretend

our relationship is perfect. If we'd been close, she would have come to me as soon as she discovered she was pregnant. But we have to move on. My being bitter or angry won't help." She shifted to gaze out the window, her eyes taking on a distant look. "I learned a long time ago that harboring bad feelings only makes a situation worse. No one is perfect. We all make mistakes. We must forgive one another and move on."

She faced him again, an apologetic smile tracing her lips. "Sorry, I didn't intend to lecture you. You, above all, accept people for who they are."

Mike gripped the paperweight, wariness battling curiosity. "What makes you say that?"

"I can tell by the way you treat Glenna and me. You don't judge us. You accept the situation and offer your help, like a good doctor should."

"You're very kind." Heat flooded Mike's face, and he was sure he must be blushing. Not something he did often.

"We appreciate you, Dr. Mike."

"Thanks, Ellie. Your words mean a lot."

She clutched her purse. "And now, I'd better get off my soapbox. I've taken up far too much of your time. By now, Glenna's ready and waiting for me. We're going shopping for baby clothes."

Mike came from behind his desk and walked her to the door. "She's lucky she has you."

Ellie's eyes shone. "And I'm lucky I have her."

After Ellie left, with still a few minutes remaining until his next appointment, Mike strode to his office window. He gazed at the parking lot, at the rows of parked cars, at the aspen trees waving in the breeze. The landscape faded, and Ellie's words blazed a trail across his mind.

You don't judge. You accept and help us.

Guilt niggled him. That wasn't exactly true, not about the judging part, anyway. He did judge. He just kept his censure carefully under wraps.

People weren't perfect, she'd said. Of course, he knew that. Yet, he'd always thought Rose perfect. He'd wanted so badly for her, above all, to be without flaw. He wasn't sure why. Perhaps because his birth mother had been so imperfect in her betrayal.

Yet, as his internal vision shifted, he realized that by expecting Rose to be perfect, he'd demanded the impossible. She was a human being and therefore flawed, just like everyone else.

He traced his fingers along the edge of the windowsill, the metal rim cool to the touch, thinking of his birth mother and the resentment he'd always harbored toward her. How did he know she hadn't done the best she could, given who she was and the circumstances? Like Ellie's acceptance of Glenna's pregnancy, he needed to accept what had happened to him as part of his human experience. He should embrace it, not push it away.

He also needed to accept Rose's experience as a part of her. Instead of rejecting her, if anything, he should love her all the more.

Returning to his desk, he slumped into the chair and dropped his head into his hands. How blind and stupid he'd been. If only he'd had these insights sooner, he would've handled the revelation of her past differently. Now, it was too late. Rose was leaving town. Forever.

Or was it too late? He straightened his spine with new resolve. Maybe, just maybe, he had another chance to make things right.

****

Home from a shopping trip to Denver, Rose carried her purchases into her bedroom and dumped them on the bed. She stared at the pile of bags and boxes, wondering what she'd been thinking to go on such a spree.

Yet, she wanted some new outfits for her new life in St. Louis. Today's buying jag was part of her plan to reinvent herself. New job, new residence, new clothes equaled New Rose.

Dipping into one of the bags, she pulled out a pair of chocolate brown slacks, a white tee top decorated with tiny embroidered flowers, and a brown twill jacket with wide lapels and a fitted waist. She ran her fingers over the corded twill, while breathing in the fresh smell of the new fabric. The outfit would be perfect for work or a casual social event. Assuming there would be social events. Yes, there would, she vowed. Her new life would include both work and play.

She spread out the rest of the clothing, holding a couple outfits to her body and parading by the full-length mirror. Then she began folding the items and packing them in boxes for the movers.

As she worked, some of her euphoria ebbed away. Did she really want to leave Red Rock? She'd miss Sara, Jackson, and Ryan. And Molly and Karli.

And Mike.

Especially Mike.

That's all over. Forget about him.

And yet, a minute later when the doorbell chimed, the first thought that popped into her head was, *Maybe it's Mike.*

Holding her breath, she went to the door and peeked through the peephole. Not Mike, but Sara with Ryan in her arms. Rose's shoulders sagged with relief. Or was it regret? Her emotions were so jumbled she couldn't sort them out. Shaking her head to clear the confusion, she opened the door.

Sara grinned at her. "Hope you don't mind us popping in spur of the moment."

"Not at all. Come on in." Rose stepped aside to let them enter.

"We came to town to buy new shoes for Ryan."

Managing to keep her pink canvas tote anchored to one shoulder, Sara put the baby down on the carpeted floor. "Ryan, show Auntie Rose how you can walk."

Holding out his arms, Ryan teetered a few steps forward in his shiny white athletic shoes. Then his knees buckled. Sara leaped to grasp his hands before he landed on his bottom.

Rose hunkered down to eye level with Ryan. "Good job, Ryan!" Her heart constricted. Oh, how she loved her little nephew and how she would miss him when she moved.

"Mama's proud of you, too." Sara swept him up into her arms and nuzzled his neck.

"Ga ga." Ryan grinned and with chubby fingers patted Sara's cheek.

Pleased to have a diversion from her chores, Rose fetched a blanket from the bedroom and spread it on the living room floor.

Sara settled Ryan on the blanket, and then pulled wooden blocks, a few toy cars, and a stuffed bear from her tote. She spread the toys out on the blanket within Ryan's reach.

With the baby occupied, Sara dipped back into her bag and removed a plastic food storage box. "I have a couple other reasons for stopping by, and this is one." She handed the box to Rose.

"Cookies, right?"

Sara's laughter rang out. "Am I predictable or what? Yep, these are made with granola, and I'd like to have your opinion."

"My pleasure." Rose lifted a corner of the box and sniffed. "They smell yummy. Shall we have some now?"

Raising a hand, Sara took a step backward. "I've had way too many already. Save them for later, why don't you?"

Rose carried the cookies to the kitchen, and then

returned to the living room where she joined Sara on the sofa. "You said you had two more reasons for stopping by today."

Sara's eyes lighted as she darted a glance at her son. "Right. I wanted to remind you Ryan's birthday party is this Sunday."

Thinking of the gifts she'd already wrapped for her nephew, Rose nodded. "I haven't forgotten."

"You're coming, aren't you?"

Sara's voice held a tentative tone. Wanting to reassure her, Rose said without hesitation, "Of course. I wouldn't miss it."

"You do realize Mike will be there."

Rose heaved a sigh. "I figured he would be."

"And that's okay with you?"

In truth, the thought of being near him again, even though he obviously didn't care about her anymore, filled her with sadness. "I wouldn't expect you to exclude him just because he and I are no longer a couple."

"That's what I figured, but I wanted to make sure."

"You're always so thoughtful." Rose reached over and touched Sara's arm.

Sara pushed a lock of hair back behind her ear. "I try to be. I know you did what you thought best, but I can't help wishing things between you two had turned out differently."

"So do I." Rose fussed with a loose thread on the sofa's arm. "I feel I owe you an explanation for my actions."

"No, you don't." Sara raised a hand, palm outward. "I know in the past I've pushed you to confide, but I've since decided your reasons for not staying with Mike are none of my business."

Rose leaned forward and said in earnest, "But I want to explain. Really." Telling Sara her story would test her newfound courage and strength.

A moment slid by, and then Sara said, "Well, okay. I've always said I would be glad to listen. That still stands."

You must never tell. Like a broken record, the familiar warning popped into Rose's mind.

This time, she had no trouble pushing aside the warning. Yes, if she wanted to, she could tell. And she wanted to confide in Sara.

Still, the possibility of rejection and censure trapped the initial words in her throat. Gripping the sofa arm, she took a deep breath and forged ahead. "Everything started a long time ago, back in high school..."

When she'd finished, Sara scooted over and gave her a hug. "Oh, honey, oh, I'm so sorry!"

Relief washed over Rose, and she leaned into her sister-in-law. "Thanks, Sara. I hoped you'd understand."

"I do. Now I know why you were so upset when Kurt showed up at the class reunion. And why you broke up with Mike two years ago." She tilted her head and added, "Jackson doesn't know, though, does he?"

"No, he doesn't. Our mother made me promise to tell no one, and that included Jackson. The lie about me getting a scholarship to a private school my senior year wasn't so far-fetched, though. I was always a serious student, and I made good grades. I don't think Jackson blinked an eye when he heard the plan. Maybe someday I'll tell him." She paused and pressed a hand to her forehead. "But maybe not. Unlike me, he had a good relationship with our mother. I'd hate to spoil that."

"Jackson's a pretty strong guy. I think he'd understand. But, if you do decide to tell him, you'll know when the time is right, like you did with me today." Sara paused then added, "You did finish high school, though, didn't you? You must've, because you went to college."

"Yes, I did finish. After I gave up my baby, I called my Aunt Nelda."

"The aunt you were supposed to stay with?"

"Yes. She took me in and home-schooled me, as she'd planned. I was able to get my diploma, so I could go on to college. I took the first year at a community college near Aunt Nelda's then returned to Colorado and Denver U." Rose would always be grateful to her aunt for helping her through a difficult time.

Sara leaned down to hand Ryan a toy car that was out of his reach. "There you go, sweetie." She straightened and shook her head. "I don't understand Mike's reaction. I'd have thought he'd be sympathetic. He's such a caring person."

Mike's reaction was the sticky part of Rose's confession. She took a moment to carefully form her reply. "All I can say is he has strong personal reasons for not accepting me," she finally told Sara. "I can't reveal those without his permission. But I wanted you to know my side, anyway." She twisted her hands in her lap. "Are you sure you don't feel differently toward me now?"

Sara's eyes widened. "Of course, I'm sure! Whose life is not without some regrets? I certainly have mine. I still can't help wishing, though, that you and Mike could've worked things out." She let out a sigh. "I always thought you two were made for each other."

Heaviness weighed on Rose's shoulders. "There was a time when I thought that, too. But no more."

After Sara and Ryan left, Rose returned to her packing. Although baring her soul gave her a sense of power and release from long pent-up emotions, the loss of Mike was a huge price to pay. She could only hope her upcoming move to St. Louis would, if not heal, at least dull the pain.

****

Mike parked his SUV at the end of a long line of vehicles in the Phillips' driveway. Tucking Ryan's birthday present under one arm, he stepped from the car and headed along the flower-lined walkway to the front porch. From the backyard came the sounds of Western music and the smells of barbecued meat and roasted corn.

Several guests stood on the porch, sipping drinks and nibbling cheese and crackers from a plate on the log table. "Hey, Mike's here!" one of them said.

Mike stopped to shake hands and exchange greetings. When he left them and entered the house, Sara broke away from a group by the fireplace and hurried toward him.

"Mike! Good to see you!" She gave him a hug and a kiss on his cheek. "I'm glad you decided to come, despite—well, you know."

A twinge of uncertainty niggled Mike as he patted Sara's shoulder. "Yes, I know Rose will be here. Don't worry about me. I wouldn't miss celebrating Ryan's first birthday."

Truth be told, he'd debated about whether or not to come. Although he'd decided to contact Rose before she left town, he wasn't sure a party was the best place for what he had to say. But, neither had he summoned the courage to call and arrange a private meeting. He was afraid she'd refuse to see him. Here, at least, they were thrust into the same environment. Still, he'd no idea what would happen when they crossed paths.

The moment arrived sooner than he'd expected. As he stepped away from Sara's embrace and glanced over her shoulder, his gaze landed squarely on Rose. She stood across the room talking to a man he recognized as Jackson's horse trainer. Dressed in a short denim skirt and a white tee top, her dark hair curling around her face, she looked sexy as hell. His temperature shot up a notch.

As though some sixth sense had told her he'd arrived, she turned, and their gazes collided. Her eyes lighted with familiar warmth, and the hint of a smile touched her lips. He was about to return her smile when her mouth drew into a grim line, and her eyes went cold. She offered him a brief, stiff nod, and returned to her conversation with the horse trainer.

Although over in seconds, the exchange left him shaken. Aware he still held Ryan's gift, he turned to Sara. "Ah, where shall I put this?"

"Over here." She led him to a stack of gifts by the fireplace, and then to the portable bar, where he ordered a soft drink from the bartender.

Sara moved off to greet new arrivals, leaving him to mingle. Drink in hand, he worked his way through the crowd and into the kitchen where he paused to greet Anna Gabraldi and her three helpers, up to their elbows in salads, baked beans, and trays of assorted vegetables. He drained the last sip of his drink, tossed the plastic glass into the recycle can, and stepped out the back door.

The air held a hint of approaching autumn but was still plenty warm for an outdoor party. Sara and Jackson had gone all out for Ryan's big day. Colorful balloons and streamers hung from the trees. Half a dozen long tables covered with red and blue cloths were set for dinner. The Western music he'd been hearing came from a combo set up on a portable dance floor. Several couples were dancing, while onlookers clapped and tapped their feet.

Sara appeared at Mike's side. "How're you doing?"

"Just great." The lie lumped in his stomach. Maybe he should leave. "Where's the birthday boy?" he asked, reminding himself that he was here for more reasons than just to connect with Rose.

"He's over there." She led him toward a shady spot near the barn, where a pony ride for the younger guests was in progress.

Mike spotted Ryan, all decked out in cowboy gear, astride one of the ponies ambling around in a circle.

Jackson walked beside his son, supporting his back and clasping the child's hands around the reins. "Hey, Mike!" he called as they approached.

"Jackson." He nodded and waved to Ryan. "Happy birthday, young man. Looks like you're gonna be a cowboy, just like your dad."

"Can you say 'birthday' for Uncle Mike?" Sara walked over to her son and tipped up the boy's cowboy hat.

"Bir-day?" Ryan grinned at his mother.

Mike, Sara, and Jackson, along with the other pony riders and guides, clapped and cheered. Mike stood aside with Sara while Jackson and Ryan and the others circled one more time.

Then Jackson swept the child from the pony's back and joined them.

While they were talking, Mike's glance caught Rose headed their way. Prepared to speak to her this time, his shoulders tensed. But when their gazes collided, she veered off toward the house. He exhaled but the tension remained. If he intended to say his piece on this occasion, he'd better do it soon, before the party was over. Next time he saw her, he'd make his move.

Mike approached the barbecue pit, where Molly, wearing the traditional chef's hat and white apron, stood over the racks of ribs and burgers. Smoke curled into the air then drifted away in the breeze.

He waited until she finished brushing barbecue sauce on a couple ribs, and then asked. "How're you doing?"

She set the brush in a nearby pan. "Okay, I

guess. Buck's passing left a huge hole in my life, but I've still got Karli. Thank God for her." A smile tugged at her lips.

Mike propped one foot on the patio's low brick wall. "Will you be staying on here at the ranch?"

Picking up a long-handled spatula, Molly flipped a burger. Grease dripped onto the coals, sizzling and sputtering. "I'm not sure. Sara and Jackson said I'm welcome to stay, but, right now, I don't want to be here without Buck. I may go live with my sister and her family in Chicago. For a while, anyway. I haven't decided yet."

"We'd all miss you, but a change of scene might be the best for you and Karli."

Mike wandered on. When he reached the barn, he glimpsed Rose heading down the path to the duck pond. She was alone. His mouth went dry. He sucked in a deep breath and headed after her. Was this the moment he'd been waiting for?

Chapter Seventeen

After she'd passed the barn, Rose slowed her steps. The duck pond had been her destination, but now she had second thoughts. She really shouldn't leave the party and go off by herself. But wherever she turned there was Mike. No, he wasn't stalking her, but their paths crossed all too often. Whenever he came within her radar, the pain in her heart twisted a little tighter. How would she make it through the rest of the party? They still had to eat dinner and open Ryan's gifts, which added up to a long evening.

She heaved a deep sigh. Much as she loved her nephew and wanted to celebrate his first birthday, coming tonight had been a bad idea.

But she was here now and leaving before the party was over would be rude. She'd grant herself a few more minutes alone and then return to the house. Stepping up her pace, she continued down the path. At the duck pond, she sank onto the wooden bench and leaned back against the slats. A soft breeze ruffled her hair and cooled her cheeks.

At the pond's far end, from under sun-drenched branches of the weeping willow, two ducks, a male and a female, glided into view. The male's glossy green feathers shone as though hand-polished. Without a care in the world, the pair drifted serenely around the water. If only her life could be so simple.

"They look happy, don't they?" a voice behind her said.

Mike.

Rose's heart skipped a beat. The one person

above all she'd sought to avoid.

"I was just thinking that," she said, keeping her focus on the ducks, determined not to let him know his appearance had unnerved her.

"We're often on the same wavelength, you and I."

"On some things, maybe. Unimportant things."

"I'm not so sure of that." He rounded the bench.

When he came into view, she stared a moment at his black boots, then let her gaze slowly rise. Jeans on long, sturdy legs, blue shirt covering broad chest and wide shoulders. Lastly, his face—square jaw, expressive lips, straight and narrow nose. And finally, his eyes. Eyes focused intently on her. She held his gaze long enough to feel the familiar pull, the unspoken connection that always existed between them.

"Mind if I sit down?" He gestured to the spot beside her.

She shrugged, as though not caring one way or the other. "Suit yourself."

He sat. A couple feet separated them, but the space felt like mere inches. After so many weeks of separation, his sudden nearness kept her senses humming.

Leaning forward, he propped his elbows on his knees. "I need to talk to you, Rose."

His husky tone signaled danger. A little chill slithered along her arms. "Why?"

"Because I—" He straightened and cleared his throat. "I want to apologize."

Surprise chased away her apprehension. He wanted to apologize? What good would that do? Lifting her chin, she said, "I don't want your apology. I don't want anything from you." Intending to escape, she scooted to the edge of the bench.

He held up a hand. "Wait. You listened to Kurt's apology after fifteen years. How about giving me the same consideration? And, okay, maybe this isn't the best time or place, but it might be the only opportunity I have before you leave town."

She couldn't argue with his reasoning, especially about Kurt. Settling back onto the bench, she said in a resigned voice, "All right."

He twisted around so that he faced her. "I'm sorry my attitude about women who abandon their babies increased your pain, Rose."

"Why wouldn't you have that attitude, considering you were one of those babies? I understand that."

"Yeah, but I've been pretty harsh in my judgment of women in your situation, when I had no right to be. Instead of dealing with my past and working through it, I let my experience color my beliefs about other women in the same situation as my mother." He paused to tunnel a hand through his hair, and then continued, "I need to forgive her and move on."

Rose took a moment to absorb Mike's words, which were more than the simple apology she'd expected. Finally, she said, "That sounds like quite an insight. May I ask what brought you to this conclusion?"

"Something Ellie Jordan said when she and Glenna came into the clinic for an appointment the other day." He spread his hands. "Not the first time I've learned from my patients. Instead of making Glenna and the whole family pay for her mistake, Ellie accepts the situation. She realizes the future won't be easy, but at least she's willing to do the best she can for Glenna and her child."

"I'm glad things are working out for them."

"That's the point," he said, scooting closer. "A tough situation can be worked out. Even ours."

Now he'd gone too far. She crossed her arms over her chest and shook her head. "No, no. It's too late for us."

"When two people love each other, it's never too late. I love you, Rose, with all my heart and soul." Reaching for her hand, he clasped it with both of his. "And you love me, too. I know it. I dare you to look me in the eye and tell me you don't love me."

His bold challenge brought telltale warmth to her cheeks. Her throat dry, she turned away, hoping he wouldn't notice. "No, I—"

"Come on." He grasped her chin and guided her face toward him. "Look at me, Rose."

Her heart thudding, she edged her gaze upward. The oh-so-familiar warmth flowed between them, as sweet as honey.

Mike's lips curved into a satisfied smile. "Yes, there it is—the same look I saw in your eyes when you came into the E.R. after the train accident. The same look I saw when I first walked in the door today. That look of love is what kept me going all these months and what gives me the courage to go on right now."

Uncomfortable under his steady gaze, Rose shifted on the bench. "Okay, so maybe there's still a spark between us—"

"More than a spark—"

"That still doesn't change that I'm not the perfect person you thought I was." His forefinger ran along her cheek, sending little shivers over her skin.

"Yes, you are the perfect person—for me. You always have been, and you always will be. You are thoughtful, kind, and generous. You love helping people, as I do." His finger traced along her jaw. "We belong together. I told you that before. I still believe it, now more than ever. All we've been through has made us stronger."

She nodded, aware that he steadily chipped away at her wall of resistance. "I do feel stronger these days. Now that I've shared my secret, I'm not carrying such a heavy burden. I want to work on forgiving myself, and my mother, too, like you are doing."

"It won't be easy, especially when something happens to trigger the old hurt and anger." A smile tugged at his lips. "But I believe with time and effort we can both be free of the past."

She heaved a sigh. "That would be wonderful, wouldn't it?"

"It would, and together we can find our way. I love you, Rose." His hand cradled the back of her neck. "I want to spend the rest of my life with you."

His tender words filled her with new hope. "Oh, Mike! Do you think we really could make our relationship work? Do you think we can have our own family?"

"I know we can." Gazing deeply into her eyes, he said, "Rose Phillips, will you marry me?"

His tone was the most solemn she'd ever heard him use. Heart racing, her first impulse was to shout, "Yes!" But then the old doubts crept in. She bit her lip and looked away. "There are so many things to work out."

"I know, but answer one simple question. Do you love me?"

Did she love him? Blood pounded through her veins. Of course, she did. Gripping his arm, she cried, "Yes! Oh, yes, I do!"

"Then have faith that we'll deal with whatever comes along."

"But what about my job? I'm all ready to move."

"I don't think your moving to St. Louis is a good idea now." He leaned closer and his lips grazed her cheek in a gentle kiss. "But if you want to continue working for the railroad, fine. As long as you come home to me."

Home. She longed for a home, a husband and a family, but where should her home be? In St. Louis?

Or here in Red Rock, with Mike? Her heart raced, her hands were clammy. To calm herself, she shifted her attention to the ducks gliding peacefully around their home. The pair belonged together, no doubt about that.

Mike insisted they belonged together, too. Was it true? When she searched her heart, she knew it was. Taking a deep breath, she said, "Mike, I'd be honored to be your wife."

A grin spread across his face. "Yes! I've waited so long to hear those words."

He pulled her into his arms and covered her lips with his in a warm, delicious kiss. Longing filled her. She'd missed his kisses so much. Hard to believe she'd now have all of them she wanted.

Moments later, nestled in his arms, she said, "Am I dreaming?"

A low chuckle sounded. "No, this is real. We're going to be married, my love, and spend the rest of our lives together." He inclined his head, his cheek brushing hers, and found her lips again. When the kiss ended, he said, "And now, how about sharing our good news with Sara and Jackson and the others?"

Rose giggled, thinking of the startled expressions on everyone's faces. "Won't they be surprised?"

"I doubt it," he drawled. "I've a feeling they've known all along this moment would eventually come to pass."

****

"No, you can't come in here!" Sara slammed the bedroom door in Mike's face.

Glimpsing a peek at Mike's stunned expression, Rose giggled. "The superstition that the groom can't see the bride before the wedding is a little harsh in this case, isn't it?"

Sara shrugged, and then smoothed the collar of

her beige silk matron-of-honor's dress. "I'm big on tradition. Besides, he'd be in the way." Glancing at her wristwatch, she added, "We don't have much time. Pastor Robinson's due in twenty minutes, and he's never late."

"I'm glad Pastor is able to perform the ceremony, even though it's Thanksgiving Day."

She and Mike had discussed their wedding date at length. Neither wanted to wait long. They wanted to use the trip to Jamaica he'd won at the hospital auction for their honeymoon, and still join Sara and Jackson at their Aspen condo for Christmas.

Thanksgiving seemed appropriate, because they both had so much to be thankful for. Adding their union to the day's traditional festivities would be perfect. When Sara and Jackson suggested they have the ceremony at the Rolling R, they'd readily agreed.

They'd worried the date might be too soon after Buck's death, but Molly assured them she'd attend. "You two have waited for this long enough," she'd said. "Go for it."

And so, they did. Together they picked out their rings. Rose gazed at the two-carat diamond on her finger. She loved how it sparkled in the light. Even more, she loved what it symbolized—her commitment to her future husband. Along with her wedding band, she would wear it the rest of her life.

They also had to decide where to live. For now, Mike's condo would be their home. But they'd already begun looking at property on which to build a future home for the family they planned to have.

Sara strode to the closet where Rose's wedding dress hung on the open door. Removing it from the hanger, she brought the dress to Rose and helped her slip it over her head.

The smooth fabric slid coolly along her skin, and Rose let out a sigh.

Sara zipped up the back then twirled Rose around to face the full-length mirror. "Take a look at yourself," Sara said, leaning over Rose's shoulder. "You're gorgeous. The dress looks even better on you than it did on Gimble's model."

Rose gazed at her mirror twin. A fancy wedding dress wasn't her style, so she'd chosen one of ivory silk with simple yet elegant lines. The scooped neckline flattered her slender neck and the knee-length skirt showed off her legs. "Yes, I'm glad I chose this one, and that you helped me pick it out. I've always admired your fashion sense."

Sara patted a wrinkle from Rose's skirt. "Thanks. I do love clothes and shopping." She pressed a forefinger to her cheek. "Okay, what's left? Shoes, of course." Plucking a pair of ivory pumps from a box on the bed, she handed them to Rose.

"And my necklace and earrings," Rose said, holding on to the bedpost for balance while she slipped on her shoes. "Then we're done."

Sara was combing Rose's hair into place when someone tapped on the door.

"Pastor's here," Jackson said.

Rose clutched her stomach. "Oh my, all of a sudden, I'm scared."

Sara put down the comb and gave Rose a quick hug. "You'll do fine, honey. Come on, now, everyone's waiting for you. Especially Mike."

"Yes, Mike." The thought of her beloved husband-to-be prompted Rose to action. Stealing a last glimpse of herself in the mirror, she followed Sara out the door.

Beaming like a proud father, Jackson waited for Rose at the bottom of the steps. "You look beautiful, Sis."

"Thanks." She planted a quick kiss on his cheek. Rose picked up her bride's bouquet of pink carnations and baby's breath, and then took

Jackson's arm. They stepped into the living room to the strains of recorded organ music and the warmth of a fire crackling in the hearth.

Her gaze skimmed over the group gathered to witness the ceremony. In addition to Molly, Ryan and Karli, were Rose's apartment house neighbor, Nancy; Mike's partner, David, and his wife, Sorvina; and Rose's boss, Stan, and his wife, Grace. Anna Gabraldi stood by the door leading to the dining room, dabbing her eyes with her handkerchief.

Rose and Mike had purposely kept today's group small. Later, there would be a reception at the Red Rock Hotel for all their friends and associates.

At the far end of the room, along with Pastor Robinson and Sara, Mike waited. A few moments later, she stepped into place beside him. Their gazes met, and Rose's heart swelled with love. How fortunate she was to be marrying this wonderful man.

Pastor Robinson cleared his throat and began, "Dearly Beloved..."

When the ceremony was over, Rose closed her eyes as Mike bestowed his first kiss as her husband. A thrill rippled through her. Then they turned to receive hugs and congratulations from their guests.

Later, after they'd finished a delicious Thanksgiving dinner, the party moved back to the living room to enjoy the three-tier wedding cake Sara had created. The top had an arbor of pink icing roses to shelter the traditional bride and groom figurines.

In a daze of happiness, Rose sat beside Mike on the cozy love seat.

"You're beautiful," he whispered. "I can't wait until we're alone and I can show you how much I love you."

His warm breath tickled her ear and sent delicious chills down her spine. She squeezed his hand. "I can hardly wait, either!"

Jackson tapped a spoon against his wine glass. "Attention, everyone." When the group quieted, he raised his glass and said, "Here's a toast to my sister, Rose, and to my best friend, Mike, who are now man and wife. Together may they enjoy a long and happy life."

Everyone chimed in with, "To Rose and Mike!"

After they'd all sipped their drinks, Mike raised his glass. "I'd like to toast our friends and family gathered here today. Thanks for hanging in with me and Rose until we finally got it right." He paused for a round of laughter then continued, "I want everyone, most of all my beautiful bride, to be assured that this time, we're together forever!"

Amid the cheers and applause, Rose turned to her husband. Eyes brimming with tears of joy, she whispered, "Yes, my love, this time, forever!"

The journey to this moment had been long and sometimes painful. But now Rose was certain only love and happiness lay ahead.

Sara's Granola Chocolate Chip Cookies

1/3 cup butter
1/2 cup light brown sugar
1 egg
1 cup flour
1/2 tsp. baking soda
1/8 tsp salt
1 tsp. vanilla extract
1 cup Pecan and Praline Granola*
2/3 cup chocolate chips

Preheat oven to 375°F. Lightly grease baking sheet.
    1. Cream butter and sugar with mixer. Beat in egg. Add vanilla extract.
    2. Combine flour, baking soda, salt and granola. Stir into butter mixture. Combine thoroughly.
    3. Add chocolate chips.
    4. Drop by the teaspoonful onto baking sheet. Gently flatten. Bake 8 to 10 minutes or until golden brown.
    5. Remove from sheet and cool on wire rack.
Makes approximately 2 dozen cookies.
*For variation, use a different flavored granola.

A word about the author...

Linda Hope Lee has written contemporary romance, mystery, and romantic suspense. Also an artist, she works in watercolor, colored pencil, and pen and ink. Collecting children's books and anything to do with wire-haired fox terriers occupies her spare time. She lives in the Pacific Northwest, a setting for many of her novels.

Visit her website at www.lindahopelee.com

CPSIA information can be obtained at www.ICGtesting.com
Printed in the USA
BVOW011556121011

273472BV00006B/3/P